THE NOTES

CATHERINE CON MORSE

Crown
New York

Text copyright © 2024 by Catherine Con Morse
Jacket art copyright © 2024 by Hsiao-Ron Cheng

Visit us on the Web! GetUnderlined.com

Educators and librarians, for a variety of teaching tools, visit us at
RHTeachersLibrarians.com

Library of Congress Cataloging-in-Publication Data
Names: Con Morse, Catherine, author.
Title: The notes / Catherine Con Morse.
Description: First edition. | New York: Crown, 2024. | Audience: Ages 12 and up. | Audience: Grades 10–12. | Summary: "A reserved Chinese American teen at a Southern performing arts boarding school comes into her own under the tutelage of a glamorous new piano teacher while grappling with her first love, adolescent and academic pressures, and mysterious, personal notes"—Provided by publisher.
Identifiers: LCCN 2023041086 (print) | LCCN 2023041087 (ebook) | ISBN 978-0-593-71138-5 (hardcover) | ISBN 978-0-593-71139-2 (library binding) | ISBN 978-0-593-71140-8 (ebook)
Subjects: CYAC: Pianists—Fiction. | Interpersonal relations—Fiction. | Boarding schools—Fiction. | Schools—Fiction. | Chinese Americans—Fiction. | LCGFT: School fiction. | Novels.
Classification: LCC PZ7.1.C6456 No 2024 (print) | LCC PZ7.1.C6456 (ebook) | DDC [Fic]—dc23

The text of this book is set in 11.3-point Adobe Garamond Pro.
Interior design by Cathy Bobak

Printed in the United States of America
10 9 8 7 6 5 4 3 2 1
First Edition

Random House Children's Books supports the First Amendment
and celebrates the right to read.

To Mom and Dad, who—against their wishes—
dropped me off at arts boarding school.
And to El, who has been listening to my stories all her life.

Content Note

Certain passages in this book mention struggles with mental illness and self-harm.

Chapter 1

WE SAW DR. LI BEFORE WE MET HER. IN THE DINING HALL, she wore knee-high black leather boots and sunglasses so large they practically rested on her cheekbones. It was early September in Green Valley, South Carolina, but even our winters didn't call for boots like that. Jenny and I watched as she nudged a tray along with just the tips of her fingers, as if wanting to touch it as little as possible. She stood on the colored tiles in front of the green beans spotted with bacon, the mashed potatoes and their vat of gravy, the dripping kernels of sweet corn. In her black sheath dress, a black leather tote on her shoulder, she looked out of place, her outfit more fit for an office than a school. Somehow, already, we could sense her disappointment. Maybe it was the way she had walked into the room, the sigh when she entered, the pause in front of the trays before resigning herself to take one and approach the counter. *Well, if this is what I have to work with,* she seemed to be saying, *so be it.*

"Whatchoo want, baby?" said Barbara, the dining hall manager. She wore plum-colored lipstick and spoke to Dr. Li in the same way she did us, her *whatchoo* like a sneeze, then a dip into the long, low *want,* ending in a high, soft *baby* that nearly sounded like *babe.*

Dr. Li did not seem the least bit taken aback about being called *baby.* She said, "I'll have some of this, please," and pointed to the wet, dark green mass that we knew to be canned spinach. Her voice was cool and quiet. When she spoke, it was nearly accentless, unlike my mother, who spoke English fluently but not without some remnant of her native Mandarin.

The spinach was slapped onto the plate. "What else?" said Barbara.

"That's it," said Dr. Li.

"That be all?"

"Yes, thank you."

The plate, a bright orange plastic disk, was passed over, and Dr. Li set it on her tray. One hip cocked, one black boot pointed toward the tables, she carried her tray to the salad bar, her shoes clicking on the tile. She stood over the soup and lifted the ladle, inspecting the contents of the tureen. Chicken noodle.

At a table by the windows, Dr. Li sat down and took her sunglasses off. I saw that her eyes were dark and her skin pale and smooth. Her long hair, set loose to the humidity, had begun to curl just the slightest bit at the ends. She ate the spinach quickly but neatly, as if wanting to get it over with. Of course, it hardly needed chewing and, in fact, was a weekly offering we all avoided. It would be reheated and re-salted for a casserole on Saturday, when the dining staff took the leftovers from the week and baked them twice between sheets of flour. Dr. Li didn't know yet that meals were never this calm at Greenwood, but today—three days before the fall semester—was an exception. When school was in session, dinners were frenzied affairs, lunches worse. We simultaneously needed to eat everything and say everything. Now it was well past lunchtime, nearly two-thirty. The dining hall was empty.

Just then, Jenny waved a hand in front of my face. "Earth to Claire," she said. She adjusted her glasses and bent her head toward mine—our faces so close that her light brown ponytail brushed my shoulder—and looked where I was looking.

"I wonder if the Asian Student Society will ask her to sponsor them," said Jenny.

"They don't already have a sponsor?" I asked.

"Somehow, they function without one, since there are no Asian teachers. Well, there *were* none, anyway."

"Where did you hear that?" I asked.

"Everyone knows. Where have you been? Living under a *Rachmaninoff?*"

I groaned.

It annoyed me that even Jenny knew more about the Asian Student Society than I did, given that I was Asian and she wasn't. I had applied to the Society last spring and been rejected. I was pretty sure I knew exactly why, could trace my failure back to first-year Halloween. I'd dressed up as Holly Golightly from *Breakfast at Tiffany's,* a movie that I later found out was on the Society's list of boycotted films. Of course it was: Mr. Yunioshi was a bucktoothed, bumbling Japanese caricature played by a white actor. I cringed at the memory of my elbow-length gloves and fake cigarette holder.

"If you know so much," I asked Jenny now, "tell me this. Why was Dr. Li wearing sunglasses inside?"

Jenny considered, then said, "She's either drunk or stoned. All the really good ones have to get stoned because of stress."

When Jenny said things like that, I wanted to be more like her. She always sounded like she knew exactly what she was talking about, even when she didn't—maybe even more so when she didn't—and I envied that.

Dr. Li headed back to the counter. She didn't look stoned to me. "Excuse me," we heard her say. "Do you have any bread?"

"There you go, babe," said Barbara, and held out a dinner roll with her tongs. "You'll love it here," she continued. "These students are like my own kids. Pretty soon you be feeling that way, too."

"That's lovely," said Dr. Li. But it sounded like she thought the opposite was true.

♩♫

Every fall, we attended the Annual Faculty-Student Assembly in Elizabeth D. Halpern Recital Hall. This year's was my third. Dr. Hamilton, who presided over the assembly, had studied musicology at Penn decades ago. He had been making "introductory remarks" for what felt like half an hour. "And that is why, young artists," he was saying, "you must stay the course, despite how often we artists are marginalized."

"But with all due respect, Dr. Hamilton, have you ever thought maybe we *need* to be marginalized?" Rocky Wong called out. " 'An artist is always alone—if he is an artist,' " he quoted.

I craned my neck and saw Rocky high-five everyone around him. We'd been in the same piano studio for the past two years, so I knew he loved going on tangents to delay class—but he'd never interrupted Assembly before. That was the seniors' job. But this year, Rocky *was* a senior, and he looked the part, too: he leaned back in his chair with his feet up, and I could see his familiar gray Converses from where I was sitting.

"Yes, that's Henry Miller," said Dr. Hamilton. "Feet down, Mr. Wong. You've made an interesting point, in spite of interrupting me. If the artist is truly a master, are they necessarily, alone?" He sighed. "But that, young artists, is another conversation for another day. Put all your technologies away. I hereby call to order the forty-fifth Greenwood Annual Faculty-Student Assembly."

"Or Annual Fucking-Stupid Assembly," Jenny muttered beside me. "Am I right?" She patted me on the back. "Don't look so nervous, Claire. No one really cares about this stuff."

I gave Jenny a look. I was the music rep this year, which meant I was supposed to go up to the stage to ask Dr. Li a question when she was introduced.

Dr. Hamilton went on. "This year, I am pleased to announce that the special topics for music history include 'The Renaissance in Music and Art' "—at this, a few groans from the audience, except for a few who whooped—"and, in the spring, 'The Four Bs: Bach, Beethoven, Brahms, and the Beatles.' " This was met by cheers from nearly everyone, and then Dr. Hamilton went on to announce the electives for the other arts concentrations: visual arts, drama, and dance.

"Now, let us begin our assembly with the Greenwood Pledge. This year's representative from the theater department—an honors student in chemistry, English, and French—is Lauren Culpepper."

We clapped. Beside me, Jenny said, "Of *course* it would be Lauren Culpepper."

Toward the back of the auditorium, Lauren stood up. "Present at Greenwood," she said, enunciating. "Please rise."

Jenny and I stood, our seats clapping back along with everyone else's, so we heard a collective shuffling as everyone got to their feet. Then Lauren led us in reciting: "We pledge ourselves to our calling, our art. We seek to serve with our gifts, and to stretch our talent as far as it will go, as we stand on the shoulders of the masters before us."

"Thank you, Lauren," said Dr. Hamilton. "Now, I am honored to introduce our new faculty members. We have two of them this year. First, from the dance department, Paul Yanko."

From the front row, a small, lithe man made his way up and waved at us.

At the same time, a dancer walked quickly toward the stage, her feet in the same splayed position as Yanko's.

"Thanks, Mr. Yanko," said Dr. Hamilton. "This is our dance representative, Adeline Felts."

"Mr. Yanko," Adeline said after shaking his hand, "when did you first know that you wanted to be a dancer?"

Paul Yanko cleared his throat. "Well, I remember the first time I saw *The Nutcracker* on TV. From that moment, I was hooked. I *knew* that I had to dance!"

Beside me, Jenny whispered, "Oh, brother."

"Oh, come on," I said. "That wasn't that bad."

"Thank you, Mr. Yanko," Dr. Hamilton said. "Now it's my pleasure to introduce our other new faculty member, Tina Li. Dr. Li will take over our piano program this fall."

Jenny patted me on the back. I stood and made my way toward the stage. My heart was beating fast. From the front of the recital hall, I scanned the seats for Dr. Li.

When I stepped onto the stage, Dr. Hamilton gave me a small smile. "Dr. Li?" he said. We waited. It was so quiet that when someone sneezed, we heard a whispered "Bless you."

A few people giggled. A phone buzzed.

After several seconds, students began to cough and shuffle in their seats, much like we did between movements of a sonata. It felt as if we'd been waiting for a long time. Maybe a full minute passed, and finally someone—I think it was Rocky again—said, "Well? Where is she?"

"Quiet, please," said Dr. Hamilton. "Dr. Li? Come on up."

But no one moved. I looked toward the music faculty. No one appeared to be getting out of their seat.

"Dr. Tina Li? Piano?" Dr. Hamilton said.

"Maybe she's asleep," a brass player suggested.

"*You* were asleep," someone else said.

"Order," said Dr. Hamilton.

One of the teachers stood, propped her glasses up on her head, and looked around the hall. Then she looked at Dr. Hamilton, shook her head, and sat back down.

Dr. Hamilton said, "I'm calling the right name, aren't I?"

No one laughed. People were beginning to murmur.

Dr. Hamilton said, "I'm sorry, Claire. It looks like she didn't make it today."

I turned toward the piano section. Even from where I stood, I could see Jenny looking at me, then at the others, with her eyebrows furrowed. I knew what she would be saying after we were dismissed: *What the hell? Where was she?*

People began talking among themselves.

"Can *I* skip Assembly next year?"

"I hope nothing happened to her."

Then they were saying "Shhh!" and "Listen!" And everyone fell silent as they heard, just faintly, a trickle of piano notes coming up from the vents on either side of the hall. I recognized the piece immediately: it was the opening of the Beethoven E major, one of the last piano sonatas he wrote. Just the first two bars. Someone was playing them again and again. They unfurled softly and rapidly, like spools of silk. The hall was built directly on top of the practice rooms. But why hadn't this happened before? Because until now, all music students and faculty had been present for any event that took place in Elizabeth D. Halpern Recital Hall.

We were quiet as we listened to the first two measures again. And again, and again.

Chapter 2

THE NEXT EVENING WAS WARM AND SOUPY AND LOOKED like rain, but we didn't care, because it was Clubs Night. Jenny and I walked arm in arm, pushing past backpacks and instrument cases, taking in the smell of sugar and sweat and trees. In front of us, the Greenwood Chamber Choir was singing Mozart in full concert dress, while at the Artists for Science Club, tiny light bulbs spelled *AFS,* buzzing and blinking, connected with copper wire.

"Join us in the search for truth and knowledge!" Lauren Culpepper chirped from the AFS table. "Or at least join us in learning about crickets and their mating habits."

"Join us in the search for truth with a capital *T,*" Daniel Giambalvo countered across from her. "Better than cricket sex." His table was piled with books and had a banner that read *Greenwood Philosophers Guild.* He looked the part, too, with his full beard and glasses.

"GPG seems harmless," Lauren said to us, "but they made me

stay up all night reading aloud from *Being and Time* until I fell asleep standing. That's how I got in."

From yet another table, Jessie Washington called out, "You want truth? Get your *Greenwood Gavotte,* twenty-five cents! Printed on one hundred percent recycled paper." She waved newspapers at us, and I fished a quarter from my backpack while Jenny grumbled, "It doesn't cost anything to read it online."

Jessie said, "We have to pay for ink and shit with our club allowance money, and it doesn't roll over into next semester—"

"But it's school news. We're reading about stuff *we* did."

"Jenny Stone, you know very well that there's some local news in here, too."

"Yeah, yeah," said Jenny. "Sign me up. I want to be a reporter again."

Although her official title was staff writer, Jenny had mostly been relegated to making crossword puzzles about school history and writing tiny obits for inanimate objects, like textbooks that were no longer in use and last month's seasonal dining hall offerings: *The advent of allergy season begets a farewell to peppermint hot cocoa,* and *Despite the unknown nature of its contents, we are deeply saddened by the loss of the Summer Refresher. Made of (most likely) lemon water, fruit punch, and artificial sweetener, Refresher is survived by a grandchild known to all as Watered-Down Lemonade.*

Jenny handed me a copy of the paper. On the front page was a blurry photo of Dr. Li, midstride in front of the music building as if she'd been caught by the paparazzi. The headline above it read *New Piano Teacher Missing at AFSA.*

"You call that news?" Jenny said.

But I grabbed the paper and inspected the photo. A faculty member—and a brand-new one at that—had missed one of Greenwood's most important ceremonies to practice her own rep; I could think of few things more newsworthy. The article didn't say much more than what we already knew, and I couldn't see Dr. Li's face, but she was wearing the same tall boots we'd seen in the dining hall. The way she'd played the same two measures over and over, as if trying to improve upon perfection: I'd never heard anything like it. "Aren't you curious about why she wasn't there?" I asked.

Jenny put her hands on my shoulders, steering me toward the tables ahead. "I'm curious about why you're thinking so much about a teacher. Don't waste your time."

We walked by Artists for Animals, who were handing out pamphlets about why veganism was sexy. I'd heard that their first club meeting was always a dinner of baked tempeh while watching *Meat the Truth*. The year before, I'd watched a handful of people join the group, but several of them left by Christmas. This was the South, after all, and it was hard to say no to barbecue.

But there was one group that was noticeably silent. It did not ask anyone to join; in fact, its table was empty except for a banner painted with *SOCIETY* in black letters. This was the Asian Student Society, and it was famously, historically, exclusive. It was not to be confused with the AAPI Student Union, which was welcoming to all—even non-Asian students could join their boba and board games nights. The Asian Student Society was different. It had received special permission to stay small: it could never have more than six people at once. Its members moved together and ate together and sometimes even napped together, lying around in the North Campus Garden like a piece of performance art, their dark hair spilling onto the grass, hot in the late summer sun. They met in a secret place on campus, where they did secret things. Last spring, several members had walked around campus holding plastic spoons up to their noses. It lasted a week and then stopped. Nobody ever found out why. I heard that they played music together, though I'd never witnessed it myself.

"I don't see what the big deal is," said Jenny. "So they're exclusive and no one really knows what their weird rituals are. Just like the Ivy League. And the Ivy League can jump up and bite me in the ass."

"I like how you added that part about jumping up," I said. "No, seriously. Simply biting you in the ass wouldn't have been enough."

Jenny knew me better than anyone, but she couldn't understand that I felt guilty—guilty that my parents and I spoke English at home and they called me Claire instead of a Chinese name, even though I had one. Once, my mother boasted to me that she and my father were so much more westernized than any of their Chinese friends: some of them, after years of living in the US, had hardly learned any English. "And I don't think that's right," my mother had said. My parents were friends with their white neighbors, who rarely asked about or mentioned any differences between us—except once, when Mrs. Humphrey, who lived next door, had wrinkled her nose and asked "What *is* that?" when the smell of sesame oil came wafting from the kitchen. We had Chinese calligraphy and paintings in the living room, and on weekends my mother volunteered at Little Lingos, teaching Mandarin to elementary school students. We got our hair cut by Mrs. Kim, who was Korean, because my mother insisted that no one else in town would understand our hair. On weekends, we sometimes drove an hour from our house in Thomasville, North Carolina, to Charlotte, to buy dumpling wrappers and chili oil and a thirty-pound bag of white rice.

Still, it could be easy to let ourselves forget. Forgetting meant that we would be invited to birthday parties and New Year's Eve parties at the Humphreys' and the Bennetts', that we would not be taken advantage of because of our shoddy English, that no one would say that we dressed funny or accuse us of not being sociable. So easy, sometimes I forgot until I looked in the mirror—or until someone stared at us at Mutt's BBQ or yelled "Konnichiwa!" at the mall. Then I was painfully self-conscious of how different we looked. We all had the same thick black hair. Mine was stick-straight and just touched my shoulders, and I never knew what to do with it—if it wasn't in a ponytail, I tucked it behind my ears. I had the same wide-set eyes and high forehead as my father, and my mother's slightly upturned nose, which Jenny called cute.

Before Greenwood, my only Chinese friend was Olivia—I knew her from piano lessons. Olivia wore her shorts too long, with cartoon characters I'd never seen before, the color always just a shade off from what was in. Only later did I realize they were clothes from Taiwan. We didn't go to the same school, and I was grateful because that meant no one would get us mixed up with each other or assume we were sisters, both of which happened often if there was one other Chinese girl around. When I had dinner at her house, I'd been embarrassed when Olivia's mother had picked up mixed nuts with her chopsticks, and when instead of asking me to pass the rice, she'd reached across the table, her arm hovering inches above my plate.

Later, Olivia had said to me, "My brother said you're kind of whitewashed." When I looked surprised—too surprised to be hurt, she said, "It's not a bad thing. Your family has a Christmas tree. You know what I get on Christmas morning? A check."

It was only after my first semester at Greenwood that I realized it could be different. At Greenwood, the Asian American students didn't hide behind J.Crew stripes or avoid being friends with each other. Miyoung Kim brought BB cream from Seoul and shared with us a jar of kimchi that stank up the entire hallway. I heard Rocky using Mandarin now and again with Ellie Giang, the phrases musical and animated. Rocky wore Chinese prayer beads on his wrist, and when I found the bracelet in a practice room, he'd thanked me profusely, telling me it belonged to his grandfather. The Asian Student Society made fried rice out of Thanksgiving leftovers from the dining hall on Black Friday, and crowded around K dramas in the rec room, yelling at the TV as if watching a football game. For Lunar New Year, they played a version of Secret Santa using lucky red envelopes (their club mascot). Last spring, Rocky had given me one of those envelopes containing a single dollar and a haiku by Bashō, which I still kept in my desk drawer. According to their website, the Society sought to be a "safe space where your troubles, secrets, and fears can be poured out and sealed." They had a confidence in themselves and a fierce bond with each other from this, it seemed, and I wanted that, too. Growing up, I had often hidden my Asianness. So I felt I didn't fit in with other Asians, maybe didn't even deserve to, because of how long I'd been hiding. To be a part of the Society would mean that despite everything, I was one of them. That I belonged.

I was not hopeful now that anyone would show up at the ASS table, as Jenny called it. She'd pointed out its unfortunate acronym once, and Rocky, who was usually happy to make a joke about anything, had met her with a stare so deadly that Jenny never said it within earshot of any members again. Now Jenny took me by the elbow and we made our way over to Artists for Science to look at earthworms under a microscope. Their bodies glowed green as they slithered on the glass. "They've been injected with a deadly bacteria, and I mean *deadly*," Lauren Culpepper explained. "We're watching them fight it off right now. This can help us learn more about our *own* immune systems—"

That was when it started raining, a steady rain that came all at once and pelted the sidewalks and windows. Umbrellas flew open and everyone scattered.

"Save your books!" someone yelled. "The cupcakes!" said another. We ran through the courtyard, where the trees were dripping and thunder cracked. We heard the doors opening and slamming shut, the squeak of wet sneakers. Soon Jenny and I were under the dining hall awning, right outside the cereal dispensers. Our flip-flops squished. From the window, I watched Barbara wiping the counters in preparation for Saturday breakfast. Beside us, the rain fell harder, pooling in the plastic chairs. I saw Adeline Felts running for cover, and Scott Dessen, her dance partner, swooped in and lifted her up. She held her arms out as if it were a ballet performance.

From where we stood, I could see that the music department was still lit inside. Just outside the door, a lone figure stood. She had tied a scarf around her hair. Holding a newspaper above her head, she ran to a gray Mini Cooper, the only car left in the faculty lot.

Chapter 3

STUDIO CLASS WAS NOT A CLASS IN THE TRADITIONAL SENSE. There were no desks or textbooks or exams, no papers or projects. We simply met with the other pianists and our teacher and played for each other, then offered encouragement and advice. When Jenny and I showed up at Dr. Li's studio, another student was pressing her ear against the door, trying to hear. She turned to us and grinned. "I love hearing my teacher practice," she said, with an accent that gave her away as an international student.

This was one of those times when Rocky would have cheerfully called out, "Music nerd alert!" and opened the door for all of us to go in. But Rocky wasn't here yet.

"Martyna Svenyatka," the girl said. "I'm a first-year. From Poland." Her eyes were eager, her hair cut in a reddish-brown bob that framed her face.

"International students, hell yes!" JT Lau exclaimed. They high-fived.

"Are you going to be able to play in that thing?" Jenny asked JT. He was wearing what looked to be a velvet cape over his jeans.

JT huffed. "I can do anything in this 'thing.' Therein lies the beauty of it." He ran a hand through his floppy dark hair, which he deep-conditioned with coconut oil twice a week.

The music inside the studio stopped.

"Someone knock," said Jenny.

"You," JT and I both said.

Martyna said, "I don't know what the big deal is. I'll do it." She cleared her throat, then knocked.

There was no reply but the sound of arpeggios being played slowly, deliberately, over and over again. Martyna knocked again, louder this time, and when there was still no response, she tried the door. When it opened, the music came spilling out for a second, then stopped. We took that as our cue and stepped inside.

The studio as we knew it had been spare. Mr. Buck hadn't put anything on the walls, and the room was full enough with its two grand pianos: a Steinway and a Kawai. But now one wall was covered in Dr. Li's own concert posters and programs: Tina Li in a long, backless dress, looking over her shoulder with one hand on the piano at Paine Concert Hall; Tina Li accompanying a violinist at Indiana University; Tina Li playing Chopin and Ravel in a benefit concert for the Young Artists Foundation of Massachusetts.

There were books and books of piano scores on the shelves and in stacks on the floor, the thin spines pressed close together. The gray-blue Henle editions of Bach were packed into one section on the bookcase. I spotted other books, too: volumes one through three of *The Oxford History of Western Music* and

Beethoven, A Life. On the Steinway was a nail clipper, an old wooden metronome with a pendulum that swung back and forth, and a clay mug filled with yellow pencils. We had all been taught never to mark a score with a pen.

Dr. Li was holding one of those pencils now. She was sitting not on a piano bench but on a red yoga ball, and made no move to stand up when we appeared bunched together in the doorway. Her legs were so long that she could cross them comfortably even while on the ball, one tall boot over the other. I had never seen a piano teacher sit cross-legged at the instrument before, much less on a ball. I liked it—it made her seem above the rules. She wore a burgundy dress and gold earrings shaped like curled ribbons. She looked at all of us and we looked back at her. Then she put her hands on her hips even though she was sitting down, which made her look a little like a circus performer.

"Sorry, Dr. Li," said Martyna, "but we are here for class?"

"I know why you're here," said Dr. Li. "Come in."

We filed in and took our backpacks off, settling into chairs in a semicircle facing the pianos.

She continued to jot something down on her score. Then she closed it and turned to face us. "Class begins," she said, "when I say it begins."

"Sorry, but it was already four—" Martyna said.

"Don't apologize," said Dr. Li. "This is our first meeting, and I am simply telling you that I will begin when I am ready."

We all nodded.

"Now," Dr. Li said, "this is Music 301: 'Performing and Critiquing Music.' In this class, my job is to make all of you into better musicians and critics of music. Now tell me, your job is to . . . ?"

The room was silent.

Dr. Li turned to the piano and struck a single note, the A above middle C, as if ringing a bell to make an announcement. She played it again, softer this time, like the beginning of a shepherd's flute song, and then again staccato, as if the keys were hot. Then she dropped her hand onto the key and it sounded so loudly that Martyna jumped.

"That single note," said Dr. Li, "can be played in a multitude of ways. How should you play it, and why should you play it that way? Your job is to make these decisions in every piece you learn, and to listen to those decisions in the performances of your fellow musicians. It is also, with respect to being a student, to be fully present when you are in class."

At her last word, the studio door flew open and Rocky appeared, a little sweaty and out of breath, but—I thought—looking cooler than any of us in his Japanese Breakfast T-shirt and black jeans. He held his skateboard under one arm.

"So sorry," Rocky said. "I was on afternoon shift at the Maple-Mart, then had to drop off an add-class form, and then the hallway traffic was kind of traffic-y—"

"Leave your skateboard out there, please," Dr. Li said.

Rocky did. When he came back in, he slid into the seat next to me. "Hey, Wu," he whispered. "First week of school and I'm already slammed. I want to take Honors Euro because it'll raise my GPA for college apps, but then again an added course could wreck my GPA. So either way I'm screwed. How was your summer?"

I kept my eyes on Dr. Li because something told me she wouldn't appreciate a pre-class chat. Not to mention, class had already started. "I'll tell you after," I whispered to Rocky. *I'll tell you after?* I sounded like a goody-goody. But I wanted Dr. Li to think well of me, especially on the first day. Rocky looked from me to Dr. Li and back to me again.

Right on cue, Dr. Li sighed loudly.

"I'm really sorry I was late," Rocky said to her. "My boss, she had me stay a teensy bit later, and—"

"Unless your hands have fallen off, it doesn't matter to me why you are late," said Dr. Li. "Even then, you should pick them up and bring them with you to class."

Everyone giggled at this except Rocky, who frowned into his lap. When he looked up, I gave him what I hoped was a sympathetic face. Then his mouth eased into a smile as if to say, *Just kidding. It's cool.*

"Musicians cannot afford to be late," Dr. Li continued. "You can all be studying something—anything—else, that's more *useful.* You could be studying law, or medicine. Or how to settle a dispute between countries, for all we know. Instead, you are choosing to dedicate yourselves to music. You've left your homes to be here for this. So you must give it everything you have, or you may as well not do it at all."

Across the room, Martyna's jaw hung slightly open.

"You may think this is a small thing, being on time for a class. But being on time means you have respect for each other, for your craft, and for me."

Martyna nodded furiously.

Dr. Li stood and opened her desk drawer. "I almost forgot." She opened her bag, took out her cell phone, and placed it in the drawer. "This will allow us to be fully present. You can have them back when I dismiss class."

Begrudgingly, we handed our phones over to her.

"Now," said Dr. Li, "I want to hear some Bach. Who's playing him?"

"I am," said Rocky.

"Try the ball." She slid off it gracefully and rolled it toward us.

Rocky stopped it with his hand. "I'd rather just use the bench, if that's okay? I've never, I mean, we've never—"

"You've never used it before? What were they teaching you last year?"

Rocky looked at me, then at Jenny.

"Never mind, that was rhetorical," Dr. Li said. "Just give it a try."

Rocky eased himself onto the ball, and Dr. Li stood and began tapping his shoulder while he sat, although he hadn't yet started playing. "You must feel the beat"—*tap, tap, tap*—"in your whole body. Try bouncing in rhythm with the beat."

Rocky moved his body, but he looked a little stiff, nothing like when I'd seen him on his skateboard, when he looked like he could do anything.

"On second thought, you are clearly not ready for the ball. Move to the bench," said Dr. Li.

Rocky carried the bench over to the Steinway and spent a few seconds lowering it because of his height. I had to do the opposite when I played. "Bach Partita in B-flat major. Prelude," he said, and then began playing: loud, triumphant, and as fast as he could go. Whenever we played too fast, Mr. Buck would say we were "pulling a Rocky Wong."

After only a few seconds, Dr. Li stood and said, "No, no, no. Stop."

We all looked at each other, as this had never happened before. Typically, we'd play something from memory, and then anyone who had a comment would make it, and Mr. Buck would say something—usually positive—about our playing, and that was it. Because usually, by the time you were ready to perform in studio class, you had the piece in your fingers pretty well already.

"You're not in the right state of mind," said Dr. Li. "That is clear even from the first few measures, which, to me, do not sound like Bach. Do you hear, in your mind, what those first few notes will sound like? Before you begin, do you imagine what your fingers will feel like on the keys? Right now, that is all that matters."

Rocky looked down at his hands.

"Breathe," said Dr. Li. "Hear the notes in your head."

On the bench, Rocky closed his eyes. He took a deep breath. Then he began to play. Dr. Li had been right: even with this small adjustment, the beginning already sounded better. The trills were less clunky, for one thing, and the melodic line had a little more sense of movement to it.

When he finished, Dr. Li said, "Stay there. And everyone else, be still. Think about what you have just heard."

We sat with our hands in our laps, eyes cast down to the floor, for a couple minutes. The only other time I had felt that quiet reverence among people was when I went to church with my parents, and in fact this was something like prayer, all of us sitting with our heads bowed, contemplating the same thing. But instead of thinking about the music, I was now dreading my own turn to play.

And then, reading from a sheet on her desk, Dr. Li said my name.

Our eyes met. I had been practicing a Beethoven sonata all summer, but now none of my practicing seemed adequate. I stood.

"Sit, Claire," said Dr. Li. "I'm not calling on you to play. I'm calling on you to critique."

"Oh," I said, settling back into my chair. My mind raced with musical vocabulary: voicing, articulation, dynamics. But talking about the piece in such technical terms seemed wrong after what Dr. Li had said. Still, that was the only way I knew how. "You did a really good job of bringing out the voices everywhere—upper and lower and middle," I said.

At this, Dr. Li looked down at the floor. She waved her hand in the air, as if to say, *Was that all?*

"Some of them came out in unexpected ways, which made the piece very interesting."

Her hand waved again, faster this time.

"And," I hazarded, "it was impressive how you could keep up the tempo for the entire piece, and the trills were great, too."

By instinct, I looked over at Jenny for help, but she just looked back at me.

"Something useful, Claire," said Dr. Li. "Every second that passes means you're forgetting what you've heard."

I felt my face grow hot. "Oh, right." I almost added *sorry,* but remembered that she didn't like apologies. I turned back to Rocky. "Something about the—the flow of the piece—"

"Yes, the shape of the piece," Dr. Li said. "Articulation is fine. Dynamics are there. But something is missing. What is it?" She looked at me.

"I'm not sure. Something about it sounds . . . rushed? But it's not like you need to slow down a lot. You just need to sound as if you actually *like* playing the piece?"

Dr. Li pursed her lips and regarded me. "If you could express things more assertively, you might be onto something."

I swallowed.

Dr. Li turned back to Rocky. "Claire is right. First, it's rushed. Second, frankly, it's boring."

From the corner of my eye, I saw Rocky flinch.

"Your interpretation lacks direction, character. You must play with more conviction of the mood you are trying to evoke. Imagine Bach playing this on a harpsichord. I didn't get a sense of personality in your playing just now."

Rocky nodded, but his eyes looked indifferent.

"Now, how about technique and tempo? Thoughts?" said Dr. Li.

"To be honest with you, Rock-o, your pedaling is wonky today," said JT.

Rocky shot him a look.

"Toward the middle," said Dr. Li, "you used pedal to cover up the weaker part. The pedal must be used like frosting. It doesn't hide a bad cake; it must only enhance a cake that has been made perfectly."

"Gotcha," said Rocky. "That was nerves, probably. I don't usually add so much pedal there."

No one said anything, but I could feel Dr. Li watching me. Then: "Claire," she said. "Say more."

Already, I knew Jenny and I would do impressions of Dr. Li later: *Say more.*

"I think, the part in the middle with the crescendo?" I said. "The notes of your right-hand chords aren't sounding completely together."

"They're very messy, in fact. While Rocky is perhaps overconfident in his playing, Claire lacks confidence in her listening."

No teacher had ever spoken to me like that before, especially not on the first day. I felt my stomach bottom out at the same time that I heard Jenny suck in her breath. She patted me on the back.

No one had ever spoken to Rocky like that before, either.

Dr. Li turned back to Rocky. "Your idea of this is quite good. But you need to respect the composer, not just play with the aim of showing off. If the audience can hear that you're showing off, they won't be very impressed, in the end. That's the very opposite of what you want to achieve."

Beside me, Jenny stiffened—trying not to laugh because Dr. Li clearly wasn't impressed with Rocky the way other teachers were. Mr. Buck had always praised Rocky, maybe even considered him a near prodigy, and I had always thought of him as the best pianist in the studio. Until now, I had never dared say anything critical about Rocky's playing.

"You have taste as well as talent, choosing this exquisite Bach partita. If you practice hard," Dr. Li continued, "your talent will soon be able to express your taste. This goes for all of you: Your talent can only grow in proportion to your ambition. Your ambition is expressed through how much you practice."

Rocky's face was stoic as he thanked Dr. Li and sat back down. After that, Martyna played the first movement of a Haydn sonata, and JT played a Barber excursion. Jenny and I would play next week, since we were short on time. I could tell Rocky was a little shaken. For the rest of class, he didn't participate as much as he usually did. But it was what Dr. Li said at the end that upset him most.

"One does not require a skateboard to get across this campus," she said. "You could injure a hand, wrist, or finger—or even an arm or shoulder, for that matter—and you'd be out of commission. A hand in a cast would set you back for college auditions, for the Student Showcase, everything."

Rocky scoffed. "But I won't injure myself. I mean, sure, everyone falls sometimes, but I haven't broken a bone since I was, like, eight. I've been skating for so long it's basically like walking—"

"Please don't talk back to me," said Dr. Li.

"Sorry, I didn't mean—"

"As long as you are in my studio, there is to be no more skateboarding. It is forbidden."

"What?" said Rocky, the word catching in his throat.

Dr. Li, however, seemed to consider the case closed. "Now," she said, "you should all be practicing on grands. I'm sure your fingers are growing lazy from those uprights. The action is completely different. Don't you ever get tired of practicing on such bad instruments?"

I had never thought of the pianos as bad. They were a little old, but it was nice just having a piano in a room for myself. At our house, the instrument competed with the laptop in the living room and the TV in the kitchen, where my mother listened to the news while cooking. In fact, my mother would be appalled if she heard anyone calling Greenwood pianos "bad." Both my parents loved to emphasize how extremely lucky I was to attend a school with such beautiful new facilities. And in truth, Greenwood pianos were better than what we had at home—which, even though it was a secondhand upright, the whole family regarded as the focal point of the living room.

Dr. Li continued, "Well, I'll do what we did at Juilliard, then. A sign-up sheet for all the rooms with grands on them. If you aren't in there practicing within five minutes of your time, you forfeit the room. The first slot will be at six, the last, from eight to ten at night."

"Six?" JT said. "In the morning?"

"You can achieve so much more in the morning, when your mind is clearer." Dr. Li smiled slightly, but she didn't look happy. "On another note, you're all working out, right?" she asked. "To build your stamina, and the strength in your arms and torso? Piano playing is very physical."

Jenny snorted, and I got the sense she wasn't sure if Dr. Li was joking. None of us said anything. At Greenwood, it was the dancers, the actors, and the Nineties Step Aerobics Club who exercised the most. We didn't have any sports teams. We didn't even have a mascot.

Then Martyna said, "I like basketball." She made an awkward

gesture with her right hand that looked as if she were tentatively petting a cat, which I realized was meant to be dribbling.

"Also an unwise choice for a pianist," Dr. Li said.

"Sometimes I do yoga," JT said. I knew that "sometimes" meant once.

Rocky, who probably exercised the most out of all of us because of his skating, was looking smug, like, *Well? What do you want from me?*

I had called it "skateboarding" once, and he'd corrected me, saying that skaters never called it that.

"So, more practice on the grands, and more exercise. Any questions before I let you all go?" said Dr. Li.

Jenny raised her hand. "We were just wondering . . ."

"Yes?"

"We were wondering where you were on Friday."

Dr. Li crossed one leg over the other. "Friday?"

"The assembly," Martyna said.

"Ah. I do remember now, receiving an email about that. But I didn't think it was actually required. I assumed it was just a formality."

"I wish that was true," Jenny said.

"Those things can be such BS. Don't you think so? You all went?" Dr. Li asked.

"Total BS," said Rocky, enjoying her use of the phrase.

"Slept right through it," JT lied.

"Not me," said Martyna. "It's tradition."

"Newbie," Jenny said under her breath. "Just you wait."

"It's just," I heard myself saying. I could feel Jenny turn to look at me, since I didn't speak up in class very much, but something about what Dr. Li had said had struck a nerve, as if she thought Greenwood traditions were beneath her. "The faculty . . . they go up to the stage and tell us what they're going to do during the year, and we talk about, you know, our commitment to Greenwood, and Greenwood's commitment to us. It's a school spirit thing."

Across the room, Martyna was nodding vigorously.

"School spirit," Dr. Li repeated. "This is interesting to you?"

Suddenly it sounded very uncool.

"It gives us an idea of the collective misery that is to come. Announces that summer frolicking is over," said JT.

"I suppose," Dr. Li said slowly, "I suppose you find this idea appealing. The idea that you're all 'connected through the arts.'" She made quotes with her fingers. "Or that you're all part of some team." She paused. "But you must know, the artist is alone."

When I looked at Rocky, his face said, *Told you so.*

"Art requires solitude, sacrifice. At the end of the day, it's just you and the instrument. When I was your age, I didn't go to a school where all my friends played music. In fact, I didn't have many friends at all. I'd come home from school and go immediately to the piano to practice."

We all shifted in our seats, not knowing how to respond to that.

Dr. Li dismissed us and we all collected our phones. Rocky and JT walked out with their heads bent over texts. I thought about trying to catch up with Rocky so we could walk together, but after all that had transpired, he probably wasn't even thinking about talking with me anymore.

Then something about Jenny caught Dr. Li's eye. She gestured to Jenny's hand. "What's this?" she asked. "Is this for an event or something?" Before Jenny could respond, Dr. Li said, "Pianists should not paint their fingernails. It looks unprofessional. Besides, chemicals from the polish can get into your skin."

"I've never heard that in all my life," said Jenny. But the next day, the nail polish was gone.

Chapter 4

I SAW DR. LI AROUND CAMPUS ON THE WEEKENDS. I WOULD have said hello to any other teacher, but she walked right by me and kept going with barely a nod. It didn't bother me. If anything, it made me feel that an understanding had passed between us. Her relationship with us was only at the piano. That was what mattered: it was important and perhaps even sacred. On Saturday afternoon, as I rounded a corner in the fourth-floor library stacks, I almost crashed right into her. She wore berry-colored lipstick, and her long, tapered fingers held a hardback book called *Bach: From Eisenach to Leipzig.*

I myself held part of this Bach series in my hand, but I knew I wouldn't read it until the week our music history term paper was due.

"I was wondering where the first volume was," she said, eyeing my copy. "It's fascinating, isn't it? Religious faith often influenced the great composers more than we know."

"Fascinating," I said, kicking myself for parroting her.

"I'm glad you're reading about Bach. He is the father of all western music and, more important, can teach us a spiritual reason to love music. For him, it was all about making music that worshiped God, reflected God, glorified God." She smiled. "It's inspiring, even if one doesn't believe in the Lutheran God that Bach believed in."

She made as if to continue walking, then said, "Make sure to take wide turns in the library. We nearly collided just now."

♩♫

"Do you ever talk to Dr. Li, like, outside of class?" I asked the pianists at dinner.

Jenny squinted at me. "Oh no. She says all these abstract, vaguely pretty things about piano and you're falling for her inspiration porn." Jenny put a hand on mine. "Don't do it, Claire. Don't let her worm her way into your brain."

"She's not abstract," I said. "She's wise. And she has such interesting things to say about music."

But Rocky shook his head. "Jenny's right. Li is frustrating as hell, Wu! She wants all of us to exercise, but no skating or sports. She doesn't want us to apologize, but she also doesn't want us to talk back. So how am I supposed to behave around her? At least other teachers are consistent."

But when Dr. Li called on me in studio class, it was like she was testing me. She must have sensed my discomfort in critiquing Rocky, who was a better pianist than me by far—easily the best in the studio—but she pushed me to do it anyway. Other teachers didn't hold me to that standard; they just let me raise my hand when I felt ready—or let me sit quietly if I never raised my hand. They didn't poke and prod, asking me to say more. But with Dr. Li, things were different.

I lay in bed that night and thought about my spiritual reason for loving music, if there was one. Once, my mother and I saw Emanuel Ax play Chopin in Atlanta, and I felt more worshipful than I ever did in church. Leaning forward in my seat, I was listening so hard I forgot to breathe, and everyone in the audience seemed to be doing the same. At rare times, when I was practicing, all the work was transformed into a sound so lovely I felt I was hearing something from God himself. Sometimes it felt like music *was* God. It was everywhere, and it could make me feel low or loved, could break me down and lift me up.

I took the 6:00 a.m. practice time slot. I wanted to know what it was that she described: "the cool morning air, warming up as you practiced, with no one to disturb you." When I quoted this back to Rocky, almost word for word, he told me that she was just ripping off Hemingway and, for that reason alone, I shouldn't try so hard to please her. "Just come to me whenever you need a Dr. Li BS detector," he said.

♩♫

At the beginning of my first lesson with Dr. Li, she ushered me into her studio eagerly.

"Come in, come in," she said. "We need to get to work. I've

noticed a studio-wide problem." She paused. "At least I *think* it's a studio-wide problem, but maybe you'll prove me wrong today. What might it be?"

"Uh," I said, "we're not practicing . . . enough?"

She frowned. "Of course that's true, but that's not what I'm talking about. Your technique. It's mediocre at best. Scales, arpeggios, chords: Have you been practicing these?"

I said I always warmed up with scales. She said, "Prove it." She rolled the red yoga ball toward me. I balanced myself on it, trying to find my center of gravity, an angle that would allow me to sit on it without thinking too much about it. Only my toes touched the floor. She set her metronome at one hundred beats per minute, which didn't seem that fast to me. "Start at C major."

She had me play four octaves up and back down again, landing a third below the key, on the relative minor, switching keys without ever lifting my hands from the keyboard. Starting with C, I ended up on A and played an A-minor scale; that led to F, so I played an F-major scale, which took me three notes down to D, for D minor, and so forth. It did not start off well. For one thing, I had never played while sitting on something bouncy, and I was preoccupied with making sure I didn't fall. For another, I wasn't used to playing scales without stopping to give my arms a break. My arms were so tight that my left hand started lagging behind my right. By the time I got to B-flat major, I had completely fallen apart. I apologized and said I would start over.

"That's fine," she said. "Frankly, you don't sound good." As if to emphasize her point, she reached over and turned the metronome all the way down to only sixty beats per minute. "Looks like we'll have to go back to the basics. Miles and miles of scales." The way she said "back to the basics" reminded me of how my mother sometimes tried to use slang that I taught her, but it often came out sounding unnatural. "You're not going to be ready for Student Showcase if you can't even play these," said Dr. Li.

Showcase wasn't until February.

"Do it again. From C major," she said. "With your right hand only. Your wrist is like a fish that's just been caught. Keep it still, but keep your body bouncing."

My scale, it turned out, was even worse than mediocre. It was supposed to come out in a cascade of sound, but instead it was wobbly and stilted. I couldn't seem to get my body in time with the music. I felt my face grow hot as I played, stopping and starting again.

"Stop *thinking* about playing, Claire, and *feel* the rhythm in your body," said Dr. Li. As she had with Rocky, she tapped on my shoulder. "In rhythm—one, two, three, four!"

And then, I wasn't sure how it happened, but somehow it did: my scale sounded much better, in time with my bouncing on the ball. It wasn't anything that I was doing consciously, but an instinct I didn't even have to think about anymore, as natural as breathing. Even though the metronome was ticking, Dr. Li beat out the pulse by clapping. When it was over and I ended up back at C, she sank into her chair as if *she'd* been the one playing.

"See?" she said. "Sometimes it takes that much work to improve even a little." She eyed the clock. "We've been here for nearly twenty minutes and all you've done is play a scale with your right hand, at the pace of your Chopin nocturne."

I winced. If she had been my mother, I would have said, *Thanks for rubbing it in.* Instead, I said, "Time for the left hand now, I guess."

I thought I saw her hold back a smile.

"Claire, if you keep it up, you can go pretty far. Your peers may be more talented, but you'll do well because you're not afraid. You become a different person at the piano. The way you handled being on the ball just now, for example. Other students have tried it and they didn't do as well."

I'd really only done well because I was curious, and because I wanted more than anything for Dr. Li to like me. But I said I knew what she meant, because what she was saying sounded much better in spite of being called less talented.

"You're a junior, is that right? Have you thought about where you'll audition for college?"

"I'm not sure yet. Maybe North Carolina School of the Arts." Jenny and I had talked about going there together.

She shook her head. "You should get out of the South. The place where you've grown up can be stifling."

I nodded. "I guess that's true."

"You don't have to agree with everything I say. They're just suggestions. If you like it here, stay. If not, no one's stopping you from leaving."

I sighed. Rocky was right when he'd mentioned that she could be sort of frustrating. "Was it stifling for *you*?" I asked.

Dr. Li smiled, the type of smile that meant I had overstepped my bounds. "Was it stifling for me? Taiwan is a small island. What do you think?"

Then it was my turn to smile awkwardly.

"What about New England Conservatory?" I asked. I didn't know that much about it, but I liked picturing myself walking to classes in the snow.

"Ah, now you're thinking." She nodded. "You'll need some gloves."

"And probably a lot more than that."

"I don't mean for the cold, although that is also the case. I'll tell you a secret."

She shifted in the chair, and I felt myself lean toward her slightly, wondering if this was going to be a juicy secret, or the type of thing that adults only *thought* was really interesting to us.

"The week before my Juilliard audition," she said, "I would wake myself up in the middle of the night—two, three in the morning—and run my entire audition program from beginning to end, from memory, with gloves on. That way, I could be absolutely sure that, if anything happened—say, I caught a cold, or I was jet-lagged—I could still play it perfectly."

This wasn't prime gossip, but it wasn't a boring secret, either. I imagined her waking up this way in the dead of night. What kind of person, what kind of teenager, would do that? Would I ever do that?

"I used the soft pedal to keep it down, but my parents hated it, of course. Especially my father. He didn't take my playing seriously and just truly did not know what to make of a daughter who was aspiring to be a concert pianist."

"That sounds rough," I said.

Dr. Li waved her hand as if to say it wasn't anything. "You

know what I want you to do, which I think will be quite good for you? Accompanying. I'll ask Mr. Yanko if you can play for the ballet rehearsals."

"Don't we already have a staff pianist?" Greenwood always hired a local accompanist for the ballet rehearsals.

"Oh, I don't think we need to do that this semester. Why go through the trouble when we have so many capable pianists here?" When she said that, I felt like she was poking fun at me—and the other pianists—a little.

"Well—" I began. I had accompanied vocalists before, but I wasn't very good at sight-reading. I also wondered if Dr. Li would be able to convince Dr. Hamilton to let a piano student take the job.

"The pay isn't very much, for all the extra practicing you'll have to do, but it would be a very good opportunity for you. And a privilege." Already she was up and scanning her bookshelves. "What's more, you'll get to play at the dance performance in November. This is exciting, Claire. It's rare for a pianist to play together with the orchestra, especially for a ballet performance." She didn't wait for me to respond. "They're doing the Movements for Piano and Orchestra by Stravinsky. Very short pieces. And an excerpt from *Sleeping Beauty*, which shouldn't be too hard, and for the pas de deux, the gorgeous *Andante* from Tchaikovsky's second piano concerto." She pulled a score down from the shelf and began thumbing through it. "Yes, this should be quite manageable." I glimpsed a smattering of sixteenth notes and chromatic passages. It didn't seem manageable at all.

"You'll play the piano part during rehearsals," she explained, "and then at the dance performance, the Greenwood orchestra will play with you. You'll be very important." She looked at me then, and again I got the sense that she was teasing me, but I couldn't be sure.

I smiled back as if to say I was in on the joke.

"At first," she said, "you'll feel like you're flying by the seat of your pants, trying to keep up with all the stops and starts. If you're wrong, everyone notices. Your job is to be invisible but perfect. When you know the music enough to listen to yourself, you'll make necessary changes to suit the dancers—changes so subtle they won't hear the difference, but they'll feel it. After this, you'll be able to play any gig you want. Weddings, funerals, even operas."

She held the stack of sheet music out to me.

I peered down at it, wondering if it was too late now to say no, this was a mistake, there was no way I was going to be able to do this—when she reached over and slid the music into my bag.

I gaped at her.

"Don't look so anxious, Claire. Trust me, you're ready for this. It's going to be good for you."

"I don't know—" I began.

"You'll learn it just as you'd learn any music, and then Mr. Yanko will tell you what to do."

It was always sort of funny when teachers used their titles to refer to each other. *Mr. Yanko* instead of *Paul.*

"Thank you so much, Dr. Li," I said. What else could I say? "I'll do my best."

"Okay," she said, and turned back to the piano to get ready for the next student.

I hesitated. My mother often said "okay" when people thanked her, instead of "you're welcome" or "no problem." She even said "okay" when cashiers told her to have a nice day.

Dr. Li turned around again. "Students should thank their teachers. But you and Rocky are the only ones who do. Maybe because you're Chinese. We're grateful people. It's in our blood."

Rocky thanked her? Even though she annoyed him? That didn't sound like Rocky to me.

None of my teachers had ever mentioned my race. Usually, being Chinese was something I tucked away until I was filling out a form, or eating at the Lunar New Year celebration in the dining hall, complete with Greenwood chopsticks and fried chicken with a sticky orange glaze. I wanted to ask what it was like for Dr. Li, being Asian in Green Valley. I wanted to ask if people stared at her when she went grocery shopping, if they stopped her on the street to ask her to join the Korean Presbyterian church. That had happened to me twice. But she had already turned back to the piano.

♩♫

At my next lesson, Dr. Li offered to meet me sometime in the dorm before six, so she could give me the key to her studio. "That way you can practice on the best pianos," she'd said.

I told Rocky about it as we were refilling our water bottles between practice sessions.

"Oh my god, Wu, she's going to make you get up even earlier? Why doesn't she just leave the key in your mailbox? I swear, she's trying to test you, or groom you, or something."

"Do you have to be so suspicious? She just wants us to be serious about music."

"I'm *damn* serious about music!" Rocky said.

"Yeah you are, Rock-o!" someone yelled from the instrument lockers down the hall.

"I just don't need a micromanaging teacher breathing down my neck," he continued. "And neither do you. You're a baby junior who'll do anything to please a teacher."

"No I won't!" I said, simultaneously appalled that Rocky was calling me a "baby junior," and sort of flattered that he was trying to take me under his wing—or was pretending to, anyway. "I think Dr. Li cares about us a lot. I don't want to let her down."

"Doesn't seem that caring to me," Rocky muttered.

I decided I wouldn't tell Rocky about the accompanying yet—he was already worked up enough as it was. "Anyway, why don't *you* take the early morning practice session?"

"Because," he said, "I stay up way too late playing *Animal Crossing*."

I looked at him, surprised. I didn't know Rocky played video games, much less one that was so . . . adorable.

"Don't judge," he said. "Almost everyone in the Society plays. And I'm going to stop soon, but for now it's an escape from the *C* word."

I raised my eyebrows.

Rocky threw his hands up. "College!"

How did he manage to look so cute even when he was stressed? "Any music school would want you, though."

"That's nice of you to say, but I'll only get to go if I'm on scholarship, Wu. Or some sort of financial aid. I'm going to *try* for all the big names: Eastman, Peabody, Colburn, Juilliard. But what if I don't get in *anywhere*? I'll be a failure. Especially since I could have stayed in Atlanta to work at the restaurant, then gone to college and majored in pre-med or whatever."

"Now you're getting ahead of yourself," I said. "You're working really hard. I'm sure you'll make it into *one* of the big ones, at the very least."

Rocky shook his head. "You know how your parents are always like, 'We gave up everything for you'? My mom seriously gave up everything. Ever since my dad left, she . . ." His voice trailed off.

"She what?" I said.

"She's been so *alone*. Her family's in Taiwan, I'm hours away, and she's always working at the restaurant—it's kind of incredible, actually, how she started out as a server and now she's a manager. But also it just really sucks. I at least have to make this count for something. If I don't make it, then what was the point of me coming here? She sure as shit doesn't want me to turn out like her, having to work in a kitchen twenty-four seven. You know, most of her paychecks went toward my lessons."

I felt for Rocky. He put more pressure on himself than anyone else at Greenwood. "You're doing your best," I said gently. "That's all your mom wants you to do. You can't control what happens outside of practicing."

"I guess," said Rocky, but he didn't look convinced.

"You'll make it," I said. "Those lessons won't go to waste." And I really meant it. Based on the difficulty of Rocky's repertoire alone, he probably had a better chance of making it big than any of us.

"Thanks, Wu," he said. For a second, I wondered if we were going to hug—but that would've been ridiculous. All we'd done was have a conversation in the hallway, which people did all the time. Rocky tapped his water bottle to mine. "Drink up," he said. "We musicians need to stay hydrated."

Chapter 5

I ARRIVED EARLY TO MY FIRST DANCE REHEARSAL SO I COULD warm up. Although I'd practiced for several hours over the weekend, it didn't seem like enough. As I ran through some of the more difficult parts, the dancers began to appear, also early, some of them chatting with each other and some of them all business. None of them paid any attention to me. They stretched into impossible contortions on the floor or pulled one foot up in the air while the other hand rested on the barre. The dance studio smelled like sweat, and floor-to-ceiling mirrors covered two entire walls. A slight wetness clung to the air, making the piano sound tinny and sharp.

"So how did she pick you?" a voice above me said.

I looked up, my fingers still pressed into an A-flat major chord, to see Adeline Felts—who people called Toothpick because she was so slender. She wore an American Ballet Theatre sweatshirt over her white dance tights, a headband sweeping her bangs off her face. "Are you, like, the best pianist here or something?"

I knew I wasn't, not by a long shot. As far as I knew, it was just a favor Dr. Li had done because I happened to be in her studio when she thought of it. But what if Dr. Li saw something in me that wasn't actually there? Or what if she'd offered it to every other pianist and they had all turned it down? I looked at Toothpick and shook my head. "I don't know how she picked me."

Toothpick frowned. I had no gossip, no insight into a new teacher. Before I had a chance to say anything more, Mr. Yanko strode to the center of the room.

"Morning, dancers! I want to see more limbs stretching and fewer mouths moving." He wore loose black pants, a white T-shirt, and thin-soled, stretchy black shoes.

Mr. Yanko approached the piano. He walked with elegant posture, his chest erect and his neck held high, his toes pointing out. "Claire, hello. I'm glad you've agreed to do this. This should be fun. All you really have to do is get used to these dancers jumping around as you play." He said they were all glad to have me, which didn't seem true since none of the dancers had spoken to me except for Toothpick.

Up close, Mr. Yanko's face looked a bit crooked. One of his eyelids hung lower over one eye and there were lines around one side of his mouth. I'd heard some people making fun of him, screwing up their faces to look like his. There was no way to hide a face, and I felt bad for him but was also impressed: in spite of it, he was a dancer and it seemed like his students respected him.

As the dancers warmed up, Yanko alternated between watching from one corner of the room, taking in the whole scene, and zeroing in on just one dancer, scrutinizing her every turn, or telling another his turnout could be stronger. Even though I knew nothing about dance, it was clear that Adeline Felts and Scott Dessen were a cut above the rest. Yanko pushed them harder: he adjusted Scott's arm a quarter of an inch, a change so tiny that I thought surely not even a dancer would be able to tell.

"You have to be responsible for yourself," Yanko told the room. "I want you to dance with conviction, not waiting for me to correct you, so that when you leave this place, you'll know what to do." Yanko told them he knew they had it in them, but that they couldn't be afraid of failure: failure was inevitable, necessary. Every single dancer they loved had failed several times.

"And please welcome Claire, our new accompanist," he said. "Let's be patient and gracious as she adjusts to her new role."

A few of the dancers looked over at me. Behind the piano, I sat and waited, trying to look casual while inside, I was alert and anxious.

"Let's start with *Sleeping Beauty*, from the top," Yanko said.

I sighed with relief. *Sleeping Beauty* was slower and I could play it pretty well.

All at once, everyone took off their layers and dropped them on the floor along the wall. Toothpick peeled off her sweatshirt, revealing the winged bones that poked out of her upper back, the muscles in her arms expanding and tightening.

"All right, Claire. This tempo, okay?" Yanko said, and tapped out a beat.

"Got it."

Yanko turned to the dancers. "Places. And five, six, seven, eight . . ."

I began to play. It was—not great, but at least okay, especially with Yanko clapping his hands to mark the beat. I wanted to watch the dancing, but it was enough work already to look up from the keyboard to the music and down again, and turn the pages in time. So instead I kept my eyes on the music and tried to play a steady beat, which Dr. Li had said was the most important thing to do when playing for dancers. When we finished with the first piece, Mr. Yanko didn't tell me whether my performance was good or bad, but simply nodded at me. I remembered what Dr. Li had said about being invisible and hoped this meant I'd done well.

Then Scott Dessen and Adeline Felts began the pas de deux. They approached the center from opposite ends, and then they embraced: Scott's hands on Adeline's waist, hers around his neck.

"Cut, cut, cut," Yanko called. "What's going on here? You guys should not be afraid to touch each other. You're supposed to be in love, remember? Start again. And, Claire? Faster."

Adeline scowled. She and Scott must have broken up recently, again.

Scott stood to the side, waiting for the music to begin. But after I started playing, he hesitated, beginning just after the chords. "Was that my cue, or . . . ? Sorry." He looked at me sheepishly. "I suck at hearing the right notes sometimes."

It wasn't their fault; it was mine. There were so many jumps at the keyboard for my hands to find, I couldn't keep up. Guiltily, desperately, I was doing what Dr. Li called "ketchup playing." You drowned foods in ketchup because it would cover up how bland or bad they were. I used the pedal liberally and left out the notes of chords, but even so, wrong notes came through, and Scott and Toothpick moved hesitantly, confused and second-guessing themselves.

"No, stay in tempo!" Mr. Yanko said, and clapped his hands to the beat. To me, he said, "If you make a mistake, don't correct it. Keep going. The important thing is to stay in tempo."

I did as I was told. But my hands scrambled to find their chords, or worse, froze for half a second over the keys, so for a beat there was no sound at all. I tried to make up for it by being on time for the next measure. Yanko called Scott and Toothpick to stop again.

"We're going so slow. And the music is off, again," Toothpick grumbled while still performing a perfectly executed turn.

I was starting to sweat from humiliation. It wasn't the same as playing for the vocalists; I hadn't accounted for the dancers leaping around me as my eyes darted up to the score and down to my hands again.

I started again, but I couldn't keep tempo. Scott kept dancing, moving along confidently while I floundered my way through the music. Toothpick joined him, but from the corner of my eye, I saw she was glaring at me.

Finally, after half a page, Toothpick put her hands on her hips. "We have to start over," she said. "Was I off," she said from across the room, "or was it the music?"

The room fell silent. My stomach curled itself into a ball, and I felt a pinprick of desperation start its way up my throat. I had never felt so disliked, so incompetent. What made it worse—I couldn't help thinking—was that I was the only Asian in the room, and I wasn't living up to what people expected. I remembered what my mother often said: that I had to perform twice as well because everyone already expected Asians to be good at piano.

I took a deep breath. "I can start again," I said.

Toothpick threw one foot up onto the barre, her eyes narrowed.

Mr. Yanko sighed. "You all stretch," he said. He came over to where I was sitting. "The pianist should always be able to pick up again. You should know the music well enough so that, if you sense you're off, you can jump to the correct measure."

"I'm really sorry," I said. "I'm not good at this."

"But you can be," he said, which only made me feel worse. "You're new. Things will be better next week."

Afterward, the dancers went to their gym bags against the wall. They gossiped and chatted as they put their sweatshirts and leg warmers on again.

As she walked past, I heard Toothpick saying, "I know, I had high hopes for her, too. I thought it was cool we were getting a student pianist instead of an old *staff* pianist."

"Will you shut up?" said Scott. "You don't have to talk about her like she can't hear you." He looked at me.

"Fine," said Toothpick. To me, she said, "You better get it right before the actual performance."

♩♫

That night, after dinner, I headed to the practice rooms. I played through the difficult parts of the accompaniment slowly, trying and trying to get them up to speed. I pictured the dancers leaping as I played, Mr. Yanko clapping out the tempo. After that, I practiced the repertoire I was learning with Dr. Li: the Beethoven sonata and Chopin nocturne and all the different finger exercises she had us do. The ascending and descending thirds, the alternating fourth and fifth fingers, and the strangest one, where I closed the piano and played arpeggios on the lid. Dr. Li claimed it would strengthen my fingers. (When she had demonstrated, her fingers had sounded as loud as a knock on the door.) I ended the session by playing the *Sleeping Beauty* excerpt once more, just to be sure. In the middle of the practice session, my mother called, and I told her—again—all about Dr. Li. I left out the part about struggling at dance rehearsal. She and my father were so pleased with my new "role model"—and they especially liked that she was Chinese.

When I'd been playing for so long that it was getting hard to concentrate, I packed up my things. Just as I opened the door, a piece of paper fluttered to the ground. I picked it up, meaning to throw it away, when I thought I saw my name on it.

GIVE IT A REST, CLAIRE.
YOU DON'T NEED TO WORSHIP HER.

I felt a chill run through my whole body, my stomach churning. The note had been directly addressed to *me*. I studied my name on the paper: The *C* was bigger than the other letters. The *L, A,* and the *I* were connected, as if the writer hadn't lifted the pen between them, and the tail of the *R* led to the *E*. Whoever had written this had been watching me, listening in, overhearing things. Maybe they had been standing right outside the door when I practiced and talked to my mother. Maybe they had overheard my conversations with the other pianists. Maybe they'd heard my lessons, heard me cave even when I didn't want to be an accompanist. I shivered, feeling goose bumps form on my arms. The note had been written on college-ruled notebook paper. I didn't recognize the handwriting—we typed almost everything these days—which was in all caps and slanted slightly left. I couldn't shake the feeling that I'd been caught, somehow.

I pictured envelopes with erasure poetry spelling out creepy messages, magazine cutouts, my name in neon marker, smiley face stamps. The phone ringing in the middle of the night. I remembered a show that Jenny liked, *True Stalkers*. It asserted that most stalkers were angry at their victims, felt rejected by them. But who at Greenwood felt that way toward me?

I couldn't think of anyone at all.

What if the writer was still nearby? What if they were watching me at this very second? I could feel my heart racing in my chest. I wanted to go back to my room, be in the same place as Jenny, maybe even call Jenny now and ask her to come to the music building and walk with me. But that was ridiculous. Or was it?

My feet felt immobile, pinned to the floor. By instinct I took out my phone. My hands were shaking as I looked up the Greenwood directory. There was a campus hotline you could call; a police officer would show up immediately. But what good would that do? The note writer wasn't here. The police would just make a record of the note—if that—and I could do that myself. Or maybe they would just dismiss it as some harmless high school prank. Or maybe you were only supposed to call them if you were in a true emergency, like if you were under attack.

My fingers hovered over the number.

Then I forced myself to take five deep breaths, reminding myself that right now, the only thing that had happened was that I'd picked up a creepy note. On Student Wellness Day last spring, our school counselor Ms. Shelley had taught us that you could trick your body into thinking everything was okay. You could picture a bright red stop sign and bring the spiraling thoughts to a stop. I tried that now, but it didn't work: I saw the stop sign, but all I could think about was the note, which I was still holding.

I forced myself to walk toward the stairs. I peeked into other rooms, grateful to not be alone in the building. Craig Meyers was packing up his violin, and he waved at me through the window. None of the pianists were around: Jenny was in the dorm, getting her hair cut by JT, and Martyna went to bed early and wouldn't have risked being out of the dorm this late anyway. Rocky was finishing a shift at the MapleMart—earlier, I'd heard him beating himself up about how he'd overcommitted. The hallway was so silent that the lights were off until I started up the stairs.

Outside, even though I knew it looked silly, I broke into a run. My heart was still pounding. In the dorm, I didn't wait for the elevator, just sprinted upstairs, still clutching the note. It was getting sweaty between my fingers.

When I got to our room, I tried to breathe. Before I could get any words out, I opened the door and locked it behind me.

"Whoa, what's up?" said Jenny. "Are you okay? Claire, you're white as a sheet."

I touched my face. My forehead was damp. I thrust the note at Jenny. "Read this, just read it."

Jenny scanned the message, her eyebrows furrowed.

"Who is *her*?" she said.

Then we both looked at each other and said, "Dr. Li."

Jenny threw an arm around me, rubbing my shoulder. "This is so dumb. It's just a piece of paper. You don't need to let it get to you."

"It—it has my name on it. Someone's, like, watching me!"

Jenny filled my water bottle and I took a few gulps, then sank onto my bed.

"Whoever wrote this is *trying* to freak you out, but what can they really do?" She took the note, tore it into four neat pieces, and dropped it into our recycling bin. "See? It's already trash."

Then Jenny had me list everyone who was in the basement when I was practicing, but I could only name Craig. She pursed her lips. "Well, it's not him, obviously." She paused. "The way those dancers talk about Li, it could have been one of them. You know who it has to be? Toothpick, trying to get under your skin."

"But isn't her handwriting all cute and bubbly?"

"Duh, she can disguise her handwriting."

"She would go through the trouble? Isn't she too busy to come find me in the music building and stick a note in the door?"

"You have no idea how weird and mean dancers can be. She's clearly trying to mess with you, make you lose focus so you won't be able to play."

I turned this over in my mind. It seemed a pretty cruel trick to try to make me fail as an accompanist when it was only going to hurt her and the other dancers, too. I wasn't about to mention that to Jenny, who was so convinced of her theory and loved finding any excuse to bash the dancers. Well, Toothpick *was* mean; she'd once used her roommate's underpants to decorate the rec room.

Just then, I remembered how at rehearsal, Toothpick had asked how "she" had picked me.

"Toothpick doesn't want to see you succeed. But you're not going to give her that," Jenny said.

Later, I fished out the paper, taped it together, and stuck it in the top drawer of my desk. If someone was stalking me, I wanted to have proof.

♩♫

The second rehearsal didn't go much better, and I had no excuse this time because I'd had the music for over two weeks. Toothpick sent more looks my way. Looks of impatience and disappointment, as if she was saying, *I prepared for this class, why didn't you do your part?* I thought of the note and wondered if she really was behind it. *Give it a rest, Claire.*

After class, Yanko crouched down beside me. "Accompanists need to be ready. This is our rehearsal, not yours. I don't mean that harshly, Claire."

I nodded. A knot formed in my stomach, and I took a deep breath to fight my tears.

"I know Dr. Li chose you for this position, which means she

must believe you're the right one for it. But I simply cannot waste any more time with my dancers. The fall dance performance is in a couple months. You must have the music ready for us to practice, or we'll have to ask another pianist." He didn't mention that I was getting paid, but I felt ashamed about that, too.

I nodded, then looked down at the keys. The white keys had yellowed considerably. They saved the best and newest pianos for the practice rooms.

When I returned to our room that afternoon, there was a note in hot-pink dry-erase marker on the whiteboard on our door.

REHEARSAL SHOULDN'T BE SOMETHING
THAT MAKES YOU CRY.

I rubbed it off before anyone else could see it. Everyone knew that hot pink was Toothpick's color.

Chapter 6

THAT FALL, ROCKY PRACTICED HIS SKATEBOARD TRICKS AT night, under the lights that beamed on the empty faculty lot. In the quiet after classes, without Dr. Li around to catch him, he glided over the pavement. I heard the wheels rushing against concrete, the soft click of the board as it left the ground. I thought that if Dr. Li could see Rocky as he flipped his skateboard in one fluid motion, she'd see that skating was as much an art as ballet or opera; it involved rhythm, timing, accuracy, efficiency, and practice: the same things we thought about as pianists.

In any case, ever since Dr. Li had banned skating, Rocky had not stopped. He was just skating at different times. Every night he was there, going back and forth across the lot. A couple days after the second rehearsal, I stopped to chat with him on the way to the dorms. He was practicing a dark slide—flipping the board, landing on it wheels side up, and then flipping it again—and had already fallen twice, throwing his hands up to protect his head, swearing under his breath.

"You're out late," I said.

"It gives me a rush to burst in the dorms right before ten."

"Right *at* ten, more like."

Rocky was on the far side of the lot now, his body a silhouette against the trees at the main entrance of campus. "I need to tire myself out," he said, coming toward me again. "It takes me forever to fall asleep, and I don't like being alone with my thoughts."

"That sucks," I said.

He shrugged. "You'll probably feel the same way when you're a senior."

"What are you thinking about before bed?" I asked, which sounded way more personal than I'd meant it to be, but Rocky was already skating away again, pretending not to have heard me—or maybe he truly hadn't.

"So I've started soaking my fingers in orange juice at night. Makes them stronger," he said.

"Wait, have you really? Or are you just saying that so I'll try it and look like an idiot? Is this orange juice sforzando?"

Last year, Rocky had invented what he called chocolate sforzando. In the dorm kitchen, he melted down Hershey's milk chocolate bars in the microwave, then stirred in Pop Rocks (strawberry was best, he said, but any kind worked). Then he poured the mixture onto a baking sheet in the dorm kitchen and refrigerated it. He cut it into neat squares and wrapped each bar in stiff brown paper, tying them with twine that he got from the visual arts department. Repackaged, they looked exactly like the local chocolate bars at the Silver Spoon. Rocky would offer them to people, who took them gratefully until they yelped and said the chocolate was exploding in their mouths.

"I'm serious, Wu. Pour some juice in a contact lenses case and stick your fourth and fifth fingers in for a few minutes each night. No pulp. The brand doesn't matter, but no pulp."

Half a year ago, it was the sort of thing I would have tried just to have more to talk about with Rocky, but now I was skeptical. I tried to picture Dr. Li soaking *her* weakest fingers (were any of them weak?) in orange juice, but the image that came up instead was of her resting her fingers in a bowl of warm, soapy water, about to get a manicure because her hands were so often photographed. Of course, she wouldn't get her nails painted, just cleaned and filed and massaged.

Now Rocky skated toward me with his hands stretched out in front of him, showing me his fingers up close. I'd seen them several times because we had been piano ensemble partners last spring, practicing Dvořák music for four hands, sitting side by side on the bench twice a week for rehearsals and lessons. His hands didn't look any different to me now. They were scraped and scabbed in places from skating and from working in the restaurant with his mother. Rocky told me he had washed dishes there after school before coming to Greenwood.

"Anyway," Rocky continued, "since you're so clearly fascinated by my finger-strengthening methods—"

"I started accompanying the ballet studio," I blurted out. I'd been wanting to talk with someone about it, someone besides Jenny. "I suck at it. Toothpick hates me and I can't get the music down and I don't want to disappoint Dr. Li."

Rocky skated away from me again, but I could tell he was thinking. With an elegant turn on the curb, he skated toward me again, and when I saw his face, I knew that I'd made a mistake.

"She gave the gig to you?" he said. "I thought she was going to let *me* play Stravinsky. She knows I could use the money."

He came to a smooth stop beside me, waiting for my response.

"She didn't *give* it to me so much as gently coerce me," I said.

"Hmm," said Rocky. "Is that a healthy relationship? Great word, by the way."

"Well, look," I continued, "we could divide the music—and the money—between us. That would be a relief, actually."

He studied me, then shook his head. "She picked you for it, so clearly she wants you to do it, for some mysterious reason." Then, softening, "You got this, Wu. You just have to sit and suffer for a while and then you'll get the notes. Besides, she's been saying I work too much and need to concentrate on school. Although she's so hard on my playing that it's like, do you want me to concentrate on school or piano? Because I can't handle both."

"You seem to be handling it fine," I said.

And it was true: since he used to be the pianist at his mother's church, sight-reading new hymns every Sunday, Rocky knew how to practice more efficiently than any of us. In classes, he knew more than we did. In his mother's restaurant, he'd learned Spanish from the dishwashers and chemistry from the chefs, history and government from the regular customers whose heated political conversations he overheard. He appeared to coast through school and music, even though, on top of everything, he was one of the few Greenies who worked during the school year. But Jenny said that this picture of effortlessness was just another part of Rocky's facade, a personality he cultivated, a performance. He did work hard—he just acted like he didn't. And that, she said, was Rocky's greatest flaw: he always had to appear like he was on top of everything.

Only once had I seen a crack in Rocky's facade, and I hadn't told anyone about it. One afternoon during my first semester at Greenwood, I'd seen him coming out of Ms. Shelley's office, his eyes puffy and red. I'd met Ms. Shelley during orientation, but I hadn't seen anyone use her services until now. I wondered what could have had Rocky so shaken.

Before I could say anything, he put a hand up. "I'm good."

I looked from Ms. Shelley's door, covered in positive affirmations, to Rocky's face. "Are you sure?"

He sniffed and swiped his sleeve over his nose. "Well, I'm not feeling so great."

"I'm sorry," I said, and splayed my hands out at my sides in what I later realized looked like an invitation to hug, which Rocky took. Unexpectedly, he threw his arms around me. He was so much taller than me that my head fell against his chest. It had been a while since I'd hugged anyone—Jenny and I hadn't yet become close, and I missed my mother's hugs—so I hugged him too, tightly. His arms felt as strong as they looked, and he smelled like deodorant.

Neither of us ever mentioned it again.

"I can't stand how Dr. Li tells us what we can and can't do," he was saying now. "Like, it's one thing to tell us what to do at the piano, but another to say I'm not allowed to skate. That's my personal life and I'm going to do what I want!"

"She's only taught at Mannes. She probably just doesn't know how to talk with us."

Rocky whistled. "Only taught at Mannes, huh? Someone's got her CV memorized. I call girl crush!"

"I'm only saying what Dr. Hamilton told us at Assembly!" In spite of myself, I was smiling, strangely caught between elation that Rocky was teasing me and embarrassment that it was about Dr. Li.

"Well, how do you feel about her telling you that you *must* take this accompanying gig?"

I wondered what would have happened if I'd protested more when Dr. Li had slid the music into my bag. She wouldn't have *forced* me—and it wasn't like it would affect my grade—but she would have been disappointed, which was just as bad.

"I feel like . . . she believes in me?" I felt myself blush. "I know that sounds cheesy. But I mean, she's just doing what she thinks is best for us," I said. "The no-skating rule is intense, but I trust her. I think she's more perceptive than we think."

Rocky glided toward me, flipped the board up, and caught it under his arm. "Geez, Wu," he said. "Where does this trust come from? She's not your *mom.*"

If my mother were my piano teacher, she wouldn't have given me extra music to learn, that was for sure. She would have told me to focus on the music that had already been assigned to me, and then join Model UN and study more for the SAT so I could get into a good college and have more skills to offer than—in her words—*just* music. But maybe that was why I trusted Dr. Li: she took my music-making as seriously as I did, if not more seriously. "Dr. Li hasn't taught high school before. Give her a break."

Rocky eyed me. "Why should I give her a break when she

won't give *me* a break? I don't need my Chinese mom teaching me piano, but here we are."

"You're right, she's the only Asian teacher in the whole school," I said. "So you of all people should get to know her better."

Rocky scoffed. "Me of all people? Why?"

"You could ask her to sponsor the Asian Student Society."

Rocky shook his head. "Not a chance that I'll ask Li to sponsor us. Besides, I'd want *you* to get in before I even think of inviting her."

Though I tried to suppress it, I smiled—big. "Thanks, Rocky," I said, but he'd already started skating another lap across the lot.

♩♫

I had barely voiced this to myself, much less to anyone else: Dr. Li's Asianness was part of her appeal. I'd never had an Asian teacher before. Maybe she'd even given me the accompanying because of that. Maybe she felt she could push me harder. Maybe there was some unspoken something between us, the same something that compelled my parents to seek out and befriend—even in a small way—other Chinese families: the only other one in our neighborhood, or the one whose kids were taking piano lessons from my teacher, or the Lams, who (unexpectedly, I thought) owned the Outback Steakhouse off of 485. But from what I'd seen so far, Dr. Li didn't seek community in that way, at least not at Greenwood. In the dining hall, when the other teachers sat at the same tables, eating in a cheerful frenzy, Dr. Li always came in after the lunchtime rush. She ate by the window, bent over a book or the

New Yorker. She didn't seem to care about fitting in. The other teachers all wore practical clothes and shoes, gamely setting off across campus for a reading of *Othello* in the amphitheater or to supervise Artists for Science as they launched bottle rockets in the field by the North Campus Garden. But even now, weeks into the semester, Dr. Li hadn't stopped wearing the types of clothes that most teachers wore only for interviews. She strode through the courtyard in blazers and boots, sweaters and pencil skirts. While it would be amazing if she sponsored the Asian Student Society, I wondered if she would even agree to it. As far as I knew, she didn't interact with students outside of class.

Last spring, I'd spent several days in constant anticipation of my acceptance to the Society. Rocky had told me that one of the members would come up to you and tap you on the shoulder three times—that was how you'd know. In the dining hall, I stayed extra alert to anyone who touched me, many of which were false alarms, because someone was always doing that, brushing your arm by accident on the way to the milk dispenser or nudging you to say, "Pass the salt, this chicken is miserable." I walked across campus slowly, waiting for Ellie Giang's distinctive long strides, for her to tap me on the shoulder and whisper, "You're in." She never did, and it turned out Lily Zhang was the new member that semester. At our rehearsal, Rocky and I didn't talk about my rejection explicitly, but even he seemed disappointed the next day, when clubs met with their new members for the first time.

Each member of the Society was fascinating in their own way, but it was Ellie who intrigued me most. Nearly every day she wore the same thing: a white T-shirt inside out and frayed jeans with holes in the knees. After her mother died last spring, Ellie's art changed. She began molding masks from her own face, which she covered in thick white plaster. The masks won first prize in the visual arts contest and were praised for their "emotional maturity." According to our old piano teacher, Mr. Buck, emotional maturity was what my playing lacked. He could hear a glimmer of it, he said, but it wasn't yet there.

Ms. Shelley had told us to be exactly ourselves and not try to be anybody else. But what if everyone else seemed more worth being? Ellie Giang played guitar on the grass, her tan legs stretched out in front of her while she sang her own songs in a sweet, sad voice. Rocky had no trouble saying exactly what was on his mind and had an opinion about everything from politics to how many pickles improved a dining hall burger. If I ever wrote songs, I wouldn't have the confidence to play them in front of people. In class, just the thought of raising my hand made my heart pound. But if I got into the Society, I was certain that the real Claire Wu would emerge, and when she did, she would surprise everyone. Even me.

Chapter 7

"DR. LI HAS A LOVER?" ROCKY ASKED. "I CAN'T EVEN imagine her with any friends." He took several large gulps from a dining hall mug, then laid his head down on the desk. He was drinking coffee way too fast, I thought. A week before, I'd mentioned to Jenny how tired he looked, and she'd said, "That's sweet, Claire, but haven't you noticed *all* the seniors look really tired?"

"Dr. Li is not exactly personable," Jenny said now. "The way she handles class gives me the creeps. We just sit around waiting for people to speak like we're at a Quaker service."

But I liked Dr. Li's rituals—the way she had us close our eyes to listen to one another, and the silence before and after playing, like music was a form of worship.

Leo Epstein's eyes widened. "Like a music cult? I love that. There's something monastic about being a pianist anyway, all that practicing you guys do alone. Have you listened to her latest album? Tchaik piano concerto? Damn, it's good. And the photos that go with it are *hot*. Her hair's different now, though."

Of course I had listened to that album. I was probably increasing her listens on Spotify by a good ten percent every day. I'd had a moment of panic the week before, frantically searching, *Can artists see who is listening to them on Spotify?* I had visited her website so many times that I remembered the dates and repertoires of her past concerts. November of last year, she played Brahms with the Knoxville Symphony Orchestra. In December, she joined the Boston Pops in a family concert, playing Gershwin at two in the afternoon, and in January, she gave master classes in Santa Barbara. I'd been slightly surprised that she wasn't playing bigger venues, like in Europe or New York. I knew all the publicity photos, too: the close-up where it looked like she had highlights, and the one where she was sitting at the piano in a long, sleeveless blue dress, her chin cupped in one hand and the other striking a single key, as if testing it out. Her arms were taut and sleek, like a dancer's or a sportswear model's. In another picture, she stood over a student, one hand on her hip and the other pointing toward the score, her mouth caught midsentence. I could only guess at what she had been saying. I'd even found her own user profile on Spotify, but it was private. I wasn't about to share that with Leo and Rocky, though. I knew how weird it sounded.

Daniel Giambalvo burst in the door and threw his sunglasses off, slipping into a desk in the very front. "I decided to have a six-minute breakfast instead of a four-minute one," he said with a huff. "I apologize." He was wearing khaki shorts with loafers and no socks, and when he sat down, he propped one long, hairy leg on top of the other. On his ankle was a practice record: tally marks in purple pen indicated how many times he'd practiced a certain passage in one session. He unwrapped his napkin and I caught a glimpse of two breakfast sandwiches from the dining hall. He took a bite, then looked up at the painting—*Venus of Urbino* by Titian—that Dr. Hamilton had projected on the wall, and very nearly choked.

So far, taking electives with the seniors had proved to be more entertaining than any of our classes had been last year.

"I shall mark you T, for 'Tardy' and 'Too Loud.' This is your third tardy of the semester, Mr. Giambalvo, a semester which has only just begun, so you had better be on time for the rest of it or your grade will drop by approximately one letter."

Daniel groaned.

"Mr. Wong?" Dr. Hamilton said.

"I have a headache," said Rocky, his head on the desk.

"Either health center or face forward," Dr. Hamilton said.

"The health center sent me to class," Rocky muttered. But he sat up, rubbing his temples.

"That's more like it. Well, young musicians! The Renaissance is a particularly rich time. Music, as well as painting, is becoming three-dimensional, full of contrast and fullness, moving away from the hard lines of medieval art. How might that be so?"

Rocky raised his hand.

"Yes?" said Dr. Hamilton.

"Chiaroscuro," said Rocky.

A few people snickered. Although Rocky's mouth moved to form the words, it was Daniel's voice we heard responding.

"Yes, very good, Mr. Wong," said Dr. Hamilton.

Daniel wasn't moving. He sat with chin in hand, mouth obscured.

"Would you like to elaborate?" Dr. Hamilton asked. "What does *chiaroscuro* mean?"

Daniel's voice said, "Light and dark," but again Rocky mouthed the words, like a ventriloquist's dummy in reverse.

"You're exactly right, Mr. *Giambalvo*."

Daniel dropped his hand and grinned.

"Please remove your feet from the chair in front of you and sit up straight," said Dr. Hamilton. "Yes, like so. We are in class, not mourning a loss at Tuesday Trivia at the Hideaway."

"Haven't lost yet!" said Rocky. "So I don't know what that looks like."

Lip-synching during lectures was a Greenwood classic. Dr. Hamilton wasn't as easily fooled, but I'd heard that Rocky and Daniel had pulled it off for almost an entire semester in another class.

Usually I loved music history, but I couldn't concentrate: I was dreading the pages of music I still had to learn and the hours of rehearsal to come, and what Dr. Li would say if she found out I was failing, the notes I might continue to receive. I'd already thought through the worst possible outcome, which was that I wouldn't be ready in time for the dance performance and they'd have to hire someone else in a hurry. I still didn't understand why Dr. Li had picked me. Maybe—the thought horrified me—she'd somehow detected I needed the money more than Jenny, whose mother was a doctor, or Martyna and JT, whose families could afford to send them to another country for school.

And did Rocky think I was spoiled from only having to go to school while he worked between classes? Had Mr. Yanko been telling Dr. Li about our rehearsals? The dancers talked to each other, and probably word would spread to their non-dancer friends as well. If I failed, what were my chances of getting into the Society? I was sure that someone like Ellie Giang, or any of the other dependable members of the Society, didn't let their teachers down in this way. There was also the problem of my parents. I had spent so long trying to convince my mother that piano could be a lucrative career path, and when I told her about the gig, she almost sounded like she approved. "One hundred dollars a week is not bad," she'd said. "It's a lucky number, after all." But if I couldn't hang on to a gig after only a few weeks, what would that say about making a living through music for the rest of my life?

I tried to focus on class. Dr. Hamilton had moved on to another painting.

Jenny raised her hand. "The contrast is pretty interesting. Her light body against the dark background. The softness is unexpected."

"Wonderful, Ms. Stone. So young, so sharp!"

Out of the corner of my eye, I saw Rocky stifling a laugh after reading something Daniel had written on the corner of his notebook. To my right, Leo was scrambling to finish our assignment from last night. His first sentence was, *As we all know, Palestrina and Monteverdi were both Renaissance composers, but they have differences as well as similarities.*

Then Dr. Hamilton said, "Ah, before I forget, we do have something logistical to address this morning."

"Yawn," someone called out.

"On the contrary, I think you will find this quite interesting. We have, in this very classroom, nothing less than a case of vandalism—a primary source, if you will, that we can inspect as scholars of history. Very recent history, I believe." He walked over to the thermostat and pointed at it with his baton. "Someone has written"—he cleared his throat—"'Cool off, Tina Li,' exclamation point, on this, our most trusty air-conditioning adjuster—using, it appears, one of the dry-erase markers intended for educational purposes."

The class tittered. Rocky said, "That's our girl!"

Jenny and I met eyes. It seemed that interest in Dr. Li was spreading outside of just the piano studio.

Dr. Hamilton continued to study it, frowning. "At the very least, try to come up with a more original pun! Now, I understand your hormonal veins cause you to do rebellious acts such as this, but that is no excuse for marking property in our school. And especially calling attention to one of your esteemed faculty members this way."

Jessie Washington said, "Preach it, Dr. H."

"Who would do such a thing?" Dr. Hamilton continued, gesturing to the thermostat. "It's not even clever, or even visually pleasing, for that matter. Not all art should be beautiful or brilliant, necessarily, but for heaven's sake at least try to do something compelling."

I thought that the appearance of Dr. Li's name—and especially calling her by her first name—on school property was pretty compelling.

Dr. Hamilton said, "Mr. Giambalvo, come up and scrub this off."

Jenny and I looked at each other again. I thought Daniel was a pretty good suspect—maybe he had come in before class. Then, too, there was Leo Epstein, who everyone knew had a crush on Dr. Li.

"Nice, Dan," said Rocky. "She *does* run hot sometimes."

"What?" said Daniel. "Come on now, Dr. H. It wasn't me, I swear."

"Come on now yourself, Mr. G. I don't care who it was, it needs to be gone." He held out a roll of paper towels.

Daniel groaned. He carefully arranged the remains of his second sandwich on his desk, then stood and walked to the thermostat, which he began rubbing furiously with the paper towel.

I wondered who wrote it. Was it the same person who had written *my* note? I had thought it might be, but now saw that this one wasn't the same all-caps handwriting. Whoever it was had to be a musician, I mused, because the other departments had no reason to come into the building.

Or was that what the person wanted us to think?

"It won't come off," said Daniel, after several seconds of trying.

Dr. Hamilton took a closer look at the thermostat. He swiped a finger across it and inspected. "So it's not one of these wimpy whiteboard markers after all. Thank you, at any rate, for trying. I'll have to ask someone from maintenance to use the potent stuff."

Chapter 8

WHEN I ARRIVED AT MY LESSON THAT WEEK, DR. LI WASN'T in her typical spot at the piano.

"Over here, Claire," she said. She was standing at the bookshelf, holding a book open to a spread of black-and-white drawings. Peering over her shoulder, I saw they were the great composers as cartoons. "These illustrations are by a friend of mine. I helped him with some of the early drafts. Not with drawing, of course. Just musical accuracy."

Up close, I could see that the book was worn; some of the pages were falling out. For a second, I got a glimpse of her life in New York, hobnobbing with other artists and musicians, sharing work with each other, sipping wine and smoking as the sun went down—although Dr. Li didn't smoke, and I had no idea if she liked wine. But Jenny always said that you weren't a true artist if you didn't drink booze or coffee, so Dr. Li had to drink *some*thing.

"Really cool," I said, glancing down at the caricatures.

Her eyes were mischievous. "Here, I'll quiz you." She pointed and I named them: "Mozart," I said, in his waistcoat playing at a tiny piano. "Bach!" sitting at an organ with his head thrown heavenward and powder flying off his wig. "Beethoven"—he brandished a conductor's baton, and his face was ferocious, his hair wild.

Dr. Li turned a few pages. "What about . . . this guy?" She pointed. This composer looked younger, but the artist had rendered his eyes as spirals.

"Schumann."

"Correct again. And do you know why his eyes were like that?"

I thought for a second. "He was schizophrenic."

"Yes. It was a terrible time for both him and Clara," Dr. Li said, as if the Schumanns were family friends of hers. "You know the concerto? It begins with a declaration, but at the same time, the choppy rhythm makes it stilted. That first chord from the orchestra is an attack. Then, out of nowhere, a tender melody on the piano. The piece is a musical rendering of Schumann's own suffering."

She closed the book. "That's why, when you play a piece like that, you have to understand what the composer was going through when he wrote it. It's a matter of respect. We have to know who our masters are in order to play them the way they intended. Beethoven, for example, he wanted to shock. And he did! You must return to feeling as if you're hearing the piece for the first time."

"Okay," I said. I had no idea how I might do that. I was beginning to notice that, unlike other teachers at Greenwood, Dr. Li often told us what she wanted us to do, but didn't give instructions on how to do it.

I peeked over at the book again. "Who's the artist?" I asked. Not that I knew any famous artists myself.

Dr. Li looked at me. "I told you: a friend. From graduate school." She slid the book onto the shelf so I could no longer see its cover. "Let's get back to your lesson."

I felt suddenly like I'd been prying. Had I sounded nosy? Or, the thought made me wince: Had I accidentally asked about her boyfriend? Or girlfriend, for that matter? Or—the word Rocky had used earlier made me cringe—her *lover*? Or maybe she really did just want to get started—teachers were always saying we didn't have enough time—and she thought I was trying to delay my playing.

She wouldn't have been wrong.

I apologized and started taking the music from my bag when she said, "Before I forget, how are rehearsals going?"

I looked down at my hands. "I'm sorry, Dr. Li, but I'm not so sure about accompanying. I think someone else might be better at it than me. Like Rocky for example."

She looked at me with surprise. "You want to give the position to someone else? Why? Because it's hard?"

"I just don't think I'm very good at it."

"So, you only want to do things that you're good at."

I pursed my lips, not wanting to agree with her—but it was true, wasn't it? My mother had lectured me on this before: I was always doing things on a whim, and then dropping them just as quickly when they didn't go as well as I'd imagined.

"And—" I hesitated. I wanted to tell her about how Tooth-pick was behaving toward me during rehearsal, but anything I said would sound like whining. "And it's really clear that some of the dancers don't like . . . how I play."

Dr. Li considered this. "I have to tell you, I didn't give you this position because you are the fastest sight-reader or the most efficient accompanist."

That much was obvious. Rocky would have mastered all of the repertoire by now. I thought of how happy he would be to receive the gig, and that thought made me so happy: finding him in a practice room, handing over the music. He might even hug me.

"This is a learning opportunity," said Dr. Li, "and I think you *are* able to get along with the dancers, and they with you. Accompanists are team players." She looked at me. "I'm disappointed to see you giving up so easily."

I could feel the onset of tears, a lump forming in the back of my throat. I looked over at the shelf so she couldn't see my eyes. On it was a bust of Shostakovich and the tightly packed spines of blue Henle edition Bach scores.

"Claire, look at me," she said.

I did, more out of surprise than the actual request. Dr. Li regarded me with her head cocked to the side. Then she put her hand lightly on my shoulder. Inadvertently, I felt myself stiffen.

She was looking at me intently, in a way that was usually impossible when we were both facing the piano. "There are always going to be people who don't like your playing," she said. "Or who don't like *you*, for that matter. It's part of being human. You can't be bothered by every person who dislikes you."

I nodded, but I was having trouble listening. For the first time, I felt sort of embarrassed for Dr. Li. She was speaking to me almost like a parent.

"The others only act confident. They're not any better than you. You're the one who wakes up early to practice. You should be confident about your abilities."

How did she know? How did she know that I felt like I could never play as fast as Rocky, or with as much color as Jenny, or the stage presence of JT? Sometimes I felt unworthy of Greenwood, like I had only gotten in because of circumstance: They needed another student from the South because so many of the others were from New York or California or outside the US. Or— the thought made me wince—they had extra funding and they needed to give it to non-white students.

"I guess—" I willed myself to say it, even if just to bring our conversation to an end. "I guess I can keep going with it."

"That's the spirit!" she said, and smiled so that I saw her teeth—which was rare—and somehow I felt even more embarrassed. "I am not in the business of giving up, and neither are my students. You'll work hard on this for a couple more weeks, and you'll be able to coast through rehearsals before you know it."

"But I've already worked on it for weeks. It's taking forever."

Dr. Li stood and opened my binder of accompaniment scores. "You're progressing far too slowly for someone of your intelligence."

I wondered how she could be so confident she could judge my intelligence, but I was pleased that she thought it was at least somewhat high. Then I wondered if she was just making an assumption about me, the way, subconsciously, I felt like Mrs. McHeusen, the music theory teacher, expected more of me because I was Asian.

"When you practice," said Dr. Li, "only do four measures at a time, like you're memorizing a phone number. Play them at performance tempo; your fingers can handle that because you're just doing a small bit at a time."

I tried out a few measures then.

"Yes," she said, "like that. The dancers won't mind if the chord isn't completely full. They're listening for cues. You can write the chord you need on the page, like a lead sheet. Other than that, Claire, there are no shortcuts in music. Most of it, as you know, is work."

I said, "Yes, ma'am," relieved we were working on music instead of my lack of perseverance, and Dr. Li reached over and picked up my Beethoven. "Speaking of which: let's get to it." She took a seat at the other piano with the score open on her lap. "Whenever you're ready," she said.

I began to play the "Pathétique," which I had been practicing all summer. I was disappointed in how it came out, clunky and messy, my hands not exactly together. A lot of the dynamics I'd planned on were lost; our conversation had thrown me off.

When I finished, she said, "Your attack is too stiff. Hold out your hand." She got up and sat beside me on the bench, so close that her sleeve brushed my arm. I held out my right hand, and she dropped her forearm into it. "Feel that? How heavy my arm is?" It was heavy, and completely limp, as if it didn't belong to her. "You have to put all your weight into your arms. Hold nothing back."

She put her hands out, and I dropped my arms into them.

"You're holding tension in your arms—that will only lead to pain. Relax. Yes, like that. Do it again. Good. You have to sink into the keys for that first chord. Let it ring."

She kept her hands on my arms as I turned again to the keyboard.

"Begin," she said.

I played the first chord, but this time, the sound was somehow deeper than before, and I was pushing into the keys as if trying to get to the wood beneath them.

In terms of sound, it was simple. It wasn't one of those funky chords that Beethoven could throw, the kind that made Dr. Hamilton swear we could trace jazz all the way to him. It was the most straightforward opening he could have written, but a big one: eight notes sounding all at once and held for five slow beats. Playing it now, after relaxing, felt completely different than before. My arms felt stronger, looser. I plunged them into the keys.

"See how big the sound is?" Dr. Li said. "If you always play chords like this, not holding any tension in your shoulders but just letting them fall into the keyboard, you will have a magnificent sound."

I did it a few more times. Then she said, "Claire, you have talent. You all do. But you need that little something extra: obsession. You need to be obsessed with music. Nothing else can be as important as this. Do you know why Beethoven is the greatest, greater than anyone who came before him or after him? His obsessiveness. Just look at the fifth symphony: he takes the simplest motif and writes this forty-instrument powerhouse out of it. It's not a futile obsession, though, the way some people are obsessed with money, or power, or fame. When you sit down to practice, you're trying to create something beautiful, something to give people hope. You have to think like a musician now."

I nodded, but that wasn't what my mother said. She said I wouldn't get into a good college if I wasn't well-rounded, and she didn't want me going to a conservatory because it wouldn't be attractive to the job market. In fact, what Dr. Li was saying sounded sort of unhealthy. I thought it was the kind of thing that would appeal to Rocky, though. I could see him aspiring to it.

"This is what I want you to do," she said. "Play this chord several times a day, exactly as you just did. Do it for me once more now."

I did.

"Again," she said.

I did.

"Aha," she said. "Now you are sounding like a pianist."

When I stepped out, there was a note waiting for me on the floor, cut into a perfect square:

RELAX.
HER OBSESSION
DOESN'T NEED
TO BE
YOUR OBSESSION.

As I read it, I felt all the air leave my body. I folded the paper in half and stuffed it into my bag. Again, I looked: down the long hallways, in the practice rooms. But everyone was at their instruments, deep in concentration, not paying any attention to me at all.

♩♫

That evening, I went to the music building. Dr. Li had suggested I borrow the yoga ball for practicing, so I moved the bench aside and settled onto the ball. I turned the metronome to eighty beats per minute, bounced along with the beat, and took the Tchaikovsky just four measures at a time. At first, I was pleased at how quickly I was making progress, but then it seemed like it would take all night—and many more nights. There was a particularly difficult passage in the middle that I had to go over several times, first my right hand, then my left, very slowly. Then the two hands together. I worked on it until I got up to one hundred beats per minute, even faster than performance tempo. That was good, but it was only four measures, and there were hundreds more to go. That night, and for several nights after, I stayed in the practice rooms as long as I could, and didn't leave until eight minutes before ten o'clock. Then I ran as fast as I could across campus to make it in time for curfew.

Chapter 9

DR. LI WAS RIGHT. BY THE FOURTH REHEARSAL I HAD PRAC-
ticed so much that I had basically memorized the material. Looking up and down from the keyboard, turning pages, and catching
glimpses of Mr. Yanko and the dancers didn't throw me off. I hadn't
been sleeping very much and my grades were beginning to suffer,
but Jenny had let me copy some of her chemistry homework, and
Rocky poured me my first coffee (mostly milk and sugar). On Friday nights, I treated Jenny to dinners at the Hideaway, where she
teased me about Rocky: how he always complimented my playing
more than anyone else's in studio class, and stared at the back of
my head in music history. I had a hard time believing that either
was true.

Toothpick had dips and turns during the Tchaik *Andante* that
were achingly slow, so slow that I was impressed she didn't topple
over or wince in pain. When she finished, she stood with one hand
on the barre and the other on her hip, keeled over, sweat dripping

to the floor. Then she would ask me if we could do her part again. Now that the music was better, the dancers all congregated around the piano during breaks. They liked using the instrument as a prop for their bodies, leaning against it with one leg extended behind them, absentmindedly plucking the strings of the instrument as they delivered news to each other. They talked about everything as if it were hugely important: how there weren't enough oranges at breakfast, how they had gained two pounds and that may not sound like much but it was actually a lot on such a small frame, how Yanko had given them a crappy part and they'd felt depressed about it all weekend. Toothpick complained about Dr. Li—that upon her arrival all the other teachers had gotten even stricter (if this was true, I hadn't noticed anything in particular). That she had knocked out Ms. Shelley as HFF: Hottest Faculty Female, a category created by Amy Cellars. "What is she even *doing* here?" Toothpick said.

During one of these breaks, it was Toothpick who told us all about Mr. Yanko: how American Ballet Theatre had promoted him to principal dancer when he was already twenty-nine. "In dancer years," Toothpick said, "that's basically geriatric."

Amy Cellars perched next to me on the bench.

"Amy, are you listening?" Toothpick asked, in an impression of Mr. Yanko. Amy giggled.

Toothpick told us how Mr. Yanko woke up one morning to find his face locked in a smirk, pushed up on the left side. He was told it would clear up in a couple weeks. Instead, it grew worse. For a few days he could only communicate by writing on a yellow legal pad. Bell's palsy. No company wanted a dancer with a face that looked like it was in pain. His had been an art of the body, and years of training had made it so that he walked a dancer's walk whether he was performing or not.

"And you know what else?" said Toothpick. "I think Tina Li and Yanko are MFEO."

"What's that mean?" I said.

"Duh," said Toothpick. "Made for each other. Just watch them, you'll see."

Scott tapped Toothpick's shoulder, pointing his chin toward the window. Mr. Yanko was approaching.

"All right, everyone," he said when he entered. "Get ready for part two of the *Sleeping Beauty* waltz. We'll be adding some new steps today."

Despite Toothpick's theory, they seemed to be nothing more than friends. Still, after Toothpick told me, I couldn't help picturing them kissing in the music building elevator with Yanko against the buttons, random floors lighting up orange. What did it feel like to kiss a man whose mouth couldn't fully close on one side? Would she end up kissing teeth? His were stained from the black coffee that he told his dancers not to drink (they did anyway). And what was it like to be Dr. Li? To turn heads when you went to the MapleMart—not because you didn't look like everyone else, although that was part of it, but because there was something about you that set you apart: the way you held your body, the way you dressed, the way you commanded authority with your walk.

♩♫

At lunch that day, Toothpick and Amy passed by our table, arm in arm.

"Claire!" Amy yelled over the clatter. Everyone at our table looked up. "New theory," said Amy, "and this by no means cancels out the other one, but actually supports it." Toothpick pulled at Amy's arm, and Amy started to speed up her words. "Tina Li was injured. And that's why she can bond with Yanko so well. They both had these physical ailments that led to—ow!—stopping. See you later!" They were both gone before Amy could say more.

"Wow, Claire," said Jenny. "You jumped up the popularity ladder overnight."

Rocky looked annoyed. "Is Li really worth so much of your attention? Whatever happened to only thinking about teachers when we're, you know, in class?"

But Martyna and I pulled out our phones and discussed. Injury made the most sense: It explained why she was so strict about Rocky not skating, so particular about how we warmed up and practiced. She didn't want us to risk getting carpal tunnel or tendonitis, end up unable to play. Had she practiced incorrectly herself? Or had there been an accident of some kind? I shuddered to think of Dr. Li going an entire year without playing.

We saw in Dr. Li's programs that she'd learned Saint-Saëns's Six Études for the Left Hand and played it at a number of concerts. In the repertoire section of her CV, a portion of her rep was not easier, necessarily, but gentler, and wouldn't require so many fast repetitions, like the Kinderszenen by Schumann and several of the Songs Without Words by Mendelssohn.

"That's why she and Mr. Yanko get along so well, then,"

said Martyna. "They've both been through something difficult. They've both suffered."

I wondered what they talked about when they were together, if they talked about the careers they'd left behind in New York—or the lovers.

"If she *has* suffered," said Rocky, "I don't see it in her. Not an ounce of empathy or compassion. At my last lesson, she said it sounded like I hadn't practiced at all!" He snorted. "Probably because I wasn't playing it the way *she* would have. But my interpretation was solid."

"Maybe now that she has a friend, she'll lighten up," said Jenny, spreading mayo on her sandwich.

But I didn't want Dr. Li to lighten up. Her high standards made me feel like what we were doing was important, even necessary. I was practicing more than I ever had in my life, and after a lesson, I felt both exhausted and inspired.

♩♫

At our next rehearsal, when Mr. Yanko left the room to smoke, Toothpick appeared beside me immediately, brandishing her phone in its glittery pink case. "I found something. About Li. You have to see it for yourself."

I raised my eyebrows at her. "You did?" I didn't think Toothpick cared so much.

"We've all looked her up," said Amy.

"You haven't found what I have, though," Toothpick said.

On her website, I'd read some of Dr. Li's CV. It began with

what I already knew about her education, and then continued with honors and awards and every teaching position she'd ever held—even the one-time, random master classes at colleges. It listed her address (it was still in Manhattan; she hadn't yet changed it to where she lived in Green Valley), the conferences she'd attended, and every single time she'd made an appearance at any performance, anywhere, even accompanying gigs for churches, weddings, musicals, and ballets. It was single-spaced in small font and nearly six pages long. I'd slogged through the first half page and skimmed the rest.

"She is one accomplished bitch," said Toothpick. "But you know what's missing?"

"Uh," Amy Cellars said, "a social life?" at the same time that I said, "Clear formatting?"

"You're both wrong. What's missing is an entire year. Her life just completely stopped, then started again."

Amy threw her head back and laughed. "Get out of here. Now you're just playing with us."

Toothpick's face hardened. "I'm *not*. I've put in the work and figured something out. Something crucial."

I felt a twinge of jealousy. *I* knew Dr. Li in a way that the dancers didn't—I was a pianist, after all—but it was Toothpick who'd found something out about her that no one else knew. I'd looked through Dr. Li's various concert programs and reviews, scrutinized her photos, watched and rewatched her videos. I'd even seen the one where she sat in an empty concert hall and told the camera that arts funding was being cut from public schools in the Bronx, and would we consider signing a petition today?

Somehow I'd thought of my own interest as special, but now I felt like I had a crush on the same celebrity that everyone else did.

"What do you mean, it's *missing*?" I asked. "Like, she left the year out?"

"It's not that she forgot to add it. She just didn't do anything that year. Highly suspicious," said Toothpick. She ran her index finger over her phone screen. "This CV starts when she was in graduate school and was teaching and winning awards in school or whatever—and then there's no mention of the following year *anywhere*. It just, like, stops."

"Oh my god," said Amy, shoving Toothpick in the shoulder. "You are *obsessed.*"

"But that's normal, isn't it?" I asked. "It's not like she could win awards every year."

"It's not just awards. Everything stops: teaching, performing, everything."

"So people have gaps all the time," said Amy. "Maybe she was sick and then got better. Maybe there was a death in the family."

"People don't stop working because of *death,*" said Toothpick.

I couldn't help saying, "So death kindly stopped for her?"

Then Amy shoved *me,* and I couldn't help feeling weirdly flattered: the dancers didn't go around pushing just anyone. "Get out of here, Em Dickinson," she said.

Toothpick ignored us. "I think she was fired. She had an affair with another professor and they let her go quietly."

"They wouldn't let that go quietly," said Amy. "That's not how academia works." She drew out the word *academia,* relishing it as if she knew so much more than we did. Her parents were both professors.

"But that's not the only thing. There's evidence," said Tooth-pick, thumbing through her phone. "Photographic proof."

The three of us peered at Toothpick's phone. In the photo, a twentysomething Dr. Li was smiling a small, mysterious smile. I could see smoky eye shadow around her eyes, a few stray pieces of hair framing her cheeks. A lanky man with brown skin and dark curly hair was standing with his arm around her. They looked to be at a benefit or a gala of some kind.

"'Tina Li and Diego Montes,'" I read.

Toothpick zoomed in close on Dr. Li's face. "I should ask her what she uses. She has such good skin."

"Ooh," Amy said, looking at her own phone. "*Professor* Montes. He was an adjunct professor of illustration at SUNY for a while. Now he—oh my god, he lives in Savannah with—oh my god. With his wife and *daughter.*"

She and Toothpick both squealed in unison.

"Tina Li's a home-wrecker!" said Toothpick.

"It makes sense, doesn't it?" said Amy. "She left so abruptly because she didn't want to create a scandal."

"That still doesn't explain an entire year away from piano, though, does it?" I said.

"Schools hear about these things. No place would hire her after that," said Amy. She put a hand to her heart. "Tina Li, my *queen!* So badass."

"I know, right?" said Toothpick. "She risks it all for love, and now she comes to little old Green Valley, seeking sanctuary."

I didn't think it was very badass at all—if it was even true—but just then, Mr. Yanko appeared in the doorway. "Break's over," he said. "Places!"

The dancers fled from the piano, and Mr. Yanko walked over to where I was sitting. "You've improved," he said. It took me a second to realize he was talking about my playing. "Whatever you're doing, keep doing it. It's working."

♩♫

Later that day, about half an hour before curfew, I ran into the dancers again. Toothpick and Amy Cellars stood in front of the double doors that led to our rooms. Arm in arm, they kicked their legs up high like they were doing the cancan.

"You have to dance, dance, dance to pass! You have to dance, dance, dance to pass!" they chanted.

A group of onlookers, mostly theater kids in black, watched as students and a couple dorm parents shimmied and bopped and jigged their way through. Anne-Marie was known as the fun dorm parent, and she was living up to the name, jumping up and down and throwing her hands in the air. The boys' dorm parent, Stefan, was trying unsuccessfully to shut the whole thing down. Electronic dance music—rising synths and persistent, thumping bass—blasted from someone's laptop on the floor.

Jenny and I got in line behind Martyna and Rocky.

Martyna turned around and clasped her hands together. "I love this! Don't you? It's the quintessential Greenwood experience!"

"These damn dancers," said Rocky. "What's Toothpick up to now? Creating the Greenwood TSA?"

"This could be initiation for Nineties Step Aerobics Club," Martyna whispered. "And I'm determined to get in."

Rocky sighed heavily. "And poor Claire here is already around dancers twenty-four seven, because of Li."

"Rehearsals are going well, though!" I said.

"Yeah, but you had to give up sleep to get there," he muttered.

Then it was Martyna's turn, and she did something approximating the Macarena—but with a lot more footwork—to the whoops and cheers of the drama students. Jenny followed, doing the one dance move that she always did in our room: fake ballet, with her toes exaggeratedly pointed and her arms high above her head. Toothpick glared at this, but still raised her arms to let Jenny pass under and into the dorm.

Then Rocky was up. "Your turn," Toothpick said.

"No thanks," Rocky said. "Some of us are just trying to get through."

"True dat," said Daniel Giambalvo. "In life, as well as in this dorm."

"But you have to dance to pass!" said Toothpick.

"Yeah," said Amy. "You gotta dance if you wanna go to your room."

Toothpick poked him in the arm and said, "Day-ance, Rocky," drawing out the words as if they were a song.

Was it possible to simultaneously admire and hate Toothpick? Was it not enough that she had Scott, she had to flirt with Rocky, too? Rocky only looked down at her hand and scowled.

"Yeah, we want to see you dance, cocky Rocky!" someone else yelled.

"Fine," Rocky said. He threw his backpack on the floor.

"Give the man space," Daniel said, and we all backed up a bit.

Rocky squatted in the middle of the floor and nodded to the beat. Then slowly, he raised himself up so he was balancing on just one arm. He moved as fluidly as an eel, and so fast that he seemed to be made with not four limbs but six or seven. He was spinning—not the neat, graceful spins of the ballerinas, but up and down and in and out, like a slinky that someone had set loose on the stairs. His mouth was slightly open, but his face was taut with concentration. Everyone started clapping in time. I knew I had a big smile on my face, and I didn't even care: I'd never seen Rocky dance like this before, and I was enthralled. He was normally so outspoken about his various talents that I was surprised he'd kept this one to himself. The more I felt like I knew him, the more I found there was to learn. When the song finished, Rocky came to a panting stop, and then he bowed, deeply, the way we'd all been taught to do after a performance.

"Happy now?" he said, sweating.

"You may pass," Toothpick said, smiling her flirtatious grin, as if what he had done was merely adequate.

To my relief, Rocky pushed through with hardly a glance her way.

My own dancing wasn't so great—mostly I flailed my arms and stepped from side to side, resembling a drunk octopus—but Toothpick said, "Not bad, for a pianist," and let me duck my head under her arms. Then Toothpick let go of Amy and started making her way to the girls' side of the dorm, as if she'd been waiting on me.

"What?" someone said. "What about us?"

"Yeah, we wanna dance."

"Then dance, obviously," said Toothpick, lifting a hand as if to say, *How is this my problem?*

I was almost to the stairs, but Toothpick was only a few feet behind me when she said, "You still have to prove yourself at the performance next week, pianist."

♩♫

One of our favorite things to do was to crawl under a piano and lie there while someone else played. The sound was far better there than from any speaker or even concert hall. It seemed to come from everywhere at once, rushing over your body like water. Leo Epstein would set aside his cello for a minute to lie on the carpet under one of our pianos as we practiced. "Nothing soothes the soul like your own private concert," he said, wiping his eyes after a particularly moving Bach. One evening we were lying there while Jenny was practicing, and we found another one of the notes taped to the underside of the piano:

> DR. LI ONLY <u>SEEMS</u> WORTHY OF A
> SOCIAL MEDIA RABBIT HOLE.

Leo reached into his pocket. "I picked this up earlier today," he said, holding out a note of his own. "I guess it's part of this whole, uh, thing?"

I looked at it.

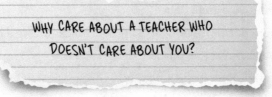

Leo held up two fingers and pointed to his eyes, then to me.

"Ugh," I said, then lay down again. "Toothpick and her mind games. She's trying to turn me against Dr. Li while also helping to research her."

Leo looked skeptical. "While *also* aiming to tear you down as an accompanist *and* leaving notes for other musicians?"

"They're sophisticated mind games," I said.

Leo shook his head.

"Hey, guys," Jenny said from the bench. "What's going on down there?"

♩♫

I wasn't the only one finding notes in the music building that week. They were on the floor in the hallway just outside our practice rooms, tucked into sheet music on our stands when I rehearsed with the orchestra for the dance performance. Martyna even found one on her desk in music history. Just before choir rehearsal—choir was a mandatory class for all musicians—we found another one. It was taped to the wall of the music building stairwell, close to the floor, in letters so tiny I had to squint to make them out. Leo peeled it off, and we all peered at it.

CLAIRE BEWARE. LI DOESN'T REALLY CARE!

"Huh," said Leo. "Nice rhyme." He patted me on the shoulder. "Are you *sure* this is Toothpick?" he said. "Doesn't she have better stuff to do, like practice her first position and make protein powder smoothies, or whatever it is dancers do?"

"Who else would it be?" said Jenny.

"Let's forget about it," I said. "I just want it to be over."

"Whoever it is, they're smart," said Leo. "Knows your schedule."

"We're a tiny school," said Jenny, "and Claire's predictable. It's not that hard."

♩♫

That night, we played Ping-Pong after choir rehearsal. It was refreshing to lunge and run for balls and use a vocabulary that we weren't using in rehearsals. To compete with each other with our bodies, not our brains and our ears. I loved slamming a ball down or sending it zipping from left to right across the table. I played a steady game, and what I lacked in skill I made up for in concentration, in staying calm. I wasn't great at drop shots or spins, but I irritated other players with my defense. I could always return the fast balls that the other player sent my way, leaving them swearing to themselves. That is, except for one rainy day last spring when I played Rocky. Although we had several long volleys, he beat me twenty-one to eleven. We played two more games and he beat me at those as well, though my scores had been better than our first game. I wasn't surprised—the Society often held its own tournaments, taking over the rec room for hours at a time, blasting music while they played. Afterward, Rocky met me at the net like a tennis player, shook my hand,

and said he'd see me in the practice rooms. We hadn't played together since.

Martyna and I had only just started a game when I scampered under the table for the ball and saw it there: a piece of stiff yellow paper, shaped like a star. Unlike the other notes, this one wasn't handwritten, but was as small and neatly typed as a piece of letterhead stationery. I picked it up and read:

Break a leg
at the performance.
Even Tina knows
you've been
working hard.

Chapter 10

DR. LI HAD TOLD ME NOT TO THINK ABOUT IT AS ONE BIG performance but to concentrate on each part, to try and be fully present for each piece. "All you have to do is play the notes. Do the best you can. It might feel like a lot of pressure, like one super-high-stakes show, but you have been preparing for this. Just think about playing one measure, and then the next. Whichever measure you're in is the most important one."

Backstage before the performance, she gave my shoulder an awkward pat. "How are you feeling?" she asked.

When I said, "Good," she said, "Not just good. You're psyched!"

I forced a smile and wondered if she'd picked that up from another teacher. Many of them were also coaches for extracurriculars like the Debate Team and intramural sports. Would Dr. Li ever help out with an extracurricular? Like, say, the Asian Student Society?

For the dance performance, I wore the typical accompanist

uniform: all black—black pants and a black blouse and black shoes. Jenny told me that I looked hot in black, and I had to admit the color was flattering. In an attempt to make my hair bouncy like Dr. Li's, Angela Chung had done something to it with a hot-air brush, and I put it up in a loose bun so it wouldn't get in the way when I was playing. Usually I just wore it in a ponytail with a ribbon for performances, and I liked how the updo made me look older. I wondered if Rocky would be at the dance performance, but it would be impossible to see the audience from the pit. When I squinted at myself in the mirror, in my black top with the scalloped neckline, I thought I sort of looked like Dr. Li.

In the wings, the orchestra members and I goofed off. We poked each other, yanked bow ties out of place, emptied trombone spit valves onto shiny black shoes, slid funny pictures of Billie Eilish in between the Tchaikovsky and Stravinsky. But the minute we stepped into the orchestra pit, we fell silent. We became pristine, filing into our seats, unsmiling in our concert black. In our chairs, we waited for the hall to darken, the applause to begin. The seats were full of parents, prospective students, locals, and talent scouts.

Down in the pit, there was only music, our mouths quiet for once while our instruments alone made the sounds. We communicated with a lift of the brow or the chin, a nod, an intake of breath. We were sitting too close to each other, and beads of sweat formed on our foreheads and seeped through our shirts and dresses. The orchestra players took their breaths in time with the music, one eye on Dr. Hamilton as he conducted, the other on the scores, all of us listening to each other with a concentration that could only come from this much adrenaline. There is perhaps a bit of magic involved in performance, and sometimes, being onstage, you hear something in the music that you hadn't heard before, and decide to do something different. A phrase leans a certain way, or a chord makes more sense *staccato* than *portato*. And you know that the audience senses that you are enjoying yourself—even if they don't entirely know why. I knew it wasn't magic that made performances go smoothly, but the hard work, as Dr. Li liked to say, of practicing so much that playing the piano was as easy as walking onto the stage and brushing your teeth.

I started to play the Stravinsky, and although my hands were trembling for the first few measures, by the middle of the page I was completely ready. Martyna was sitting to my left side, turning pages for me. Accompanists didn't typically memorize their music, but I had so nearly memorized it that even when Martyna was a beat late for one of the turns, it didn't affect me. I just kept playing—no time to think about nerves or pressure anymore: it was happening and it was all going fine. I knew the music inside and out and so did the dancers. We could trust each other. And even though I couldn't see them, it was as if I could: under the hot lights of the stage, the dancers—who we had so often made fun of for being shallow, stupid, vain—became artists. In so much satin and tulle, in corsets that had been sewn to fit the exact measurements of their bodies, they leapt and twirled and were lifted into the air, then fell into each other's arms with precision and grace. Adeline Felts slowly rose en pointe and lifted one leg up in the air so her whole body depended on the single foot that spun now once, twice, three times, and if she was in any pain at all, her face didn't show it. The audience gave a smattering of claps, far fewer than I thought she deserved, but with each successive turn (and here the strings played high and fast) the applause grew louder and louder, and I heard someone shout, *"Brava!"*

All of us in the pit stomped our feet to clap, a roar of stomping that came from a place the audience couldn't see, and then Dr. Hamilton turned and we received applause as well. I felt simultaneously tired and refreshed, as if I'd finally reached the end of a long hike. While playing, I'd been hyperaware of my body, as Dr. Li had taught me: Was my back straight? Were my shoulders down? Was my pinkie finger sticking up or curled under? Performance had a way of doing that. You had to give it your full concentration, because you knew that otherwise, your nerves would take over.

Dr. Hamilton high-fived us all on the way out. "Don't go to the practice rooms!" he called after us. "Go out and celebrate!" And then backstage, the smell of sweat and hair spray, everyone disassembling their instruments into their gleaming parts and laying them inside their cases.

Daniel had his cello on his back. He shrugged inside his suit, pulling at his bow tie. "Man, I need to get out of this thing," he said.

Bobby pins, bandages, and costume fuzz were scattered across the floor behind the stage. The dancers trotted off arm in arm, carrying gym bags stuffed with clothes and accessories over their shoulders.

Jenny appeared beside Martyna and me. "Nice job, roomie," said Jenny. "You sounded great. And, Martyna, good page-turning."

Martyna beamed.

"The woodwinds were good tonight, right?" I said. "Much better than in rehearsal."

"I couldn't tell, because that one girl . . . what's her name"—Jenny snapped her fingers—"dates that guy, Pete something . . . her bassoon was so out of tune."

"Are bassoons ever in tune, though? They always just sound like ducks to me," I said.

"That's oboes," said Jenny.

"I thought the entire show was fantastic," Martyna said. "Great job, Claire."

I craned my neck, wondering if Rocky had made it. He probably had better things to do, like hang out with the Society.

That was when Dr. Li herself appeared, walking toward us with her big black tote on one shoulder. "Yes, wonderful job, Claire. I'm proud of you."

"Thank you," I said. I couldn't help smiling. Dr. Li never told any of us anything that sounded even faintly like she was proud of us. "And your hair looks lovely," she added. She never said anything like that, either. I hoped she couldn't tell that I was trying to make it look like hers.

"I hate to do this to you last minute," she said, "but I'd like to schedule another lesson tomorrow. Would that be all right? We've spent so much time on your accompaniment and we're behind on your repertoire. I'll be on campus anyway."

Of course, other teachers at Greenwood didn't have classes on Saturday, but this was different; it was music. Besides, with Dr. Li, did I really have another choice? I agreed to it and Dr. Li said she'd see me at 9:00 a.m. Then she made a quick exit, pretending not to notice that a few straggling dancers were gaping after her, incredulous and pleased that she'd come to their performance. I could already imagine Toothpick thinking that she'd only come to support Mr. Yanko.

"A lesson on Saturday?" said Jenny.

"Well, it's too late now to say no."

"Really? Because I could still run after her for you."

I smacked her lightly on the shoulder.

Jenny slipped her arm around me for a hug. "You didn't get any notes today, did you?"

I shook my head. With the nerves and the dress rehearsals, I'd momentarily forgotten all about them.

Jenny looked triumphant. "Then it *has* to be Toothpick. She couldn't write anything on the day of her performance, which happened to be the same day as yours."

She unzipped her bag and gestured for me to take a look: champagne. They never checked bags at Greenwood, but if they did find alcohol, you could be suspended from school or even kicked out. Last year, Jimmy Landrum had kept a handle of vodka in his fridge, stored in water bottles, for the entire year. If anyone had suspected, no one said anything. Besides, brass players did drink a lot of water. Jenny tucked a sweater over the champagne and we walked to the dorms, where we did our best to act natural. In the lobby, Hank—the security guard who had worked at Greenwood for ages—was sitting at the front desk.

"You all just come in from that dance recital?" he said. He looked at us over the top of his glasses.

"Yes, sir," we all said. Jenny prided herself on being a favorite of the front desk staff. When she talked to them, she slipped into a southern accent that was more pronounced than her usual twang. Meanwhile, it seemed like Hank didn't know what to make of Asian students in Green Valley. One time, when we were chatting in the dorm lobby, he complimented my English.

"You've never been to one of the dance recitals before, have you, Hank?" Jenny asked.

Martyna looked nervous, and I hoped my face wasn't matching hers.

"What am I gonna do at a ballet? I'd rather come see you three ladies and my man Rocky. Only seen piano like that on TV."

"Oh, stop it," Jenny said, flashing her biggest smile.

"Y'all have a nice time tonight. Don't stay up too late now."

When we got to our room, we realized we had nothing to drink from. I offered to get cups.

"And get us some ice to fill up the sink. You know, for the champagne," said Jenny.

I went downstairs using the back stairwell, because the dorm parents usually used the front stairs. Already, the air was laced with the smell of weed. Students would blow it out the windows on the first floor, with the lights off, so that no one who was walking around outside could tell exactly which room it was coming from. The rooms that faced the lawn were best since it was dark there. When I entered the hall, obscure rap music emanated from a room at the other end. Amy Cellars was sitting on the floor, watching something on her iPad.

"Hey, pianist," Amy said. "Love your hair! Get over here. You deserve a toast." She gathered her legs in one at a time and stood up, bringing to mind an ostrich. When she wasn't onstage, Amy moved as if she were still getting used to her body.

"Thanks," I said. "It's okay, I was just about to go to the dining hall."

"You haven't eaten yet? Because neither have I. Maybe you could bring something."

"Well, I'm just getting ice—"

"Come on. Everyone wants to tell you what a great job you did! Join us for a while. Please?" She was sitting outside of Toothpick's room. I'd never been inside before, and if she *was* the one behind the notes, I didn't really want to be around her when I didn't have to be.

"No, I really should get going," I started to say, but Amy was making her way toward me now. "Goody! I'm kidnapping you. We never hang out with music people."

"I'll just say hi really quick," I conceded, and Amy looped her arm through mine.

Chapter 11

"LOOK WHO WE FOUND!" AMY CALLED OUT. WE STOOD IN the doorway of Toothpick's room.

A few people turned around and waved.

"Congratulations, dancers!" I shouted over the noise.

"Heeey, Claire," Scott Dessen said. He was sitting on the bed closest to the door. "Can it get any better than this?" He pointed his beer around the room.

The music was so loud I could feel the bass in my chest. Dancers were everywhere: some still in their full costumes and makeup, wearing flip-flops now instead of pointe shoes, others in sweatpants or pajamas already. They drank from red Solo cups and poured refills for themselves and other people. By the window, two dancers were kissing. Jackie Lund, one of Toothpick's friends, stumbled all over the room, opening and closing drawers as if looking for something. Dancers laughed and yelled at each other and contorted themselves into impossible positions, using the furniture for balance. A single lamp bathed the room in a warm pink glow, and a sign that read *Anything less than exhaustion is unacceptable* was taped to the mirror above the sink. A couple hung their top halves over the windowsill, breathing smoke out onto the empty parking lot. Their heads came together to whisper, then parted to take a drag. Other ballerinas lay draped on the twin beds. One of them swung her legs up so they stretched across Scott's knees. Her hair was pulled taut into a bun and her makeup, bright and exaggerated for the stage, was smeared around her eyes. Her arms and legs were impossibly long, and through the thin nylon of her leotard, I caught the unmistakable outline of ribs. Hot-pink nail polish flecked her toenails.

She burped and smiled. Her cheeks were flushed. "Welcome to my little room," she said, and twirled her fingers. I realized then that it was Toothpick, unrecognizable in her makeup, transformed for her role.

Amy reappeared. "We're going out for revelry and lewd activity."

"In *that*?" said Toothpick.

"Oh, shut up. We're just going outside to meet Giambalvo and his piano friend," said Amy. Turning to me, she said, "How do you handle it? All those boys in the music department. Giambalvo is wicked hot. And he is such a laugh riot."

"Which piano friend?" I asked. But it had to be Rocky. I worked to keep my expression neutral.

"They're not that hot," said Toothpick. "You just have your Greenwood goggles on."

"You're one to talk," said Amy. "Hanging around with this guy all the time." When she said "this guy," she gestured to Scott.

"I have to. He's my dance partner."

Amy said, "Whatever," and then she left.

Toothpick regarded me. "We're celebrating, but a lot went wrong tonight."

My stomach jumped. "What happened?"

"Well, for starters," Scott said, "she fell." He pointed a finger at Toothpick.

Toothpick's eyes flashed, then narrowed. "You dropped me."

Scott put his hands up. "I had you."

Toothpick sat up, then pushed herself off the bed.

"Oh, please. Why would I do that?" said Scott. "Give me one good reason why the hell I would drop you."

"A reason! You were being careless, you jerk. You dropped me!" She looked at me to see who I believed.

"Are you okay?" I asked.

"I'm used to it."

Scott rolled his eyes.

"See this bruise?" said Toothpick.

I looked. There was a blue-green circle the size of a cherry on her shin. "Yeah."

"That's from the time he dropped me last week. In dress rehearsal."

"Bullshit," Scott said.

"You weren't listening to the music. You were supposed to have your arms out until the crescendo into the secondary theme, and you dropped me."

"I'm sorry," Scott said, and then he tried to kiss her, but she leaned against the wall, rubbing her temples.

"Why are girls always so complicated?" Scott spoke to the wall.

"And you too," Toothpick said, looking at me. "Maybe if you'd gotten the music down *earlier*—"

"Hey," said Scott, "she's had it down for weeks. Blame me all you want, but not Claire."

Toothpick burped again, a dainty, ballerina-style burp, if there was such a thing.

"Gross," Scott said, and Toothpick smacked his arm.

I was debating leaving then—I felt like I wasn't wanted there, and besides, Jenny would be waiting for me—when Toothpick said, "Have beer," in two neat syllables, and held a cup out to me. She couldn't have been the one writing the notes. Otherwise, why invite me to stay longer? Or was this just part of her game? I took the cup and had a sip. I'd had champagne before—my parents let me have a splash with orange juice when we were celebrating. But this was my first beer, and I didn't like it. It tasted like corn. Still, holding the cup made me feel more relaxed, like I was part of the group now.

I could smell cigarettes on Scott's clothing. Plenty of the dancers smoked because it helped them eat less. Normally I didn't like the smell of smoke, but for some reason, coming off Scott Dessen—with his floppy honey-colored hair and his shoulders, in his white shirt that somehow smelled like trees—it was bizarrely attractive, adultlike.

He grinned, showing perfect teeth. "You're our accompanist for the rest of the semester, right?"

"As far as I know, yeah. Why?"

"I heard that Li was going to hire someone to do it so you

could practice your repertoire more." The way he said it made me wonder if he really had heard this from other people, or if it was just something he'd tossed off to see my reaction.

"I doubt it, since she's the one who got me the gig. And I think she wants me to learn accompanying."

"Sounds like a good teacher," said Scott. "But—" Scott scanned the room as if Dr. Li herself could show up there. "But Toothy over there told me she's an ice queen. Like she seems really pissed off all the time."

"Oh, she's really different once you get to know her," I said.

Scott raised his eyebrows at this. "Oh yeah? You're getting to know her?"

"A little."

He patted the bed beside him. "Take a seat, tell me what you know."

I didn't want Scott Dessen to be the first boy I sat with on a bed, especially in a girl's dorm. I could never imagine Dr. Li even setting foot in a messy room littered with red Solo cups. I asked myself who was more attractive: Scott or Rocky? Scott was so popular that people paid attention if they saw him talking to you. But Rocky was smarter, and funnier, and—I'd only been able to articulate this recently—he had a very square jaw.

Besides, Rocky wasn't here, and the fact that he was almost always somewhere else made him more intriguing.

By the window, one of the ballerinas started dancing, slowly and fluidly. It wasn't like ballet: there was something loose and wild about it, like she was making it up on the spot. Jenny and I used to improvise on the piano, playing our own pieces for each other.

But ever since Dr. Li arrived, we'd only had time to practice other people's music. I balanced on the edge of the mattress, making space between a biology textbook and a gauzy purple corset. The ballerinas leaned out the window with their heads close together. If they had been typical high schoolers, it wouldn't have been a bad scene at all—just girls whispering and smoking—but for some reason, maybe because they lived so stringently, I felt sad for them.

I was just about to tell Scott about how Dr. Li had scheduled a lesson on a Saturday when there was a thump at the window. The smoking dancers screamed and sprang apart.

A familiar male voice said, "You know you can smell that stuff from, like, a mile away, right?" Two large hands appeared on the sill, followed by Rocky's face. He poked his head in and surveyed the room, then climbed in through the window as if he did that sort of thing all the time. Daniel Giambalvo and Amy Cellars followed close behind, Daniel not nearly as graceful as Rocky, with Amy giving his leg a shove.

"Hey, I didn't invite you!" said Toothpick, hands on her hips, ready for Rocky to banter with her.

Rocky didn't take the bait. "Congrats on tonight!" he said to her, and then made his way through the room. When he saw me, he looked at Scott, then at me again, as if wondering what I was doing hanging out with dancers. He filled his own cup and high-fived Scott on his performance, completely ignoring the two or three ballerinas who were ogling him from across the room.

Then his eyes fell on my cup. "Whoa. Take it easy, Wu."

I looked down at it. Most of my beer was gone. "I'm about to leave anyway," I said. "Lesson in the morning."

"On a Saturday?" said Scott. "Tina *is* crazy."

"She's *not* crazy!" I said, in a tone that sounded a lot like Jackie Lund when she was being flirtatious. "After accompanying you dancers, I just need to get caught up."

Rocky's face fell. "You have a lesson *tomorrow* morning? What are you still doing in here? She's going to chew you out."

"It'll be fine," I said. The alcohol had started to creep in some. I never said lessons were going to be fine. "It's Chopin. I've been practicing for months."

"How could that bitch schedule you for right after the performance?" Rocky said.

I crossed my arms. "Geez," I said. "She's not a bitch."

Rocky sighed. "She's a bitch, but she's also such a beast. Still, Wu, you should probably go to bed, like, right now."

"It's not a big deal. I agreed to it." When Dr. Li had suggested the weekend lesson, I hadn't minded. Sports teams had games on weekends at other schools, didn't they? So what was one lesson? If anything, it made me feel special, like I was getting extra training.

"Damn, pianists," said Toothpick. "You really are her loyal disciples." She looked from me to Rocky, then me again.

"You didn't have to agree to it, though," Rocky said. "She weaseled her way into your brain, didn't she? She made you feel like you *had* to. Geez, it's like she thinks she's God's gift to us."

"I'm behind on repertoire!" I said. "That's the only reason why I said yes. And an extra lesson *is* a gift. She only needs to give one a week."

Rocky looked skeptical. "Just don't let it become a pattern," he said. Then he took the cup out of my hand and drained the final sips himself.

"Oh, so you can drink, but I'm not allowed?" I said.

"It's different. I need to take the edge off. You'll understand when you're a senior."

"It's true," Toothpick said. "I need a refill myself."

Rocky leaned toward me. "My anxiety levels are through the roof. And, I'm going to guess"—he lowered his voice to a whisper—"that this is your first drink, ever."

I nodded.

"Wu," said Rocky. "I'm trying to look out for you. Head to bed. *Now.*"

"You can't tell me what to do," I said. I crossed my arms and pretended to be mad, hoping it looked like something Toothpick would do, but more effective.

"You need to hit the hay as soon as possible. I just don't want you to face Li's wrath." He put his hand on my back, steering me toward the door. In spite of everything, I felt myself smile, my stomach somersaulting. "I'll babysit these dancers while you rest up," he added.

"You want anything from the dining hall?" I called over my shoulder, trying to act like Rocky touching me was a completely normal thing.

Scott said, "Can you bring us some cookies? I'm starving."

"Yes to the cookies!" Toothpick sang out.

"Don't waste your time, Claire." Rocky opened the door and pushed me gently into the hallway. Then he put a hand on my shoulder, and I had to catch my breath. "Did you do something different to your hair?"

Over the course of the night, several curls had come loose. "Angela did it," I said. Angela was always asking to do my and Jenny's hair, so I was glad to give her the chance. "Do you like it?"

"Honestly?" said Rocky. "I liked it better before."

I stiffened. "Why'd you mention it, then?"

"Sorry, I just meant—I mean, it looks nice now, but I prefer it how you normally wear it."

On the floor above us, a door slammed shut.

"Anyway, look, I wanted to show you something." He stuck his hand in his pocket and held out a folded-up piece of paper by the very edge, as if it was something disgusting. "I found this in my bag yesterday."

I unfolded the note.

SHE MADE YOU STOP SKATING,
SO WHY YOU
STILL PARTICIPATING?

"You have to admit," said Rocky, "they have a point. Even if it was sort of invasive to drop this into my bag."

"*Sort of* invasive?" I said.

"Okay, it was straight-up stalker behavior."

Still, I couldn't help feeling relieved that Rocky was one of the writer's victims, too.

When he took the note from me, our fingers touched for the slightest second.

"You're going to hate me for this," said Rocky.

"What?"

He took a breath. "Does it ever occur to you that it could be Jenny?" When he saw the look on my face, he plowed ahead. "I mean, I know she's your best friend and all. But that could make it even harder for her to tell you what you don't want to hear."

I laughed. "Do you *know* Jenny? She tells me plenty I don't want to hear."

"But isn't it weird how she keeps trying to pin this all on Adeline? When it's like, I'm sorry, but I don't think Toothpick cares about you enough to go through all this. You know who does? Jenny. Besides, who else knows your schedule so well?"

I shook my head. "She tells me her thoughts on Dr. Li so often to my face, it doesn't make sense. It's just not something Jenny would do."

Rocky shrugged. "If you say so. But just think about it, Wu. Maybe she's trying to tell you something."

"Thanks for showing me," I said. "You better go. You'll get caught." Boys weren't supposed to be in the girls' dorm.

"You did great tonight. But tomorrow, you cannot afford to be late. You must give it everything you have," Rocky said, imitating Dr. Li's cool speaking voice.

"Don't worry, Dr. Wong," I said. "I won't let you down."

I walked over to the dining hall in the humid night. There were a few people still sitting beneath umbrellaed tables in the court-yard, and I saw their eager bodies leaning forward, then sitting back to laugh. A couple musicians sat alone, still in their black perfor-mance clothes, lingering over cold mashed potatoes and macaroni. After the performance, a familiar sense of collective triumph hung in the air, triumph meshed with some disappointment. I didn't know how to explain it, but I knew everyone else felt it. That was why the dancers always drank too much and got upset at each other. They felt that all their hard work had been for something that wasn't good enough yet, thought it had to lead to something bet-ter. It could be lonely, too. Dr. Li was right when she said art required isolation: no one else could do your practicing for you; only you could know what you wanted to sound like.

Inside the dining hall, Jenny was already filling cups of ice. She had taken a mug her first year and had yet to bring it back, claim-ing it would be a Greenwood vintage collectible in the future. Toward the end of last year, we'd all received a memo telling us to return our cups and silverware to the dining hall because they were especially low on glasses.

"What took you so long?" Jenny said. "Martyna already went back to her room."

"Sorry, I was talking to Rocky." I paused. "He got a note, and he thinks you're the one writing them."

We looked at each other, and then we both burst out laughing.

"Is it weird that I'm sort of flattered?" said Jenny. "If I wanted to warn you about Dr. Li, I'd just do it. In fact, I do it all the time."

"That's what I said."

"You were talking to Rocky in the dorm?"

"The dancers were having a party and he was there."

"The dancers?" She handed me a cup. "I swear, those kids eat ice cubes for dinner."

"Well," I said. "You know how we feel pressure to learn at least one concerto before we graduate? That's how they feel about their weight. It's necessary for dance."

"Geez, Claire, you're in deeper than I thought. It's necessary for them to freaking starve themselves?"

I thought about Toothpick, how she weighed herself every day, sometimes more than once a day. They had their own glossary of terms for it. "Feather-light weight, super-float weight, whole-wheat-no-butter weight," I'd heard them say. "The idea," Toothpick had told me, "is that it looks effortless and light. The lighter you are, the easier it is to hoist yourself up and keep yourself going."

To Jenny, I said, "Not starve themselves. Just watch what they eat."

In our room, Jenny expertly opened the champagne, having learned from her older brother. She poured some into our cups, then laid the bottle reverently in the sink filled with ice cubes. I felt a wave of guilt about not practicing that night. I crunched on my ice cube with sudden vigor, as if to block out the interminable nocturne that repeated itself in my head. It was the tricky part— the right hand trill toward the end—that replayed itself. My face felt warm. I looked in the mirror and saw that my cheeks were bright red. "My skin is blotchy."

"It's Asian glow," said Jenny. "How much did you have to drink? And now you're going to have champagne. You're turning into quite the lush, Claire. Also, your hair still looks amazing."

I sank down onto my bed.

"To drinking with good hair," said Jenny, and held the dining hall glass, half full, up in the air. I wondered if Rocky's cheeks grew red when he drank.

Jenny said, "Maybe this experience will help you get into Ellie Giang's club. It's a start, anyway. I heard that the ASS members can drink like fish."

"My lesson," I groaned. "I'm not going to be able to warm up. I'm doomed."

"Quit being theatrical," Jenny said. "You don't know how to hold your liquor."

Jenny disappeared for a minute, then brought the trash can over to my bed, as if I were a sick patient. She poured my champagne into hers. "It's cheap, but it's not that cheap." She filled my cup with water at the sink and put it on the nightstand. "Drink this whole thing," she instructed. Then Jenny crawled into her bed to read one of the horror novels that she liked, the champagne in one hand and the book in the other. But I couldn't fall asleep even after Jenny turned out her light, so I practiced Chopin, my fingers trilling on the mattress.

Chapter 12

AT MY LESSON THE NEXT MORNING, I THANKED DR. LI AGAIN for coming to the dance performance.

"It was my pleasure," she said. "You played wonderfully. And the ballet was quite good."

She was wearing sneakers, but not the kind you'd wear to do actual exercise—they looked like leather—and her hair was damp. Dr. Li never came to campus with wet hair. I'd have to tell Jenny about it later.

I started with the Chopin nocturne, which normally I found poignant and tender, but that morning it sounded sentimental, even clunky. Beside me, I could feel Dr. Li flinch at every note that I landed on too loudly, but she let me keep playing until I had made so many mistakes that I wished she would stop me. When I finished—completely botching the trill I'd practiced before falling asleep—she said, "Is something the matter, Claire? My god, your hand is shaking."

I looked down. On the keys, my left hand was trembling slightly after its attempt at sextuplets. Jenny had given me a concoction of coffee and egg whites that she said would cure any hangover, but instead it had given me the shakes.

"Are you sick?" Dr. Li asked, eyeing me. "If you're not feeling well, I don't want you in here."

"No. I'm okay."

Dr. Li continued to look at me, as if waiting for me to say more, come out with it. The room was achingly quiet. Everything that had seemed important last night was unimportant now. What seemed important was piano, but my body was in no rush to do anything at all, much less play. "I'm not sick or anything," I said, for some reason needing to make this clear.

Dr. Li put a hand on my forehead. "You're not warm." She studied my face. "Your eyes look puffy." She narrowed her own eyes. "Did you pull an all-nighter?"

"No. I just didn't sleep very well."

She eyed me a little longer, looking me up and down, from my hair—clearly unwashed because it was still holding some curls from the night before—to the slip-on shoes I'd scrambled into that morning. Then she said, with something like a mother's intuition, "You drank." It was more a sentence than a question, so there was no use in denying it or pretending otherwise. When I nodded, she smiled slightly and said, "See? I can tell."

She looked at my hands. I could hear the clock on the wall behind us, marking the seconds.

"I should let Dr. Hamilton know. Or take whatever the

appropriate disciplinary action is, here at Greenwood." Other teachers knew exactly what the next step would be, but Dr. Li, I realized, hadn't been here long enough to know the school handbook, if she'd even read it at all.

I nodded again, shame and dread blooming in my stomach like a drop of ink in water. For my parents to find out I was drinking at school—I didn't want to picture it.

"I didn't have to come to campus on a Saturday. And now I wish I hadn't." She gestured to my Chopin score. "For this."

At these last words I hung my head. She wasn't yelling the way my mother did when really mad, her voice filling the whole house. But somehow, the calm coldness of Dr. Li's voice was a thousand times worse. "Piano is the most important thing in your life, or it should be. Maybe that sounds too intense to you. But I am simply telling you what my own teacher told me when I was your age."

That made me look up. Of course Dr. Li would have had a teacher as demanding as she was now.

"Chopin, and all these great composers, and this great art itself, you had better give it your all, or just quit. Just do something else altogether. This music, this lifestyle—you owe it to the music world to give it everything you can. Do I make myself clear?"

"Yes, ma'am."

"I won't tell anyone, but you won't do this ever again."

She rested a hand on my shoulder. "I suggest eating a big breakfast, lots of carbs, and then taking it easy. Take two Advil."

I looked at her.

"Make sure you drink plenty of water, all right? You are dismissed."

It felt like we had been in there forever, but as I tucked my books into my bag, I caught a glimpse of the clock. We had only been in the lesson for twenty minutes.

♩♫

On Monday, in my favorite practice room, I found a note stuck to the bottom of my bench, which I'd only seen because I'd dropped my pencil. One long strip, curling around itself like an apple peel:

IT'S NOT LIKE DR. LI WILL LIKE YOU MORE BECAUSE YOU
MAKE YOUR HAIR LOOK LIKE HERS.

So, even though I'd played well at the dance performance, the notes hadn't stopped—not for me or anyone else. In fact, over the next few days, they seemed to double, appearing everywhere we looked. After she'd agreed to a lesson on a Saturday, Martyna received notes that read:

DOES AN EXTRA LESSON MEAN SHE'S CARING . . .
OR CONTROLLING?

WAS THAT WEEKEND LESSON FOR YOUR BENEFIT . . .
OR HERS?

And JT received one saying:

YOU HAVE TO TAKE CARE OF YOURSELF, BECAUSE LI SURE AS
HELL ISN'T.

Outside the dorm, the path winding to the dining hall com-pelled everyone to read the message, in multicolored chalk, all the way up to the door:

TINA CAN'T BE STOPPED AND NEITHER CAN
THIS PATH.

And once we'd eaten our egg sandwiches and gulped down our orange juice, the lettering continued on the brick just outside, leading to the building where we had music history first period:

BUT IS THIS THE PATH YOU WANT?

In the early morning, I walked right on the letters, as if to show Ghostwriter that I didn't care, I wasn't affected. Beside the enormous question mark, one of the art students wrote in small yellow chalk (clearly taken from a classroom):

YES, AND BUZZ OFF

And then someone else wrote:

who asked you?

When it rained a few days later, the chalk only partly washed away, leaving yellow streaks in cracks on the sidewalk like pollen after storms.

It was Jenny who pointed out that the visual artists were the ones with access to multicolored chalk. Then again, Ghostwriter could have borrowed it, or ordered it online.

♩♫

One day toward the end of November, Jessie Washington handed me a note in the dining hall. She had gotten it from Leo, who had gotten it from Daniel. It had been glued to the bottom of Daniel's water bottle, but they all figured it was meant for a pianist, if not specifically for me:

> BE YOUR OWN PERSON. DON'T LET TINA LI
> TAKE OVER YOUR LIFE.

"So, okay, whoever's doing this is obviously entitled to do whatever—free speech and all that—but in the meantime, how's a guy supposed to get a clean lunch around here?" said Leo, plucking a note from between the two halves of his chocolate chip bagel. "They're lucky I don't toast these things!"

We all peered at his note.

> DOES LI EAT CARBS?

So. Ghostwriter had a sense of humor.

"What we should do," said Jenny, "is take out our notes and compare them. Take a nice, long look at the evidence."

That was when Jessie asked me to join her at the gluten-free section—which was always the least busy—saying she needed to show me something in private. Beside the trays of cauliflower-crust pizza, Jessie took a note out of her backpack, cupping it with one hand the way some people shielded their exams. She pointed it toward me and I started to read, but then she took out another, and another.

"Hold on, you're going too fast," I said.

"That's my point," she said, now holding six or seven in one hand like playing cards. "When was the last time there was stuff everywhere, and I mean *everywhere,* on this campus?"

I looked at her. "Um, when Logan Sanders was advertising his senior recital?"

Jessie frowned, shaking her head. "Does the title 'Hair Story' ring any bells?"

Then I remembered: last spring, Angela Chung had made an outdoor art installation out of her own hair. We didn't know it was hers at first, but word got around.

IT'S NOT LIKE DR. LI WILL LIKE YOU MORE BECAUSE YOU MAKE YOUR HAIR LOOK LIKE HERS.

"But Angela's my suitemate," I said. "Why would she be targeting me?"

"Pissed-off roommates do weird shit sometimes," said Jessie. "If there's something you haven't talked about, you might want to."

"That's not how it is. We're friends."

Jessie lowered her voice. "Look. I'm sorry, but it adds up: She's the type who's weird enough to do something like this. You never know with these theater folk."

At the table, I told Jenny and Leo what Jessie had told me.

"It's a piece of performance art," Leo said solemnly. "We're in it right now."

♩♫

After my truncated weekend lesson, I was more determined than ever to do my best for Dr. Li. She had been gracious with me when she definitely didn't need to be—Greenwood took its honor code seriously, and we knew students who hadn't been allowed to walk at graduation, or had even gotten expelled, for drinking. So I practiced even more, and tried to be a model student: I spoke up a lot in studio class even when my voice shook; when Rocky or Jenny cracked jokes, I stifled my laughs; and in the music building, I avoided doing anything that wasn't practicing, just in case she happened to walk by.

She used to say nothing when we saw each other, but now she made a point of saying, "Hi, Claire," which should have made me feel more relaxed, but only made me feel more on edge, like she was watching me closely now. Practicing in her studio, I got straight to work and took a few short breaks at most. Rocky rolled his eyes when I told him, saying that Dr. Li had let me off the hook just because she wanted me in her good graces so she could take advantage of me later. But that made me wonder, what would he say if Dr. Li *had* consulted the Greenwood handbook? Probably that she was a straitlaced, unempathetic teacher who didn't remember what it was like to be a teenager.

Jenny found the whole thing hilarious. Dr. Li probably drank a ton herself, she said, and sooner or later I'd have to let up, because was I really going to act like Dr. Li was my personal god?

♩♫

Rocky suggested responding to Ghostwriter, leaving a note for them to find, but Jenny said that would only encourage them more. We'd started keeping a list of suspects on our mirror in dry-erase marker (Daniel Giambalvo because he was a goof, Lauren Culpepper because she wanted attention), but given Greenwood's history of eccentric students, it was hard to eliminate anyone.

Watching my classmates, I noticed things about them I never had before: Toothpick painted her nails with a clear polish that was supposed to make them taste bad, but this didn't stop her from biting them. Leo Epstein squinted at the board when he wasn't sitting in the front of the classroom; he must have needed a new glasses prescription. Amy Cellars read a book in the amphitheater right after dinner on weekdays. Anthony Lee and Lauren Culpepper looked at each other a lot in choir. Jackie Lund wore pink eye shadow some days and had the high cheekbones of a classic actress, like Katharine Hepburn. Craig Meyers said grace before every meal, even breakfast, bowing his head before he ate a bowl of Cheerios and half a grapefruit. And once, I saw Daniel Giambalvo lean ever so slightly forward as he took notes in class, trying to smell Jenny's hair.

Sometimes, I couldn't help inquiring into my classmates' lives as a way of looking at my own. Were my arms as toned as Angela's when I wore a tank top? Were my contributions to class discussions as eloquent as Ellie Giang's? And would I ever be as confident as Jenny, able to say what I was truly thinking, not caring what other people thought? I loved Jenny, even when I envied her, or wanted to be more like her. And I wished I could comfort Ellie, who always looked like she was in so much pain, at the same time that I was so curious about her. My favorite mystery, though, was Rocky. The more I felt I knew him, the more I found there was to learn.

♩♫

I had my lesson with Dr. Li later that week, and she kept me late to make up for Saturday's twenty-minute disaster. She didn't mention anything about what had happened, and with the dance performance over, I had been able to give my full concentration to my repertoire during the week.

As usual, she didn't give me much praise, but at the end of the lesson, she said, "You're in good shape, Claire," and that was enough for me.

I found Jenny, Martyna, and Daniel in the dining hall after the lunch rush. They weren't speaking, but looking down at the table intently. When I got closer, I saw that they were bent over their notes, scanning them like they were playing an intense card game. I pulled a chair up beside Martyna. "Right on time," she said. "We are just beginning the analysis."

I hadn't seen Daniel's notes before. They all had the date on them in the same purple ink he used for his practice record, teeny tiny in the top right-hand corner. I wished I'd done the same with mine.

"It's interesting," said Jenny. "A lot of Daniel's notes are funny. Like saying that Li is too hot and stuff like that." She slid some of her notes to the center. "But a lot of mine are vaguely . . . insulting? Li being a control freak is a recurring theme."

"What does Ghostwriter have against Dr. Li?" said Martyna. "Sure she's hard, but she's the best!"

Jenny sighed loudly in Martyna's direction.

"I've noticed a pattern that doesn't have to do with content," said Daniel. He pulled some of his notes off to one side, mumbling the dates under his breath. "Yep. On Tuesdays, the handwriting is messier."

We all peered down at them. Sure enough, they looked hastily done.

"So?" said Jenny.

"So," Daniel said, "it's the same day that the Society has SET Brek." When we all looked at him, puzzled, he groaned. "Super Early Tuesday Breakfast? It's the day when Rocky wakes me up at five. He doesn't mean to, but he does. Every time. Whether he throws his alarm clock on the floor or trips over his shoes." Daniel took a long slurp of his drink, then looked at us. "It's got to be someone in the Society."

One by one, the Society members' faces popped into my mind: it couldn't be Rocky, who had been receiving notes himself; not JT, who just wouldn't do something like this (would he?); not Lily, who I didn't know very well—

That left Ellie and my suitemates: Angela and Miyoung.

I took out my binder and laid down some of my own notes, placing them in a line beside Jenny's. Anyone far away would have thought we were doing a tarot reading. There were the earlier ones on scraps of notebook paper, the typed yellow one in the shape of a star, the most recent one with curled ends that refused to lay straight.

Jenny picked up the star. "Ellie Giang," she said. "She has business cards. You wouldn't think she'd be the type, but she does. She sells her sculptures and pottery at a farmers' market in the summer."

"So?" said Daniel.

"The cards are yellow, like this. I mean, it looks and feels like the exact same paper. She gave me one of her cards once." Jenny shrugged. "Networking, man."

"Guys," said Martyna, "I didn't want to say this before, because it sounded like, how do you say—a stretch?—but when I put some of my notes together with my roommate's, the last letters spell *Ellie.*"

Jenny patted Martyna on the back, and I had to stifle a smile.

"But why would Ellie be trying to take down Dr. Li?" I said. "And me?"

"Lots of reasons," said Jenny. "She's jealous of you because you get to have an Asian teacher mothering you at Greenwood. Or that Li reminds her of her own mom. When my grandma died, my dad didn't come out of his room for days. Grief can push people to the extreme."

Martyna nodded. "The visual artists have those fancy paper cutters. They can make stars."

"It adds up," Daniel said, rubbing his beard. "She's in the Society—so, messy handwriting on Tuesdays—and she'll try anything once, you know? I respect the shit out of her for that."

Suddenly I remembered how, at Assembly earlier that week, Ellie had turned to me and, casually as anything, said, "I hope those notes aren't getting to you too much. I know you're getting hit hard." Then she went to her seat. I hadn't thought about it again except to think that it was kind of her. The meeting went on and on: Student Council did a skit about how we could reduce our carbon footprint by decreasing our food waste, Daniel Giambalvo announced the last Ultimate Frisbee game of the fall, the American History Club did a presentation on how to celebrate Thanksgiving in a respectful way. Then it was over and everyone went to lunch. I forgot all about it, but now I was seeing it differently.

Had I completely flunked that, by not saying anything other than thank you? Or was I supposed to be cool about it?

Then I knew, with a realization that settled into my chest: it wasn't just Angela or Ellie alone—it was the entire Society. An initiation. I couldn't believe I hadn't thought of it before. One person would be cover and another would be making sure the coast was clear. Together, they created plausible explanations for why they were walking around campus before the sun was up—or after the sun went down. One person wrote all of them, but surely they got ideas from the rest of the group. That meant Rocky would be in on them—or maybe not. Maybe only a few members of the Society participated. Or Rocky was in on it, but he had to pretend like he wasn't. I hardly saw Ellie—we weren't in any classes together this semester—which made it extra easy for her to slip notes in places I'd frequent when I wasn't there, and then never have to speak with me about them. The same went for Angela, who also spent most of her time in the art studio: although she lived next door, I only ever saw her in the evenings.

♩♫

I started to look for the notes when I was alone, as if by predicting them, I could find patterns, clues. Maybe in finding out what the Society was trying to say to me, I could figure out how to respond. When I practiced, I peeked under the bench to see if one was waiting for me. I scanned the cups and the toaster at breakfast, checked under my plate at lunch. In the morning, remembering suddenly before I got to the shower, I cracked open our door in case one had been left out in the hall. But it seemed that the more I searched, the less I found. It was a game: I was onto them, but they were onto me, too. I kept the notes in a neat stack in a side pocket of my choir binder, arranged in order of when I'd picked them up. I started to read the notes more closely, underlining certain parts, circling words, noting where they had been found.

I didn't tell Jenny that I thought I was being tested. It seemed crucial that nobody know but me.

After class, when I would usually be in the practice room, I propped our door open and sat there, waiting to see if one of the Society members would come by.

"Ghostwriter isn't stupid," said Jenny. "She won't drop a note when you're just sitting there. She's like Santa Claus . . . in a sad, twisted way."

Jenny was right, of course.

Only Amy Cellars passed by, and it was clear from her eyes, unfocused behind her glasses, that she was high.

"Do you have any Cheetos?" she asked me. When I shook my head, she said, "By the way, I'm sorry your friend is doing that to you. Jealousy makes people weird sometimes."

"My friend?"

"You know. You got the gig and she has to hear about it all the time. Who else could it be?"

It took me a second to realize she was talking about Jenny.

"If it's not her, it's got to be one of the weird clubs, like Artists for Animals, or that one Asian club." She paused. "No offense."

In the morning, a note was taped to the window by my bed, an exact copy of the one from a couple weeks ago, except with added punctuation:

BE YOUR OWN PERSON! DON'T LET TINA LI
TAKE OVER YOUR LIFE!

I headed to Dr. Li's studio to practice that afternoon. She handed off the key with a rare smile. "I had a quite productive time in there just now, myself," she said. "I hope yours is just as fruitful. And I'm sure it will be, given how your last lesson went."

I thanked her, elated.

Inside the studio, I did something that I'd been wanting to do for a long time. Dr. Li's walls were covered in concert posters. In every one of them, she looked perfect, wearing a different dress. Her performances were in concert halls, in colleges, in churches. In every photo, her face seemed to say she knew people would be admiring it on such a poster. Her name was followed by the composers we all loved so much: *Tina Li Plays Beethoven, Rachmaninoff, Liszt.* She looked at me as if watching, as if telling me that she had made it, and that if I worked hard enough, I, too, could have that life. I got up close and studied each one. Then, buoyed by this new inspiration, I practiced.

When I finished, there was a note on the floor right outside the studio. I picked it up and read,

MEET AT THE
NORTH CAMPUS GARDEN
ONE HOUR BEFORE SUNSET.

My heart sped up, with fear or nerves or something else. Ghostwriter was onto me, then. They'd seen that I'd been trying and trying to catch them, and now they were going to come out and reveal themselves.

I found Jenny in a practice room and showed her the note.

I didn't want to meet Ghostwriter alone—even if it was my initiation.

In the studio, I tried to continue practicing, but I couldn't concentrate. I could see the sky changing color through the window. Around four o'clock, I packed up my music and headed out.

Chapter 13

IN THE NORTH CAMPUS GARDEN, I STOOD BENEATH A TREL-
lis that had the last of fall leaves clinging to it. After a while, Lily
Zhang and Cassandra Maverick passed by, clutching their books
to their chests, steps in sync, so deep in conversation that they
continued talking with each other even as they waved at me. A
couple minutes later, I heard male voices: Rocky and Daniel,
Rocky kicking a soccer ball.

"What I wouldn't give to be in your studio," Daniel was saying. "I bet you're learning a lot just through osmosis."

It was impossible—unless you were practicing—to be completely alone at Greenwood. Your roommate was always in the
room, and even if you went for a walk in town, you were bound to
run into other Greenies. I'd seen people try to eat lunch at a table
by themselves, reading a book or just scrolling on their phones,
and inevitably others always joined. And the North Campus Garden wasn't really a place to commune with nature—or wait for an

anonymous note writer—as much as it was a spot for people to find you outside.

"Do you think that's true, Wu?" Rocky asked, as if I'd been part of the conversation all along. He picked up the soccer ball and held it under one arm.

"Sure," I said. "I think Dr. Li does things that we can't yet understand—or at least that's what I'm hoping."

"Do you know what she assigned me the other day? Debussy Arabesque number one. My thirteen-year-old cousin is playing that!" said Rocky.

"But you can play it a lot more beautifully that your cousin," I pointed out.

She had assigned me an easier piece as well, a Copland prelude that was so still, I had groaned to Jenny that it involved more rests than actual playing. But Dr. Li had said it was suggestive of the American prairie, spacious and wide, and required the discipline of listening, of knowing when I had spent just enough time with each chord, of the surest touch that allowed each note to ring. Attention to detail, note by note and even rest by rest, was more important than being flashy, she'd said.

But Rocky said, "I don't want to play some dumb piece—"

"It's not dumb. It's Debussy."

"Okay. I don't want to play some easy piece beautifully. I want to play something that makes people piss their pants in the recital hall, because they are that impressed."

"Ew!" I said.

"Hell yeah," said Daniel, and fist-bumped Rocky.

After a couple minutes I heard the crunch of leaves being

stepped on, and through the trees I saw a familiar pair of canvas sneakers.

"You know what, this is creepy as hell," Jenny said, approaching us.

"Oh, good afternoon to you, too," I said. Stepping around me, she patted my head as if we were playing Duck, Duck, Goose.

"Wait, what's creepy?" said Rocky.

Jenny gestured toward me. "Claire here is meeting her stalker." She glanced up at the sky. "Oh, any minute now."

"What?" Rocky looked at me. "No way." He slid his backpack off and set it on the grass. "Who's ready to catch a ghost?"

"I don't know," I said. "I kind of wanted only Jenny to be here—"

"Nope, no way am I missing this," said Rocky. "The big reveal."

"I wish I could stay, but I have chamber rehearsal with Craig and Jessie, and I'm always late," said Daniel. "That's what they tell me, anyway."

Just as Daniel was leaving, Leo Epstein came running toward us, wearing his Viking hat and panting. "Guys, phew! I'm glad I made it on time." He removed the hat, wiped sweat off his forehead, then replaced it.

Rocky said, "You're the one doing this, aren't you, Epstein?"

"No!" Leo said, putting his hands in the air. "I just overheard Stone saying she was headed here and you know, I've seen some of these notes and—and I have this theory." He paused. "Everyone in the Greenwood Philosophers Guild, what do they have in common?"

"Uh," said Jenny, "besides having too much time on their hands?"

Before I could respond, Leo snapped his fingers and said, "They're all . . . weird. And I mean that in the best way possible. It makes sense they're all channeling their angst through these notes."

Rocky said, "It's got to be someone who knows your comings and goings pretty damn well."

Leo adjusted his hat again, then pushed his glasses up on his nose. Had Rocky been sent here to test me?

Rocky said, "All for Stone, hands up." He raised his own hand, but no one else did. Leo, however, looked at Jenny with wide eyes and nodded, like he had a newfound respect for her now that she was one of the suspects.

Jenny gave Rocky's shoulder a shove. "Ow!" he said, but he was grinning.

We were all silent, pondering. On the other side of the garden, someone let out a whooping sound, and I watched a red Frisbee sail through the air.

"As I've been saying all along, I think Toothpick is the one doing it," said Jenny.

"But why would she spend so much time on this?" I said. I thought about Toothpick, asking me to play the same part of the music again and again, pushing herself to exhaustion.

"Look, Claire, I know you think she's the most badass dancer and everything—" Jenny began.

"I never said that."

"—but she has to squash anybody who threatens her."

"It's not impossible," Leo said, stroking his chin, on which two or three brown hairs had begun to sprout. "But do we think she's so insecure about herself that she would pull something like this?"

I shook my head. "She's the prima ballerina."

"So?" said Jenny. "Success doesn't make you happy. Hemingway blew his brains out."

I shuddered.

"Thank you for that image," said Rocky.

"So I guess the person who's been writing them isn't going to come here and explain herself?" Jenny asked, looking at her watch.

Leo said, "Unless it's one of us."

We all looked at each other. Then Jenny and I burst into laughter.

"Don't look at me," said Rocky. "I was just playing soccer with Giam*balls*vo."

Jenny rolled her eyes. "Honestly, I don't even care who it is anymore," said Jenny. "I just want it to be over so we can all get on with our lives. And so we can make this person's life hell."

It began to grow dark and cold in the garden, and we eventually all sat down on the grass, hugging our knees to our chests and zipping our jackets.

"I don't think anyone's coming," Leo said after a while.

"No shit, Sherlock," said Jenny. "I'm heading out. You coming?" She nudged me.

"I don't know." I was disappointed, and a part of me wondered if Ghostwriter was hesitating because there were too many people around. I wondered if this was part of the test, if I was supposed to stay after everyone had left. "You can go back without me," I said.

Jenny looked at me, then at Rocky. "Okay," she said. "See you later."

Leo got up, too. "I'm telling you guys: if it's not the GPG, then I don't know who it can be. Although I gotta hand it to you, Stone, Toothy is not a bad idea." Jenny huffed, then they both left, Jenny walking fast ahead of Leo.

Rocky tore up blades of grass and threw them into a small pile between us, and I watched the evening sky fading to pink above the trees.

I couldn't take it anymore. "It's the Society, isn't it?" I blurted.

"Wait, what?"

"Please tell me. You have to tell me. Is it Ellie and them doing this? And you too?"

Rocky put his palms up. "Sorry, nothing to reveal here."

My heart sank. But then I said, "Are you being paid to say that?"

Rocky laughed. "I wish," he said. "Hey, look, I swear . . . on Chopin's grave that it's not the Society."

I sighed, looking at the garden.

"You okay?" Rocky said.

"I just thought I had it figured out." I cupped my chin in my hand and stared down at the grass. "Then it's because I don't speak Chinese, isn't it?" This had crossed my mind before. My mother's friends sometimes tried speaking to me in Mandarin. We'd start out with the usual pleasantries—*how are you, I'm well, thank you*—and they thought my pronunciation was so good that it would deceive them. When they asked me a question I couldn't understand, they'd appear confused, looking from me to my mother and me again. I always felt ashamed. I was envious when I overheard Ellie and Rocky speaking to each other in Mandarin, then laughing, sharing a joke in a secret language. "Everyone else speaks it, but I can only say things like 'My name is Claire' and 'Are you my friend?' and 'I want to eat rice.'"

Rocky laughed. "Those are some pretty important phrases. But no, it's not about that. You think all of us speak it, but it's really only, like, two or three people. JT's from Hong Kong, remember? And Miyoung is Korean." Rocky shook his head. "I'm telling you, that's not it."

"Well, is it because I've never been to Asia?" I didn't even like admitting this out loud. I'd tried to talk about it with Jenny once, but she'd said, "I've never been to England. That's where my family came from, in the eighteen hundreds."

"The only family we have in Taiwan is pretty distant," I continued, "and my mom—I mean I'm sure she misses it, but her life is here now."

Rocky nodded. "I get it. Even my mom hasn't been in a while. We go because my grandparents are still there. But just because I've gone doesn't mean you and I are much different. I go there, and you know what they call me?" He paused. "ABC. People literally yell it out to me on the street. It's the most annoying thing."

I must have looked confused, because he said, "American-Born Chinese."

"How can they tell, though?"

Rocky laughed. "Oh man, everything! My clothes, the way I walk, the way I talk."

"But at least you've been," I said.

"The thing is, Wu, it doesn't change you as much as you think. Although still, you should go! The food there is so good. And the hiking. People are so friendly."

I nodded miserably.

"Just trust me on this one. You'll get in before you graduate." Rocky stretched his legs out in front of him and crossed them at the ankles, leaning on his hands like he was settling in. "How are things otherwise? How is Li treating you these days?"

Under other circumstances, I would've been pleased to be alone with Rocky, but I was so disappointed that it was hard to focus. I took a deep breath and tried to let it go. "Well, the other day I had a ten-minute lesson because she said I hadn't practiced enough and she didn't want to hear me anymore," I said. Even the memory of it, still fresh, upset me. Dr. Li had listened to my Bach, asked me what I was doing in the practice room if I wasn't practicing, and dismissed me before I had a chance to play something else.

"Slacker," said Rocky. "She's actually done the same to me, too. It was over this damn sonata. Four measures. Four measures in and she goes, 'This doesn't sound like Prokofiev. Come back when you can play.'"

I shook my head in sympathy.

"But then when I did come back and felt like I could really play it, she didn't have a single good thing to say!" He shook his head. "It's not like we're learning anything from her. She's just trying to mess with our heads."

"I think she's trying to push us—like, she wants us to know that a performance is never perfect. Our work is never finished. Isn't that what makes her a good teacher?"

Rocky shook his head again. "She's impossible to please. Makes sense, from someone who's had everything handed to her all her life."

"What do you mean?"

"You haven't noticed? Sure, she immigrated, but she comes from some high-class stock."

"The clothes," I said.

"Those, for sure. But also the rug, and the art, and the degrees . . . And the way she talks about her mom, like, one time she said her mom wanted to be an actress? But she ended up staying home to, I don't know, decorate the house and look pretty. And I think of my own mom, and it's just so unfair."

Life isn't fair, I almost said, which is what my own mother said all the time, but Rocky knew that already.

Daniel had visited Rocky in the summer once, and told us there was no piano at the Wong home. Before he came to Greenwood, Rocky had practiced in the local Chinese church, on an old Baldwin that didn't get tuned often enough, and his first lessons had been from the church pianist, before Mrs. Wong took notice of her son's talent and found a professor at the University of Georgia who started giving him lessons at a discounted rate.

"You're right," I agreed. "It's not fair."

Rocky looked at me. "You know what? You're going to be really awesome, as long as you don't let her get inside your head. I mean, she sees something in you. Obviously. She picked you for the accompanying gig, after all."

"You would've been better at it."

He shook his head. "I can sight-read, but . . ." He rolled his eyes. "I think we all know who has more patience with those divas when they're in rehearsal. And that's probably more important, in the long run."

"Enough to get me into the Society, in the long run?"

He smiled. "You'll have to wait and see."

"What do I do if the notes never stop?"

"They'll stop."

"How do you know?"

"Easy. They'll get tired of it. Someone can't keep this up forever. Watching your every move? I mean, you're interesting, Wu, but whoever it is, they're bound to get tired of it after a while."

Rocky thought I was interesting? I tried not to look like I'd noticed. "Not soon enough," I said.

"Hey," said Rocky, "I'm sorry that they're giving you such a hard time." I shrugged, trying to act like it wasn't a huge deal, that I wasn't creeped out. Rocky leaned forward and put a hand on my shoulder. "It'll be okay. But it probably wouldn't hurt to not cling to Li's every word, don't you think?"

"I don't cling to her every word."

"Oh, really? Because it sure seems that way to me." But he was grinning as he said it. "And, look," he added. "If the notes were a test—well. If a club has to put you through the wringer just to have you join, it honestly isn't worth joining." He took his phone out of his pocket. "Shoot, I'm late. Group projects are the wooorst." He stood, but I stayed where I was. "You really want to find out who this writer is, don't you?" he said.

I knew it wasn't likely, but I was wondering if Ghostwriter—whoever it was—would show up now that it was only me who was waiting. Instead I said, "It's a nice night."

Rocky said he would see me tomorrow, and then walked to the dorms, his fingers flying over his phone. I wondered what it would be like if, instead of sitting in the garden while he walked away, I was walking with him hand in hand.

Does an extra lesson mean she's caring . . . or controlling?

After a few minutes I saw someone walking, very fast, across the courtyard. It was Adeline Felts, in a sweatshirt and her hot-pink leg warmers, finally out of the studio for the night.

Chapter 14

IN DECEMBER, WE SANG HOLIDAY CONCERTS WITH THE
Green Valley Orchestra. Onstage, we filed silently onto the risers
and held our black binders open in front of our mouths. We wore
red accents, the boys in red bow ties and the girls in red scarves.
We sang "Carol of the Bells" and "Angels We Have Heard on
High" and a classical rendition of "Silent Night," and we smiled at
the audience between songs. But once backstage, we complained
to each other that our feet hurt because our heels sank into the
cushioned risers. We wore pants under our long skirts to keep our
legs warm while we walked to the Green Valley concert hall, but
then we were too hot under the stage lights. We told each other
that these were the worst concerts of the year, cheesy holiday har-
monies that the audience sang along with, but secretly, I liked
them because they seemed to make the most people happy.

Dr. Li prepped us for our juries, the piano exams we took at
the end of each term. In studio class, she gave us short pieces to

sight-read and exercises to try. She gave us sheets to transpose to a different key, to improvise, to match pitch with our voices. At one of the classes, she gave us sixteen-measure excerpts from a Czerny étude and told us to memorize them. "You have twenty minutes. Go."

In the practice room I fumbled and swore, pushing myself to memorize it in two-measure sections, like a phone number. No one was able to memorize the entire thing except for Rocky, who wouldn't stop gloating about it. But Dr. Li, instead of praising Rocky, said, "All of you have different gifts and weaknesses, and need to approach the instrument with humility."

Rocky plopped into his chair, crossed his arms, and frowned.

Afterward, we listened to a live concert recording of Beethoven 2 by Martha Argerich and the Berlin Philharmonic, with Claudio Abbado conducting. We listened to the entire concerto, sitting huddled around only two copies of the score. After the final movement, there was applause and shouts of *"Brava!"* Some of us clapped, too.

"This is one of their many great recordings," Dr. Li said. She shook her head in awe. "Absolutely masterful." We all agreed, pondering the concerto in silence. Dr. Li gazed through the studio window, where outside the sky was slate gray and the grass had yellowed.

"So," she said suddenly, startling me. "What are your thoughts?"

None of us said anything. It seemed that discussions in Dr. Li's studio left us quiet and looking at one another, more than in any other class. Jenny had pointed out that it was because her questions were too broad.

"I think," Dr. Li said, after some time, "Argerich captures all the extremes that Beethoven would have wanted. But, as far as Abbado's conducting goes, it's more moderate than other orchestral interpretations of Beethoven. Do you know what I mean? It's more . . . chill, as some of you might say."

Jenny and I looked at each other. Whenever Dr. Li tried to sound like us, it made me cringe. She went on for a while, and then some of us bravely added a few comments—none of them nearly as insightful as hers, and then class was over.

We started packing our things when Dr. Li said, "Do you all have a few minutes? I need to ask you something."

We stopped what we were doing and looked at her. She usually took our few minutes without asking for them. I felt something shift in the room, as if we all thought she was about to confide something in us.

"The holiday Faculty Dinner is coming up," she said.

We all nodded. It was a big to-do in the dining hall, which was decorated with crepe paper streamers in green and gold (Greenwood colors), flowers and candles on the tables. The heads of each department and even some of the seniors made toasts with sparkling apple cider. Everyone got dressed up, and there were carving stations with roast beef and ham, and ice sculptures depicting Greenwood's arts disciplines.

Jenny blurted out what we were all thinking: "We just figured you weren't going."

Dr. Li cocked her head, as if what Jenny had said was amusing. "Well, of course I'm not going to the event in the *dining hall.*"

Then it was our turn to look at her questioningly.

"Why would we celebrate the holidays on campus when we can go out?" she said. "There are good restaurants downtown."

The restaurant she wanted to take us to was called Gaslight. Were we free next Friday? For such a large group, she would probably need to make a reservation. "Have you all been there? To Gaslight?"

Of course, none of us had eaten there before. Already I could hear my mother's voice in my head: Why go to a place where you paid other people to fold your napkin for you, fill your water glass, bring your food—when you could do all of those things in the comfort of your own home? Her gripe wasn't just about being waited on, it was something to do with the impracticality of fine food itself. Why put your hard-earned money toward something that was gone in an instant? My parents would rather have invested in real estate or a better car. And that, I was beginning to see, was one of the core differences between my parents and Dr. Li, and maybe also my parents and me. In my parents' eyes, fine dining was an unnecessary extravagance. But at Greenwood, glamour meant you'd made it; you'd succeeded enough in your art to be able to afford the other arts: concerts, museums, fine food and drink. Was that something to feel guilty about? In the rec room, we watched our alumni win SAG Awards wearing navy velvet tuxes, dresses made of sequins and silk. A couple years ago, Max Leopold, a senior dancer, had been invited to join the Denmark Ballet Troupe before even graduating—and that meant they paid for his flights, his room and board. Money made life easier. Did it necessarily make you spoiled or unkind or ungrateful? I wasn't sure. If Rocky's mother were wealthy, she could have eaten dinner with Rocky every night instead of spending all her time feeding other people.

At Dr. Li's question, Jenny laughed, the type of sound she made when she was stressed or incredulous. "No way," she said.

"So, we should go there," said Dr. Li, as if it were a perfectly normal thing to do. "You're all free, right? I'll make the call."

I looked at the others. Martyna was nodding eagerly. Rocky was scowling, and Jenny was staring at Dr. Li, one eyebrow raised.

"Gaslight?" JT said. "Of course we're free to go to Gaslight." He pointed at all of us. "You all better *make* yourselves free."

"Wonderful," said Dr. Li. "It'll be a nice way to celebrate the holidays together, as a studio."

Rocky had his lips pressed together, his mouth a thin line. No doubt he was assigning some ulterior motive to the invitation, or was annoyed that now, instead of eating dinner with whichever teacher he wanted, we had to spend an evening with Dr. Li. The rest of us were grinning. Martyna let out a yelp. Even though we couldn't believe our luck, we played it cool, saying we had plans that could take some finagling to cancel.

No teacher had ever asked us out to dinner before, and if they had, we wouldn't have gone somewhere so special. Mr. Buck had had a studio party at the end of the year, where we'd played Jenga in the courtyard over pizza and soda. I pictured all of us walking downtown with Dr. Li. Everyone at school would want to know about it afterward. All week, I thought about our dinner together. When I was singing, when I was doing homework, when I was practicing. What would she wear? What would we talk about? We'd never even eaten with Dr. Li in the dining hall, much less out. I wondered if it would be similar to class, all of us taking turns saying what we thought, feeling awkward around her. Or if it would be like the dining hall, all of us talking over each other and lunging for the food while she sat there calmly eating, not knowing what to do with us.

"Isn't it weird that, all of a sudden, she wants to take us out? I bet she's going to announce that she's leaving," Rocky said, when all of us pianists were at lunch.

Martyna said, "Maybe she's been talking to other teachers and realizes that we'll learn better if we feel more comfortable with her."

"More likely it's one of her intimidation tactics," said Jenny. "Maybe she wants us to confess something." Her eyes scanned the table. "Did one of you pull a prank?"

"Ha," said JT. "I *wish* I had the courage to pull something on her."

I felt a prickle of dread. Had she seen one of the notes about herself—surely she had by now—and was she going to try to figure out who was doing it? I wondered if I would receive a note or two about this very event; Ghostwriter would certainly have something to say about the motives behind this dinner. But I didn't receive anything.

A few days later, it was Dr. Li that we received emails from. Unlike other teachers, who wrote us weekly—at least—with homework assignments and due dates and reminders, we almost never received emails from Dr. Li. In our dorm, Jenny opened the message on her laptop, and we both gaped at it.

See you all on Friday outside of gaslight (76 Main St) at 6pm. After dinner, I would like to show you a manuscript of Bolcom's which is now out of print.

I ordered it from the Juilliard Store in New York. You
can come to my place for a bit to take a look

TL

There it was, so casually in the last sentence—which didn't
even have a period. That was the most bizarre part: Dr. Li was usually meticulous in her grammar, but the email had more than one
mistake. It read as if she'd dashed it off and sent it from her phone,
on her way to do something more important. It was the first email
I'd seen from her that wasn't signed "Dr. Li."

"I like how she added the address in parentheses as if we
wouldn't be able to find it ourselves. Or as if there's another restaurant called Gaslight in Green Valley," said Jenny.

"I've never heard her sound so . . . 'chill,'" I said, making air
quotes around the word that she'd used earlier.

I pictured all of us crowded around the Bolcolm score in
Dr. Li's living room. There would be palmetto trees in front and
rocking chairs on the wraparound porch, because of course Dr. Li
lived in one of the historical houses that had been made into separate apartments. It would be just a couple blocks from the Whisk,
where I imagined Dr. Li sometimes got brunch on weekends, a
coffee on weekdays. I wondered if it was a cozy little apartment,
the type of place where there were rules about the paint color
and light fixtures, a plaque outside saying when it had been built.
Maybe Dr. Li was taking an interest in us, finally, the way other
teachers did, asking about our lives outside of piano and school.
Maybe one of us would crack, would confess to writing the notes
or knowing who was.

Jenny and I counted down to the dinner every day. We looked at Gaslight's menu multiple times. We read and reread Dr. Li's email. We ordered dresses online for the occasion, then decided we didn't like them enough and stood in line at the post office on Saturday afternoon, feeling self-righteous about how we would not be contributing to fast fashion.

In Miyoung's room just days before the party, I tried on a long black skirt with a slit up the side, a peach-colored spaghetti-strap maxi dress with pleats, a sequined minidress that Miyoung had been saving for prom. A white top with off-the-shoulder ruffles, a taupe floral dress that Jenny said made me look like a milk-maid. Finally there was a sleeveless royal-blue dress with a skirt that flared out above my knees, the fabric cut out at the waist so an inch of my skin was visible on either side.

"This is the one," said Jenny.

"You don't think it's too much?" I eyed myself. In the mirror was the person I hoped I was becoming: fun, confident, and maybe even pretty.

"That color is *perfect* for your skin and hair," Miyoung said. "And I'm not just saying that because we both have black hair."

Martyna, pulling a lacy blouse over her own head, called out, "It's never too much!"

Jenny threw an arm around me, putting her cheek against mine, and whispered in my ear, "If you want to get with a certain other pianist, I think it's just right."

Chapter 15

ON FRIDAY NIGHT, JENNY, MARTYNA, AND I MET UP WITH
Rocky and JT outside the dorm, both in their performance best.
Even with our coats on, Jenny and I shivered in our dresses, tot-
tering around in the high heels we otherwise never got to wear. We
had never been inside one of our teachers' houses before. What
would it be like? I pictured a space as glamorous as Dr. Li herself, a
real adult's apartment like the ones we saw in movies, maybe even
with chandeliers. Her car was small and luxurious, so probably her
apartment was, too. So small that—

"I wonder if she has a piano at home," I said.

"Of course she has one," Rocky said. "What kind of piano
teacher doesn't?"

"One who lives in an apartment with limited space and neighbors above her and below her," JT pointed out. "I always had to
go somewhere else to practice in Hong Kong."

"She probably doesn't have very much stuff at all," Jenny said.

"New York apartments are shoeboxes. Haven't you ever watched *Girls?*"

"She's in Green Valley now, though. She should at least have an upright," said Rocky.

"Then why is she always practicing at school?"

"I think she's going to tell us something," said Rocky. "She has to take us off of school property to make her confession."

"What about the Bolcolm score?" said Martyna. I was pretty sure she was the only one of us who actually cared about it.

The entrance to the restaurant was on one side of the Avery apartment building, easily missed because there was only a tiny sign beside the door. Dr. Li was waiting for us when we arrived. Her only visible makeup was a swipe of red lipstick, which made her look cool and sophisticated next to the overly made-up women around her. Approaching her, I felt juvenile and desperate in my dress. But she met us with a smile and said, "You all look lovely." We beamed.

"Right this way," the hostess said. "I can take your coats and bags if you like?"

Rocky said, "Oh no, thanks, I'm good," and looked uncomfortable about inconveniencing anyone. In his suit and styled hair, I thought he looked even more handsome than usual, even though I liked his hair better when it was tousled and soft-looking.

Dr. Li gave her coat to the hostess. I handed mine over as well, mostly because it was something I'd never done before and it made me feel glamorous. Standing there in my dress, I couldn't make eye contact with Rocky, but I could feel him looking at me.

"Is it just me," Jenny whispered, "or are we being treated like royalty?"

We were led through a long hallway, the walls lined with abstract paintings for sale. Rocky inspected one of the prices and let out a low whistle.

The chairs at Gaslight were large and comfortable, and the table was crowded with more silverware and glasses than I had ever seen at one setting, so I waited for Jenny to sit down before I did. I sat between her and Martyna, with the boys on the other side and Dr. Li at the head. Across from me, Rocky said, "Cool dress, Wu." When I thanked him, I felt myself blush, then spent the next minutes wondering whether he was being genuine or sarcastic. Beside me, Jenny was pretending that she hadn't heard anything, which I was grateful for, because if we hadn't been sitting at a nice restaurant with Dr. Li, she would've said, "Told you so."

Our menus were taller than our choir music binders, and nearly as heavy. Out to dinner with Dr. Tina Li! But as we settled around the table I wondered, briefly, if this wasn't going to be a replay of the dining hall but with Dr. Li sitting closer to us. We would be ourselves, goofy and trying to impress each other, and Dr. Li would eat quietly, not really talking with any of us.

The waiter came to take our drink orders. He recognized Dr. Li right away. "It's such a pleasure to have you dine with us again, Ms. Li," he said.

"Wonderful to be here," said Dr. Li. "I wanted my students to experience it." Dr. Li ordered a mint julep, and it was hard to tell if that was what she usually ordered, or if she was trying to fit in somehow, be *southern,* and we all widened our eyes at each other, because our other teachers never drank in front of us.

"I'll have a virgin strawberry daquiri," Jenny announced.

"Same, but with extra soda," said JT.

"The pomegranate spritz, please," said Martyna, eyes gleaming. "It sounds delicious!"

"May I have a strawberry limeade, please?" I said. My parents and I always ordered water when we went out to eat, so I wanted to have something special, even though it sounded more like a summer drink.

Rocky ordered a Diet Coke.

"What?" he said when JT gave him a look. "I'm just watching my figure."

"You call that a figure?" said JT.

Dr. Li asked if we wanted any appetizers. There was just one we wanted, the fried goat cheese covered in crushed pistachios with blueberry compote and secret sauce. "Oh, come on," said Dr. Li. "Just that? For all six of us?"

We hemmed and hawed over the menu, suddenly shy, after we'd lunged at extra cookies in the dining hall, or showered the pasta in cheese, or gotten an extra slice of pepperoni pizza to eat while walking to class.

"Calamari?" Jenny said, looking at Dr. Li and then around at us, as if taking a stab at answering a question in class that no one else wanted to try.

We were silent, staring down at the prices.

"We'll have one of each appetizer," said Dr. Li, when the waiter returned.

I saw Rocky stiffen and furrow his eyebrows, like he didn't know how to handle Dr. Li being generous. His expression seemed to be saying, *What gives?*

When the food arrived, Dr. Li started passing it around, making sure all of us got a bite. It was as if she were an orchestra conductor confirming that everyone was contributing their part. There was steak tartare with a quail egg to crack over it, and buttered toasts to spread the meat on, shiny and pink. There were magenta-colored pickled eggs and swordfish pastrami, and fried green heirloom tomatoes, and steamed mussels in white wine broth, and potato croquettes with shaved truffle on top. There was foie gras. Dr. Li seemed pleased when I said I liked it, though, really, I was still trying to figure out what I thought of it.

"Eat up, eat up," she said. "This is one of the few times this year that you'll have *real* food."

"They force-feed the geese—" Rocky said.

"My god, it's so good, though," said Jenny.

"Amazing," said Martyna through a mouthful of it.

It was a meal that took all of our attention. Only Dr. Li knew how to eat everything properly, so I watched and mimicked what she did the same way I watched her in lessons. Thanks to a few sips of her drink, or maybe because we were in a setting that wasn't Greenwood, Dr. Li asked us about our lives outside of piano.

Martyna said she was looking forward to traveling to Poland for Christmas. She missed her family and their dog. Rocky said he was headed to the Asian Student Society holiday party next week.

"Claire's been trying to join that group for the past, like, half a century," said Jenny.

Under the table, I elbowed her.

Dr. Li looked puzzled. "It's exclusive? They won't let you in?"

"Secret rules," I said.

"Can't you put in a good word for her?" Jenny asked Rocky.

"Claire wants to get in on her own terms."

Jenny looked at me as if to say, *Oh really? Rocky knows about your terms?*

Dr. Li said, "Try again. That club doesn't know what they're missing."

I smiled at her.

Dr. Li continued. "When I was your age, I was in the American Club at school."

Jenny laughed. "Do we even have that much culture?"

"We went to see *The Squid and the Whale* at the art house cinema, and sometimes we'd get together, eat 'American food'"—she made quotes with her fingers—"and talk about what was going on here in the States." She sighed. "I was obsessed. We listened to all the big hits: Coldplay, the White Stripes, Beyoncé . . ."

I saw Jenny smile. I had trouble picturing Dr. Li listening to music that wasn't classical—especially Beyoncé.

That was how she started talking about her childhood. Dr. Li had been an only child, like me. Her father was a professor of sociology at a university in Taipei and was always working. Her mother was often away on weekends, auditioning and taking acting classes. In the evenings her mother would go out to see plays, beautifully dressed and made up. I tried to picture Dr. Li as a child, small and frowning, carrying her dinner to the living room alone to watch TV while she ate.

"My parents never really came to hear me play," said Dr. Li. "You should all be grateful. Your families travel a long way to hear you perform."

All this time, we'd been watching Dr. Li, admiring, even covetous. As much as I thought about her and her musical life, I never thought about her having parents the way I had parents—hadn't thought about her needing their support. She was a grown-up herself, after all.

Dr. Li was doing her best to feed us. When her Caesar salad came, she practically begged us to try it. A wedge of charred lettuce with anchovies on top, it was smoky and strong and garlicky, unlike any salad I'd ever had. "Come on, just have a little!" she exhorted us. It reminded me of my mother pushing me to eat everything at the kitchen table. I felt that Dr. Li was trying to teach us something, like maybe this was waiting on the other side of a life of hours and hours of practice, miles and miles of scales. It made me hungry in a different way: for money, for glamour, for the type of lifestyle that would make it easy to eat out at a place like this. To know the people who ate there, who knew how to pronounce things on the menu and which fork to use. How to dress like Dr. Li, to look stylish while also looking like you weren't trying too hard. This desire washed over me without my knowing exactly why, and then almost as immediately I was hating myself for it. When I looked over at Rocky, he was eating his short ribs while also eyeing the pile of olives on JT's plate, probably about to ask if JT was going to eat them.

Dr. Li ate methodically and thoroughly, pushing a piece of steak around in the sauce with her fork. In the dim light, she looked especially beautiful: her skin was glowing and her earrings sparkled. For several seconds, we all ate in silence. Then Dr. Li said, "I hope you all become something."

"Me too," said Jenny.

"Totally. I hope we don't fade into oblivion," said Rocky.

I wondered exactly what Dr. Li meant by that. My mother had sat me down when I got my acceptance letter from Greenwood and said that this whole music thing was against her wishes—but, fine: she would leave it up to me to make this choice. Too many Chinese mothers were controlling, and she wouldn't be one of them. She didn't want me to go so far away, but I could decide on my own, and not to blame *her* when I was "being worked to the bone" instead of having a nice, normal teenage life.

"You'll probably all teach," said Dr. Li. "That's one way to avoid fading away. Then your students take what they learned from you and pass it on to the next generation."

Rocky made a face. "I'd rather just play."

"The greatest pianists teach. It is part of this tradition, and the most noble thing you can do."

A couple of times I'd pictured myself as a piano teacher, but it felt far off, since I still needed so much instruction myself.

Dr. Li sopped up the sauces with bread and didn't care about taking the last piece. She was exuberant, urging us to try more of the gnocchi, to not be shy. It was then that Jenny, made even bolder by the new setting, and perhaps also by Dr. Li's imbibing, had the audacity to ask her the question.

"Dr. Li?" Jenny said. "How come you're not married?"

I looked down and pretended to be very interested in my

grits, butter-colored and creamy, nothing like the ones we had in the dining hall. It seemed all the other Greenwood teachers were married—but I hadn't dreamed of asking Dr. Li about it.

Dr. Li answered in a light, pleasant voice, but it was clear she was masking some other emotion. "I chose not to get married. I wanted to be a pianist. Having a family can be very distracting."

Dr. Hamilton had three kids, and Mrs. Hamilton played music, too. But he had never had a concert tour like Dr. Li. Then again, there were plenty of musicians in orchestras and chamber groups who *were* married.

"You did it for your art," JT said. "I know other musicians who do that." He nodded as if he knew all about it and was planning to do the exact same thing.

"That's right," Dr. Li said. "I didn't think it would be fair to give all my time and energy to music, and leave my family with only the little I had left."

I wondered if she'd left someone behind, heartbroken, pining after her. Maybe someone had even asked her to marry him, had bought the ring and everything, and Dr. Li had to say no—like a heroine in a Victorian novel with a surplus of suitors. How painful that must have been for her. I remembered seeing Amy Cellars crying loudly in the hallway when she'd broken up with Max Leopold—even though she'd been the one who broke it off.

Dr. Li looked at all of us again. "I don't want any of you to make that decision."

Rocky had been noisily slurping his Diet Coke, but at this, he put his glass down and looked at the white tablecloth. Everyone had stopped eating, and for the first time that evening, I became aware of the sounds of other diners—the murmur of their conversations, the silverware and glasses clinking, and the twinkle of jazz coming from the speakers. Dr. Li held her fork in the air, but wasn't putting any food in her mouth. When I looked to the side, Jenny's eyes were wide, as if, even though she'd been the one to poke Dr. Li, she hadn't expected this, and it was Dr. Li's fault for oversharing. Martyna was frowning.

JT said, "Argerich was married . . ." Then his voice trailed off as he realized what he was saying. *Was married* wasn't *is*. Argerich had been divorced twice.

We sat in awkward silence. A thought passed through me and made me shiver: that Ghostwriter would definitely write about this in their next note, and I already felt bad for Dr. Li. Then I remembered that it was only us pianists at the table, and I had already deemed it pretty close to impossible that Ghostwriter was one of us.

When the plates had been cleared, Dr. Li left the table to use the restroom. We stared as people at other tables watched her walk by. A waiter appeared and folded her napkin, then swept a few crumbs off the table with a curved silver pen-like tool that magically lifted them away.

Once Dr. Li was out of sight, Jenny leaned across the table and stuck her straw right into Dr. Li's mint julep, only ice and muddled mint now. She took the tiniest sip. "Ugh," she said, returning the straw to her glass. "I don't know how she does it. Too sweet for me, even watered down."

"Let me have some," said JT.

"Not a chance! She'll see that it's all gone."

Across the table, Rocky finished his third glass of Diet Coke and pushed a piece of bread into the white wine broth.

"Why are you doing that?" said Jenny.

"What? It's delicious."

"I meant the Coke."

Rocky tore off another piece of bread. "I need it to stay awake. I haven't been sleeping much recently."

I glanced at him. It was true that his eyes looked tired.

"Many great artists are insomniacs," said Martyna.

Rocky laughed. "It's straight-up stress. Although thanks for saying I'm great."

JT sighed. "It's glorious to be eating here," he said.

"Professors do this all the time in college," said Jenny.

"Maybe in books and movies they do. This place is wild," said Rocky. He slurped the rest of his Coke. "It's got a real stuck-up vibe, if you ask me."

"We get to go to her house after this," Martyna said in a sing-song voice, and bounced up and down in her chair. "Do you think she has pets? A garden?"

"No and no. Are you kidding me? She doesn't do yardwork," said Rocky. "Now the curtain shall come down. We'll see the *real* Dr. Li." Rocky put his palms together, then tapped his fingers against one another as if scheming.

"Will you stop it already?" said Jenny. "It's a quick visit to see the score and then we're out of there."

We saw Dr. Li approaching and immediately returned to being as nonchalant as we could. When she sat down, we thanked her several times for dinner, complimenting the food all over again.

"Oh, it was my pleasure," she said, which always struck me as a very adult thing to say. "Now we'll take a look at that Bolcolm score. Unfortunately, I don't have a lot of room in my car."

Jenny and I met eyes. I hadn't been expecting to get into Dr. Li's car.

"That's okay," said Rocky. "We can just walk."

"It would be quite a long walk," said Dr. Li.

"Oh, I don't mind. Giambalvo and I walked to Goodwill once. It was, like, six miles all together."

"What a great use of time," Jenny muttered.

"I found my favorite shirt there!" said Rocky.

"How about this," said Dr. Li. "I'll take the girls first, drop them at home, and come back for Rocky and JT."

We left the restaurant, walking through the abstract-art-lined hallway again, all of us livelier than we were when we first entered—going through the whole ritual of having our coats fetched for us again. Outside, we signed into the campus safety app, Guardian, to let staff know that we were getting a ride with a faculty member. Dr. Li signed with her index finger. Then Jenny and I climbed into the back of the gray Mini Cooper. Martyna took the passenger seat, and Dr. Li told Rocky and JT to wait for her to pick them up. "My house isn't much," she said, "but I hope you'll enjoy yourselves there."

Chapter 16

SINCE WE WEREN'T ALLOWED CARS AT GREENWOOD, IT had been several months since I'd been inside one. Still, I could tell that Dr. Li did not practice what they called, in driver's ed, defensive driving. Her small car was meant more for the city than a small town, and she drove like it, too. We ran yellow light after yellow light as if we were in a hurry. At other times she changed lanes with just a hair between us and the next car, as if trying to get out of the way. She honked, even though drivers in Green Valley rarely used their horns. Maybe she'd learned to drive in Taipei, where motorcycles weaved between the cars. My mother had said that crossing the street there was an extreme sport—and for that reason, my mother herself drove with great caution, almost never exceeding the speed limit.

From the front seat, Dr. Li said, "I didn't have time to actually see the place before I moved in. Everything happened so fast, you know. The school called and offered me the job. I figured, since

I was moving here, I might as well truly get away from the city. Dr. Hamilton told me this neighborhood was up-and-coming. In fact, his family lives not far from here."

"How are you liking it?" Martyna asked.

"I like it fine. I bought this place, so I've been able to do a few things to make it my own." She fiddled with the radio. "And you know, Dr. Hamilton wasn't wrong, it is up-and-coming. I've seen a lot of young families move in."

None of us said what we were thinking, which was that she herself was not part of a young family. Was she thinking of staying in Green Valley for a while? We passed by a long stretch of wooded areas, Spanish moss hanging from the trees, until Dr. Li pulled into a driveway and we all got out of the car. We followed her over to a white house with blue shutters. Dr. Li paused on the steps to take her shoes off before entering, and we all followed suit. Then she unlocked the door.

We stepped into Dr. Li's living room in the delicate way that girls move when they've spent far too long on their hair, but immediately forgot about it upon seeing the space. Dr. Li's remark that she'd "made it her own" had been an understatement. The entire room, cabinets and all, was painted a glossy dark blue. Books organized by color lined the wall. Everywhere there were paintings and drawings, some of them framed on the blue walls, others stacked upright in rows on the floor or against chair legs. A vase of white peonies sat on a table in front of a window. The fireplace was full not of logs, but thick white pillar candles. A few large mirrors hung over the mantle, many of them with slightly tarnished brass frames, as if they were antiques. The couch was of soft-looking black leather, accented here and there by cushions in jewel tones, and in the left corner was a black baby grand piano and matching bench—and a blue yoga ball off to one side.

"Living room, obviously," said Dr. Li.

Jenny and I looked at each other. So there *was* a piano. She had probably bought it when she arrived.

Dr. Li went over to what looked like a set of cabinets near the piano and opened it, revealing a TV inside. Then, from somewhere near the bookcases, a gray-and-white cat slinked toward us as if anticipating our arrival. Dr. Li spoke to this cat as if it were one of us. "You're late, Freddy. Stand up straight while you're walking, please." She poked the cat in the stomach with her toe, and he immediately straightened.

Jenny and I both stood taller as well. I hadn't pictured Dr. Li with any pets, but a cat—especially one that she spoke to like one of her students—made a lot of sense.

"The cat's name is Freddy?" Jenny asked.

"Frédéric, actually, as in Frédéric Chopin. I find it very fitting. Freddy can have quite a Romantic nature." Dr. Li bent down and stroked Freddy's head. "Isn't that right? Have you had your dinner yet?"

I raised my eyebrows at Jenny. Of course, I'd never seen Dr. Li speak to an animal before. I was glad she didn't do it in a higher pitch like people who treated their pets like babies. Freddy didn't look much like a Romantic to me. One of his ears and two of his feet were white, as if he'd had an accident with the milk. His yellow eyes seemed indifferent, possessing neither the melancholy expression of Chopin nor Beethoven's perpetual scowl.

"I like the color of the walls," said Jenny.

"Thank you," said Dr. Li. "I painted them myself. It's nice to have a home improvement project after teaching."

If we'd been alone, that was the type of comment that would have made Jenny and me giggle.

"You have a lot of art," Martyna observed.

"Oh, odds and ends," said Dr. Li. She seemed nervous all of a sudden, even giddy, as if she wasn't used to having people in her home and wanted to make a good impression without appearing to show off. "Some of it I got from my parents, you know, pieces they weren't using anymore. And some from flea markets, places I've traveled to for concerts. And some of them were done by friends of mine."

Beside the piano was a sketch of Dr. Li herself, a caricature in black ink. In it, she was sitting at a grand piano rendered very small, with the train of her dress trailing beyond the bench and her hair dramatically blowing behind her as she played. I peered at it. A scribbled signature at the bottom was hard to decipher, but I could make out the initials *D.M.*: Diego Montes. It *did* look similar to the caricatures of composers that Dr. Li had shown me.

Maybe the dancers had been right after all.

I drew away from the artwork to find Dr. Li looking at me, and my stomach jumped. "Now, come with me to the kitchen," she said. "This way."

As we walked through the house (or was it technically a condo?), I couldn't stop thinking about it: Dr. Li, still in love with a married man, with his artwork in her house. Or maybe they really were just friends now?

Then Jenny pointed out the large deck, visible through a living room window, and my mother's voice popped into my head, pragmatic as ever: How much did this place cost and did she like this location? How new was this development? How much would its value increase in the next ten years? Unlike in my family's house, the carpet was plush and new, like stepping onto a foam mattress. I tried to tread lightly, as if I would leave footprints. On the way to the next room, we passed a small artificial Christmas tree strung with white lights. Single file, we followed Dr. Li through the room.

The kitchen was small, but had gleaming new appliances and marble countertops. On the island there was quite a spread: a glass bowl of red punch and plenty of hors d'oeuvres awaited us. Gummy bears lay piled on a ceramic platter, and teacups and saucers were laid out.

"This is so nice," I said. The truth was, I was so full from dinner that I couldn't even think about eating anything now.

"Oh my god, this is amazing," Jenny said.

"Gummy bears!" Martyna exclaimed.

Dr. Li took ice out of the freezer and dropped it carefully into the punch bowl. Then she took cheeses, mini cheesecakes, and a "family size" tub of hummus from the refrigerator and began arranging everything on the island. Martyna helped her scoop hummus into a bowl, but I was still getting over seeing Dr. Li in stockinged feet, pulling things out of the fridge. My mother always offered way too much food to my friends, and I was starting to feel that same trickle of embarrassment on Dr. Li's behalf. I found it both touching and awkward that Dr. Li had set everything up before meeting us for dinner.

"Wow," I said. "You really didn't have to—" Then I sneezed, twice, so violently that Dr. Li started.

"Are you all right?" she asked me.

I sniffed, embarrassed.

"Damn, Claire," said Jenny.

"Excuse me. I just need a tissue," I said to Dr. Li's retreating form, and then sneezed again. She reappeared with a Kleenex box.

"Martyna mentioned she likes gummy bears, so I just wanted to make sure we had enough," Dr. Li said. Jenny and I looked at each other. Since when did she pay attention to which candy we liked? And, judging by the size of the platter, there were enough gummy bears to keep Martyna happy for weeks.

Dr. Li put her hands on her hips. "Well, I'm sorry to leave in such a rush, but I don't want the boys to be waiting long at the restaurant."

Jenny and I looked at each other again. Dr. Li never apologized.

She consulted her reflection in the microwave. We could hardly see ourselves in it, but she seemed to think she looked decent enough. We kept thanking her, and she kept waving her hand as if to quiet us down. That reminded me of my parents' few Chinese friends. They always brushed off my thank-yous and refused to say *You're welcome*. "Make yourselves at home," said Dr. Li. "I'll be back in a few minutes."

Jenny, Martyna, and I stood in the kitchen. We heard the car start up in the driveway, and then the headlights swept through the kitchen windows and disappeared.

"Holy shit," said Jenny. We all gaped at the feast on the table. Now that Dr. Li had left, we were freer with each other. "Like, who sets up a veritable *mountain* of gummy bears like this?"

Martyna helped herself to two handfuls, but that hardly did anything to the appearance of the pile.

Jenny started opening the cabinets.

"What are you doing?" I asked.

"Just curious."

Martyna had already settled onto the couch and was stroking Freddy in her lap. She turned the TV on. I picked up another tissue and blew my nose.

It turned out that Dr. Li kept liquor in one cabinet: A few amber-colored bottles and clear ones that I didn't recognize.

"What have we here?" Jenny said.

"You really shouldn't—"

Jenny twisted open the vodka and poured a splash into her punch, then put the bottle back in the cabinet, exactly where it had been.

Curious myself, I opened the refrigerator. Besides the things she had bought for us, there wasn't much else. Eggs, iced tea, club soda. A jar of Chinese chili sauce among several other condiments, a couple takeout containers. On the counter, a ceramic bowl full of lemons. I decided I would have a bowl of citrus in my kitchen when I had my own place. It looked so chic.

I closed the refrigerator. Dr. Li had bought all this food for us, and now we were too full to eat it. She would see that we hadn't touched a thing. I imagined her pushing a cart along at the grocery store. Would they like these chips? Maybe they'd want some of these. . . . Yet this was the same woman who'd sent Martyna to the dorm in tears because she "wasn't playing to her potential." I shook my head. Would she even care if the food sat there, uneaten? But she had invited us over, hadn't she? And she'd been kind, even sweet, at dinner, like a cool young aunt. I toyed with the idea of crushing some of the potato chips and arranging broken pieces on top to make it look like we'd dipped into them. Or taking some and burying them at the bottom of the trash can. Or even outside, shoving them into the dirt under a bush.

From the living room came the sound of the piano—a few random chords, then Jenny started in on Haydn. I ladled myself some of the punch and went to look at the art and books. Dr. Li had all the classics, especially the Russians: Chekhov and Tolstoy and Dostoyevsky. There were also books on piano pedagogy, which surprised me. I'd always thought she just transferred her knowledge to us in whatever way she deemed best for the day—it had never occurred to me that she read about how to teach.

"Do you think she gets lonely here? Living all by herself?" Martyna said.

"If I was a Greenwood teacher," said Jenny, "I'd give anything to have my own place away from us. No offense to my awesome roommate."

"Especially in a place like this," I said. "It's kind of far from campus, though."

"This is exactly what I would want my house to look like," said Martyna.

"Same, décor-wise," I said.

"Right," said Jenny. "I don't love that this house looks the exact same as the one next door."

I joined Jenny on the piano bench. We tinkered around, some of the four-hand Schumann we could remember, and some variations on pop songs, the same chords over and over.

Under the sound of the chords, Jenny said, "You know what we should do? We should go upstairs." We'd seen the stairs near the front door when we first came in.

"I don't know—"

"Just for a look, before she gets home."

Dr. Li was out and wouldn't be here for another half hour, at least. Martyna, on the couch, looked like she was completely sucked into the reality show she was watching, and she was picking at a plate full of snacks, which I couldn't help feeling relieved about. We left the piano and made our way to the stairs.

♩♫

Traditional Chinese-style paintings lined the walls along Dr. Li's staircase, which I only recognized because my parents had similar ones at home: minimal, delicate renderings of orchids and bamboo. Upstairs, there were three closed doors. Jenny and I stood in the dim hallway.

"I don't feel right about this," I said.

"You'll regret it if you don't," said Jenny.

"That's not true at all—" But she stepped in front of us and opened the first door.

"See? Absolutely nothing to worry about," Jenny said. "We're just seeing the bathroom that her lover uses when he's here." There was a floral shower curtain, pale blue bathmats. Jenny grinned and pointed to the sink: a tiny toothpaste, a washcloth, and a travel-sized facial cleanser.

"A *man* uses Clinique face wash?"

"Don't judge," said Jenny.

"Why would her . . . lover"—the word felt strange in my mouth—"need a separate bathroom?"

Jenny shrugged. "Beats me. I don't claim to understand the complexities of adult relationships."

We left the bathroom and went into the next room.

"Oh my gosh, I looove this," Jenny said.

The room was painted a soft blush. There were a few bright art prints and black-and-white photos propped against the wall as if Dr. Li was still deciding which ones to hang. On the nightstand was a variety of books, neatly stacked: *The Field Guide to Dumb Birds of North America*, *Pachinko* by Min Jin Lee, and a coffee table book about royal fashion. The bed-spread was white with gold polka dots, and there was a big faux fur white pillow—the kind with arms so you could sink into it and read.

"This room has such a fun vibe," I said.

"Right?" Jenny said. "It's a guest room, but it has a personality."

"Her real personality?" I said. Rocky had kept repeating that we would see the "real" Dr. Li. This couldn't possibly be what he meant. But maybe Dr. Li outside of the classroom just wanted everyone to have a good time.

"You know teachers can't be their real selves at school, right? She's probably so much funner than she lets on. Come *on*, Tina, let loose and live a little!"

It sort of looked like Dr. Li had scoured Pinterest for what made for a hip guest room. She had succeeded.

Jenny dropped to her knees in front of the artwork and rifled through it. "This is legit," she said, handing me a funky print of a blue lion on an orange background. "It's a Leo! I wonder if that means *she's* a Leo? Oh my god, it would make so much sense. That would explain why she can be so domineering sometimes. She's a diva, you know? But she also knows how to have fun."

We looked at the other prints: a giraffe wearing a tiny hat towered above several other animals; two ice-skaters glided hand in hand in Central Park; a night sky above the mountains glimmered with stars. If this was the real Dr. Li, then she had an eye for the whimsical, for pleasure in life. She wasn't just about miles of scales.

We closed the door and found ourselves in the hallway again. "Door number three?" Jenny asked, and opened it before I could respond.

It was clearly Dr. Li's bedroom. In the middle of the room was a queen-size bed with a pale gray comforter and cream-colored pillows. The room was neat and—compared to the living room—spare, an oasis away from the rest of the house, where there was something interesting in every corner.

Jenny and I looked at each other. "I'll do it if you do it," Jenny said.

With a brief running start, we flopped ourselves onto the bed. It smelled like her, the orange blossom perfume I caught sometimes in lessons.

On the pillows was a small white teddy bear.

"What do you think about this?" I asked, holding out the

bear. Now that we were on her bed, it felt less wrong to touch her things.

"Let me see it," Jenny said. "Somebody probably bought it for her."

I hoped this was the case. I hoped that someone she loved had bought it for her. But a teddy bear seemed too juvenile, and not her taste at all. I wondered if she'd bought it for someone else. A niece or a nephew, maybe. But then why would it be on her bed?

Touching the bear, I felt sad for Dr. Li in a way that I didn't understand. Somehow it made the room, which minutes ago I'd thought lovely, seem lonely.

"Do you think she has friends?" Jenny said. "In New York, maybe?"

"And in Taiwan," I said. "So far away."

"That sucks."

We lay on the bed for a while. Then a thought occurred to me: that Dr. Li had bought the bear for herself, that maybe she even talked to it at night. Had it been well-worn, at least it could be some loved thing from childhood. As it was, it sat cream-colored and pristine, blending with the pillows.

Jenny rolled over to look at the nightstand, handing me her findings one by one. Dr. Li was reading *Zen and the Art of Motorcycle Maintenance*. She had lavender hand cream as thick as butter and an alarm clock that emitted fake sunlight before playing NPR.

"Rocky was looking at you tonight," said Jenny.

I tried not to smile. "He's weird like that. Sometimes he just randomly stares at people."

"Not the way he was looking at you." Jenny poked me in the shoulder a couple times. "He was looking at you like, 'Ooh, Claire, I'm in love with you.'" She widened her eyes at my face and then my dress.

I grinned up at the ceiling. We slid off the bed—Jenny to admire a painting above the bureau and I to inspect the contents of Dr. Li's desk. She had plastic laminated cards with pictures of saints. They were brightly colored, almost gaudy, and she'd set them up on the far corner of the desk, more kitschy than religious. In addition to these, she had a few issues of *Musician's Monthly* and a fountain pen, personalized stationery, a copy of the Greenwood handbook, and a mini bust of Bach. That was when I saw it. Under the latest copy of the *Green Valley News,* a scrap of notebook paper. With one careful finger, I slid it out from under the newspaper. It had been ripped down the middle, but I recognized what I was touching: a note that had been meant for me, or else one of my classmates, that had ended up in Dr. Li's hands. Before I could consider it any longer, I read it.

LONE LI: IT'S ALWAYS
DINING HALL,
THEN LIBRARY, THEN STAYING
LATE FOR LESSONS.

YOU DON'T WANT TO END
UP LIKE HER!

My heart sank. Dr. Li had seen this? I couldn't help thinking that she'd read this and then invited us over to . . . what, exactly? Prove to herself—and to Ghostwriter—that she wasn't so lonely after all?

"Whatcha looking at?" Jenny said, and I jumped.

"Not much," I said, shoving the paper out of sight. I would have shown Jenny any other note, but this was something that I shouldn't have seen, and I was going to keep it to myself and try to unsee it. Clearly, Dr. Li had hoped no one would see it, ever. The other notes she'd let slide, but this one had struck a nerve. Was it because this one was true?

To my relief, Jenny saw the stationery and school handbook and said, "Boh-ring."

We explored Dr. Li's closet next. There were small glass bottles of perfume, a lipstick in a gold case. There was the long blue gown from her album photo, the skirt rippling in our hands. One of burgundy taffeta rustled when I touched it, and a silky black dress fell into a tangled heap when we accidentally let it slip from the hanger. We touched her clothes reverently; we thought of what it would be like to wear dresses like those. To stand backstage in a long gown while a three-thousand-seat auditorium filled up, the lights dimmed. I threw a silk scarf around my neck while Jenny buckled Dr. Li's trench coat around her waist. I wished I was grown-up, that I had earned the right to wear clothes like that without feeling I was playing dress-up. That I *was somebody.*

What did Dr. Li think about before she fell asleep? We wanted to see her sink, her silverware, her shoes, her socks. We wanted to know: Did she get on her knees and pull weeds out of her yard? What did she wear to sleep, was it as nice as what we saw her in during the day? Did she cook, take out her trash? Who did she love, and who loved her?

Jenny stood beside me and we looked at ourselves in the full-length mirror. Dr. Li's coat sleeves fell past Jenny's wrists. I saw us ten years in the future, living in our own place, on the music faculty at a school like ours, or maybe even a conservatory. We'd play four-hand Brahms in Carnegie Hall, signing programs afterward.

"You know what this lipstick is called?" Jenny pointed to her mouth, which was now the color of raspberries.

"What?"

"Orgasm."

"Gross. You put it on straight from the tube?"

"Uh-huh. It's like I just made out with her."

"I don't think she'd like that very much."

"You should try it."

I allowed Jenny to apply the lipstick, and then I sneezed. Twice, three times. Four. I had ignored my sneezes earlier, figuring it was winter, after all, but now realized that I was very allergic to Freddy: my eyes watered and itched. I went into Dr. Li's bathroom and found Benadryl, then took a single pill and was careful to replace the bottle in its exact same position, between a tube of fancy sunscreen and a box of Band-Aids. Then I cupped my hand under the faucet and swallowed the medicine in a few gulps. Jenny came in and unzipped a cosmetics bag that was beside the sink.

"False eyelashes. Hmm, I was wondering about that. What else is in here, I wonder?" She shook the bag onto the counter, and all at once, several condoms fell out.

I had seen one before, in the sex ed class that all freshmen were required to take, where Ms. Shelley had opened a condom and stretched it over a banana, to demonstrate. Amy Cellars had told Jenny and me that a penis had a life of its own. It moved around by itself, she said, with little control from its owner. The first and only time she'd had sex, Amy hadn't wanted to touch Max Leopold's penis *or* the condom.

"Jackpot," Jenny said. "Trojan Tchaikovsky." She began to unwrap one.

"Wait, what are you doing?" I said. "We shouldn't even be in here, and definitely shouldn't be messing with her . . . sexual defenses."

Jenny took one out of the wrapper, and it wasn't what I'd been expecting. It was a perfect circle. We both touched it, wrinkling our faces at the texture, all thin and slimy.

But why should I have been surprised? Of course Dr. Li had sex. All adults did, didn't they? Or if she wasn't currently, she would be prepared to.

"Look how big this one is," Jenny was saying, when we heard the soft rumble of an engine outside, and then the headlights of Dr. Li's car shone through the bathroom window. "She's here!" Jenny squealed. She swiped the lipstick off her mouth. I ran to the bed and smoothed it, fluffing the pillows to conceal the shape of our heads. Jenny gathered up the condoms and eyelashes and stuffed them into the makeup bag. We sprinted down the stairs, nearly falling over one another, and threw ourselves onto the couch. Freddy was there, curled up against the largest pillow, with a look that seemed to say, *I told you so.* Martyna shook her head at us. "You guys shouldn't have done that."

Jenny put a finger to her lips. "Not a word."

By the time Dr. Li appeared in the doorway, followed by Rocky and JT, we were sitting on the couch with our best bored faces on, scrolling through Jenny's phone.

"You're making yourselves right at home, I see," Dr. Li said.

She went to the kitchen table and plucked a single red gummy bear, then popped it in her mouth and chewed thoughtfully, as if it were a pricey chocolate.

Rocky stood in the doorway to the kitchen while JT gushed over the tiny teacups and the desserts.

"It's warm in here, isn't it?" said Dr. Li. She cracked open one of the living room windows.

Jenny looked at me knowingly.

Then Dr. Li said, "Oh, why is nobody eating anything? Come on! Eat!" She looked at us, and then at the table. I wondered what it was like when she had other guests. If a guy came over, did she buy cheesecake and set out the teacups for him? Or did she wait until he was gone before stirring sugar into her tea and taking it into the living room to practice Bach?

"We just ate," said Rocky.

Instinctively, I checked Dr. Li's face. She was smiling slightly. Normally, she'd reprimand Rocky for such a snide remark, but she said nothing this time—maybe because we were at her house and not in class, and she didn't want to get into it with him right now.

I shot Rocky a look. Did he have to be so rude?

He shrugged. "What? It's true," he said.

"But it's so nice of you," I said to Dr. Li. Feeling guilty, and wanting to make up for Rocky, I went to the table and maneuvered a slice of cheesecake onto my plate, along with a few strawberries, a chocolate cupcake with a complicated sugar decoration on top, a few celery sticks and carrot sticks, hummus, gummy bears, and two deviled eggs—far more than I intended to eat. Jenny followed suit.

"Geez," said Rocky. "What's up with you two? It's like we didn't just stuff ourselves at dinner."

Dr. Li beamed, pleased that we were enjoying the bounty she'd provided. Martyna helped herself to even more gummy bears.

"What's up with *you*?" I hissed. "It's not like you don't normally eat two cheeseburgers in the dining hall."

"Those burgers are for leprechauns." He lowered his voice to a whisper. "And what's she trying to prove, anyway, with all this?"

"Well," Dr. Li said brightly, "you can always take some with you so you have snacks over the weekend."

I waited for Rocky to mutter something about not wanting to take her bougie food, but he just scowled.

JT stood in the middle of the kitchen with his plate and turned all the way around, admiring his surroundings as if we were at a housewarming party. "I love the glass cabinets," he said, "and the way you put your beautiful pottery in there so people can see it is just perfect."

"Oh, thank you," said Dr. Li. "I'm not quite sure what to do with this space here." She pointed to an empty square of counter between the stove and refrigerator. "It's a bit awkward."

"Maybe a plant?" JT suggested. "Like a really nice, full, blooming one where the branches can hang over the sides."

"Or cookbooks?" Martyna said.

"Cookbooks! That's not a bad idea. In fact, that would free up some much-needed space on my bookshelves."

Who was this person who talked about redecorating her house with her students? This casual homeowner who had settled into a community that seemed more for small families or even old, retired couples?

Rocky rolled his eyes—clearly these topped the list of first world problems—and then proceeded to pick up a plate anyway.

I left Dr. Li to discuss her kitchen layout with JT and Martyna and took a seat on the couch. Rocky came and sat beside me, balancing his plate on his knees. Boys in their concert clothing were like men, completely different from the teenagers I saw in class, blowing spit wads and wearing T-shirts with nonsense phrases on them. At dinner I'd looked over at Rocky holding his fork and knife, no elbows on the table like in the dining hall, not even wolfing down as usual but chewing nicely, and I was delighted—he looked so grown-up. Now I was enamored by his dainty plate with several gummy bears and a mini tart, dwarfed by his huge hand. He held his cup of punch as if it were a teacup, with his fourth and fifth fingers in the air. Then he took something out of his pocket, popped it in his mouth, and washed it down with the punch.

"Whoa," I said. "What was that?"

"Oh, I've been getting these headaches." He waved it away, then said, "So, what were you guys up to while we were out?"

"Not much," I said. "Same as what we're doing now—making

ourselves at home." I smiled, thinking my answer was both mysterious and pragmatic.

Then Rocky's eyes fell on my mouth. At first, I reached up to brush a crumb away, but his eyebrows lifted. Then he cocked his head ever so slightly toward me, and under his breath said, "Hope she doesn't recognize your lipstick."

I caught my breath. I'd forgotten to wipe it off upstairs, and now I swiped my napkin over it.

"You don't have to *be* her to be a good pianist, you know."

"I wasn't doing that," I said. But if I hadn't been doing that, then what *had* I been doing?

"I just meant you only have to be yourself."

Jenny came in then and sat on the other side of me. "Ooh, are we talking about being our authentic selves? Like, what does that even mean these days?"

As we talked, I felt Rocky leaning toward me, gradually, almost imperceptibly. Soon we were knee to knee and shoulder to shoulder. On one side, I smelled the familiar scent of Jenny's Suave Essentials shampoo and conditioner, her laundry detergent; and from Rocky, on the other side, sweat mixed with the remains of too much cologne. Very, very slowly, I eased myself toward him as well. We sat like that for only a few seconds, but it felt like minutes. My heart was pounding, and I wished I weren't so congested still, and that I hadn't taken so much to eat.

Dr. Li said, "Something to drink, guys?" as she walked toward us on the couch. Then, eyeing me a bit more closely: "Are you all right, Claire?"

"Yeah." My voice had gone all raspy and nasal, despite just

having taken several sips of water from her bathroom faucet. "I think I'm sort of allergic to Freddy."

"What? Why didn't you tell me earlier?" She rushed over, and Rocky and I shifted apart. "What do you take for allergies? Would you like Benadryl? I think I have some."

"Oh, I . . . no, I don't take anything."

Jenny turned to me. "Oh man. You should definitely take some. Your eyes are starting to get puffy."

"Really, I'm worried," said Dr. Li. "Just take one Benadryl, it'll clear you right up." Gathering Freddy up in her arms, she ran up the stairs to her bathroom.

When she came down, she told me that she had left Freddy in her room and he wouldn't be appearing again that evening. Then she made a big production of filling a tall blue glass full of water and handing me the pill, which I slipped into my pocket when she wasn't looking.

"Will you be okay?" she asked, setting the glass in the sink. "You poor thing."

It sounded to me like she might be a bit drunk. She put a cool hand up to my face, lightly brushing my eyelid with her index finger. Up close, I could see that tiny creases extended from her lash lines like a bit of permanent winged eyeliner. She dropped her hand, her face suddenly stern. "Why didn't you tell me right away that you were allergic? Then you wouldn't be having such a reaction."

This probably wasn't true, but it was similar to the type of thing my own mother always said. That if I hadn't been wearing shorts I wouldn't have caught a cold. If I had been paying better attention I wouldn't have cut myself when dicing onions. It was very Chinese to turn the blame on your children for their own misfortune. I nodded.

Then I went to the couch, where JT had taken Rocky's seat— he'd gone to the piano—and Jenny was chatting away. I could tell she was in a fine mood because she liked knowing things about Dr. Li that the other students didn't. But I felt guilty about having looked through everything, as if we were searching for something.

As we watched an old episode of *Saturday Night Live* (Dr. Li's choice—she had one in particular that she wanted us to see), I spent most of the show partially curled up on her leather couch with my head on Jenny's shoulder, drowsy and loopy from the medication. She slipped an arm around me and mumbled, "Poor wittle Claire," and I watched the television and, out of the corner of my eye, saw Dr. Li laughing quietly with her legs tucked underneath her. What would she have been doing on a Friday night, if we hadn't been there?

She'd wanted us to look through her things. The more I thought about it—how she'd left us there—the more I knew it was true. She wanted us to know that, at least at this fancy school in this small town, she was someone. With this thought, I dozed off. Then the show ended and I felt I could fall asleep right in her living room, that she wouldn't have minded. By the time we got in her car to go to campus, I could breathe normally again. I sat with my forehead pressed against the cool window, Jenny beside me. We were like children again, looking out at unfamiliar houses in the dark and longing for our beds.

Chapter 17

IF DR. LI HAD NOTICED ANYTHING AWRY ABOUT HER BED-
room, she didn't say anything about it. In my lesson a few days
after our dinner, something had shifted between us. She wasn't
warm, exactly—Dr. Li was never going to be the kind of teacher
who put your birthday in her calendar or complimented a new
haircut—but she wasn't ice-cold, either. She actually greeted me
before our lesson instead of just rushing me in, getting straight to
the music.

"How was the rest of your weekend?" she asked.

"Oh, not nearly as eventful. I just caught up on homework."
I didn't want to admit that Jenny and I had slept till noon on
Saturday, then spent the rest of the day dissecting everything
that had happened on Friday night, from what Dr. Li had ordered
at dinner to Rocky "putting the moves" on me (Jenny's words), so
we hadn't done any homework until Sunday evening. I thanked
Dr. Li again for having us over.

"It was nice," she said, and then she asked me to start with Beethoven.

After my lesson, I opened the studio door to find a note fluttering down to the floor. I sighed, then picked it up and read it.

WHAT DID YOU LEARN AT HER HOUSE?
HOW TO LIVE ALONE WITH CATS?

Word had gotten around about Freddy.

It had been a while since I'd received one, but somehow, I wasn't as scared anymore. The fact that other students received notes too made me feel better. If anything, being at Dr. Li's house had made her more likable, more human, to me. And I had other things to think about now. In the days that followed, I thought about Rocky all the time: as I studied for exams, practiced for my piano jury, and rode the bus to venues for all the choir performances. Had he moved closer to me on Dr. Li's couch on purpose, or was there just not enough room on that couch for three? Was it something that Rocky did to any girl he sat next to? He was bold, and he had to know that girls liked him. I had a feeling, though, that he wouldn't have done the same thing to Jenny or Martyna. Or was I just telling myself that?

Ms. Shelley said that we always told ourselves what we wanted to believe.

The story of how Rocky Wong couldn't get enough of me was a story I told myself often.

♩♫

That week at dance rehearsal, the dancers gathered around the piano in their usual spots, but it wasn't to dump their gossip about Dr. Li. "So is it true?" said Jackie.

"Is what true?" I asked.

"You and Rocky Wong," said Toothpick. She had her hand on her hip and seemed to be appraising me. "You know, I can see it. You'd be good for him. He needs someone who can balance him out."

"As if you know so well what Rocky Wong needs," said Amy. "I'm impressed, pianist. He is hot. You'll have to report on if he's a good kisser."

Nothing's really happened between us, I was tempted to say. And nothing had—not really, not yet. Instead, I asked, "How do you know?"

"Giambalvo told me." Amy grinned.

I'd only seen Rocky a few times since the dinner, and whenever I did, it seemed like he was acting exactly the same as he had been before the party, if not even slightly more distant: he said hello to me in the halls, but then he seemed in a hurry to get wherever he was going. And he hadn't been in class on Monday—Daniel said he was skipping to practice. When he missed class Tuesday, Daniel said he was catching some much-needed R and R.

♩♫

Later that week, Rocky slid into his seat just seconds before Dr. Hamilton tapped his baton to begin his lecture.

"Mr. Wong!" said Dr. Hamilton. "A pleasure to have you here, as always. And a reminder that your two absences this week are *un*excused."

Rocky groaned. "Can't you cut a man some slack, Dr. H? All this work is kicking my ass."

Dr. Hamilton turned to the board and wrote, *Foul Language: Rocky: 1.*

Rocky dropped his forehead to his desk. "Okay, fair. I deserve that."

Then Daniel said to Rocky, "You don't have to sit with me if you'd rather sit with your friend." The way he said it was jokey and quiet, and it wouldn't have been a big deal if Jenny's head hadn't snapped up to look at me, and Leo hadn't said, "Wait, who's Rocky's friend?"

I could feel my face getting hot while my stomach was churning, my heart beating faster. So Rocky had told Daniel something! I looked down at my textbook and pretended to review material from the night before.

"It's cool, man," Rocky said. "I'm already in my seat anyway."

My heart dropped. I didn't understand how it could feel like something monumental had happened between us—or had it?—and at the same time, it didn't seem like anything had changed at all. I couldn't stop replaying how we had sat, arm against arm, leg against leg. Sometimes, walking across campus, I was so lost in thought that once I didn't see Martyna waving to me from across the courtyard.

That evening, I went to the MapleMart to get a new lipstick for choir concerts, half hoping for conversation, but Rocky only said his usual "Hi, Wu!" as he rang me up, asked me how I was doing the way he would every other customer, and immediately started checking out the next person in line. I felt foolish for even thinking we'd get to talk.

Then, just as I was pushing the door open to leave, Rocky called my name.

"If you don't mind waiting, like, ten more minutes?" he said. "We could walk together."

I watched as Rocky rang up the last customer and made sure his coworker was all set to close up. Then we set off on the short walk from the store to school, Rocky holding his skateboard under one arm.

"That was some party, huh," said Rocky. In the dark, I couldn't tell if he was making fun of it.

"It was sweet of her," I said.

"That's what she *wants* us to think," he said.

"Okay, it was *strategic* of her. That's what Jenny said. She thinks it's Dr. Li's way of getting all of us to like her. Pump up her course evals."

"Ha! Like that's going to happen." Then Rocky said, "Whatever it was, it was nice hanging out with you outside of class."

I smiled wildly into the dark. "But not as nice as meeting Freddy, right?"

"Oh god, no. Freddy was definitely the high point of the evening. Him and the gummy bears."

A few times, our hands brushed against each other as we were walking. When it happened, it was so light that I told myself it could have been happening by accident. Strolling across campus together, I could feel people's eyes on us, wondering if we were a newly formed couple or if this was simply coincidental: two pianists who had bumped into each other and were walking to the dorm.

When we arrived, Rocky opened the door and held it for me. But this was the South: boys opened doors for girls, and it was the kind of thing people did all the time at Greenwood. Just before curfew, the dorm lobby was bustling with activity and noise. Daniel carried his laundry basket while a group of dancers punched buttons for late-night snacks from the vending machine. We stood awkwardly in the fluorescent lighting, Hank watching us from the desk. I searched Rocky's face for something—I wasn't sure what. Our walk had ended so abruptly and we could still have a few minutes together. But then Daniel set his hamper down. He and Rocky high-fived, and then Hank waved Rocky over for a chat.

"Night, Wu!" Rocky said cheerfully. "Thanks for the walk." He made his way over to the desk.

"Night!" I said, trying to match his tone, not sound too disappointed. Then I headed to the girls' side of the dorm. But walking up the stairs, I unexpectedly felt my eyes well.

By the time I opened our door and saw Jenny sitting at her desk, music blasting, I was wiping tears from my face.

Jenny turned the music down. "What's wrong?" she asked.

"It's Rocky," I said. "Does he like me or not?"

She burst out laughing even while she started rubbing my shoulders. "Claire, I'm so sorry. I thought someone had died!"

"It's so frustrating. We were walking just now, and then he just said 'Night' to me the same way he does Daniel!"

"Boys are stupid."

"*I* feel stupid," I said. Obviously Rocky wasn't going to do anything in the dorm lobby; only established couples got cozy in the dorm. And why had I been expecting anything like that when, less than an hour ago, I'd almost walked out of the MapleMart alone?

"I'm telling you," Jenny said, "Rocky *likes* you. I had mixed feelings about him before, but you know what, he's a good guy. As long as you don't become one of those girls whose life gets taken over by a boyfriend and suddenly becomes super uninteresting."

"How is that going to happen when he doesn't even try to sit by me in class?"

♩♫

Then, the next day, it happened.

Jenny and I were headed to English from physics when we heard wheels against the brick walkway. We stopped to look, and sure enough, Rocky was rounding the corner of the humanities building, sweaty and out of breath. He came to a smooth stop beside us. "Hi, Wu," he said sheepishly. "And hey, Jenny. Ah, I don't usually walk from here—"

"Wait," said Jenny, "don't you have the same class with Daniel? Like, right next to the room we're about to go to now?"

Rocky swiped a hand across his brow. "That's right. We got out early and I didn't stay for the post-class convo. I came straight over." He shrugged. "It's not about anything interesting today anyway." He looked at me. "You ready? I figured we could walk together."

"Yeah, that sounds good." I felt my mouth curl up into a smile.

Jenny looked at Rocky, then at me.

"You guys go ahead," she said. "I, uh, forgot something in our room." Before I could protest, she turned and started walking toward the dorm, but I knew she would only take a few steps and turn around again. There was no way to make it to our room and then class on time.

After that, it was magical: Rocky walked me to all my classes and then sprinted down the hall to his. After practice sessions, he was waiting for me outside the door even though we'd only have a few minutes to talk. And in music history, he moved from his usual seat by Daniel to sit next to me.

"So are you two going on any actual dates?" Jenny asked. "Or is he just going to keep hovering around you like a butterfly around a . . . butterfly bush?"

I laughed. Maybe sometime soon, we'd go on an actual date, but we were so busy now that I didn't even care as long as we got to be around each other as much as possible.

I went to the MapleMart as often as I could. I'd buy a single pack of gum, or a can of blackberry seltzer that I drank while walking. Whenever I could, I stood at the end of Rocky's aisle and we talked: about the schools where Rocky would be auditioning, about his ever-growing feeling that Dr. Li was out to get him, about how she'd probably kill him if she knew he unloaded crates of soda cans and milk jugs at work, putting his hands at risk. About how usually, working there made him feel his brain was turning to mush, but recently he liked it—it was freeing, wasn't it, to do menial tasks that were straightforward and immediately accomplished their purpose, instead of the sometimes-nebulous work of making your piano-playing sound better.

"I love to perform, but don't you wish you could just give yourself a break sometimes? Seriously," he said, "wouldn't it be so nice to be a mail carrier? You just have this one job to do and it's both very important and very easy."

"Maybe you're not giving postal workers enough credit," I said. "I bet there are hard parts to the job."

"I guess. Annoying things like traffic? Lost letters? But that's not nearly as bad as Dr. Li's super-vague instructions, like 'warm the sound.'"

I thought Dr. Li gave perfectly reasonable guidance in lessons, but I didn't mind hearing Rocky out, letting him rant. We talked until there was a customer or until his boss came out and said he needed to stop talking to his girlfriend. When she called me that, Rocky didn't correct her.

♩♫

Everyone was studying, practicing, writing, rehearsing. We had tests, juries, portfolio reviews, monologues, concerts.

"You should all be able to leave here not only as music performers," Dr. Hamilton liked to say, "but as musical *citizens* who can talk about classical music on NPR, write program notes for a symphony, and, if needed, identify the piece that's playing in the epic movie you're watching with your date."

At my jury, Dr. Li didn't smile when she took copies of the scores from me. She sat between Mrs. McHeusen and Dr. Hamilton in the first row of seats in the recital hall. She told me to play a B-flat harmonic minor scale, hands together, four octaves up and down. I adjusted the bench for my height—the knob squeaking loudly in the silent hall—then breathed in deep and went for it, my fingers stronger than they had been in September, the scales smooth and fast and even. Then came Bach, followed by Beethoven, then Chopin. Then there was sight-reading—and of course Dr. Li would choose some obscure composer none of us had played: it was an excerpt from a Herzogenberg piano trio, and I made a mental note to make fun of his name with Jenny later. When it was over, Dr. Li said, "Good work, Claire." I knew I had passed.

We all rolled our eyes when we were required to sing at McGrove's Tree Farm, which wasn't even a farm at all, but a big grassy lot where you could buy pre-cut Christmas trees. Families walked past with hot chocolate, holding their children's mittened hands. The area where we sang was trimmed with fake snow. Rocky managed to snag a cup of hot chocolate for me. It was lukewarm and watery and not worth the trouble—Dr. Hebert called him out, asking if he'd procured enough cocoa for the entire choir—but I saved the paper cup on my desk for days.

♩♫

In my last lesson before winter break, Dr. Li wanted to make sure I was set up to practice well at home. I played through Beethoven and we chose new repertoire for the spring: a Schubert sonata, a few of Mendelssohn's Songs Without Words, and a couple preludes by Debussy.

"Will you practice every day?" Dr. Li asked.

"I'll try." I was still jotting notes in the margins of my score. My old teachers used to write out instructions in a practice notebook, but Dr. Li had looked at it with disdain. "Claire, you're nearly seventeen years old. You can take your own notes during lessons."

Now she waited for me to put my pencil down, and gave me a look. "Will you practice every day?" she repeated.

"Yes. Except Christmas. And I'll ask Santa for a yoga ball."

She smiled.

At the end of the lesson, I lingered at my bag, pulling a tiny box from inside my balled-up sweater. I'd spent nearly two hours looking for a gift for her the night before and finally decided on a pair of chandelier earrings from Nellie's, a boutique on Main. They were made of pale pink coral beads on delicate gold chains.

"I got you something for the holidays," I said.

Dr. Li smiled. "You didn't have to."

I handed her the box. I'd wrapped it in white copy paper from the library printer, then covered it in stars and music notes with a felt-tip pen.

"I see you're talented in many areas," she said with an amused look at the paper.

"Oh yeah," I said. "I should have applied for a visual arts scholarship instead." I kicked myself for saying that.

She peeled the tape off carefully and then took the earrings out, letting them dangle from her fingers. "They're lovely."

Seeing them in her hand, I knew they weren't right. They were casual and cheap-looking compared to the ones she usually wore—clusters of jewels or tasteful gold studs—and the color was all wrong, a pastel color in the winter.

"Thank you, Claire. I'll enjoy these." Her hands went up to one ear and then the other as she removed the earrings she already had in her ears—what looked to be diamonds or at least expensive crystals—and replaced them with the ones I'd given her.

This was when I was supposed to invite her to our house for Christmas. I had even practiced how I was going to ask her because I didn't want to come across as some sort of teacher's pet (though Jenny had said it was too late for that).

My mother had suggested it. We lived a few hours from the school, which would be a trek for Dr. Li, but wasn't nearly as far as other students had to travel. Dr. Li didn't have family nearby (as far as we knew), so why not have her over for a few days?

"Ha!" Jenny had said. And then, "No. Just no."

But I didn't think I'd mind it that much. It would only be a few days, and winter break was almost three weeks long.

"If you're embarrassed to ask her," my father had said, "then just blame me. Just say, 'My dad likes to meet my teachers. It's not you, it's him.'" He'd chuckled at himself.

I cleared my throat. "What are you doing for the holidays? Are you going out of town?"

"I'm going to New York," said Dr. Li. "I've never really liked the holidays. But I hope this is a time of both rest and intense concentration for you. Sometimes a break from the usual schedule can allow us to listen to ourselves in another light."

I figured I wouldn't invite her over after all, since she was going to be out of town anyway. I thanked her and wished her a merry Christmas.

"Have a wonderful holiday, Claire. Your Beethoven is something to be proud of. Enjoy your time at home."

When I left her studio, I saw that I had a text from Rocky. It felt like the first *real* text I'd gotten from him—ones from earlier just said things like "Please tell Li I'm going to be late" or "Save me a seat at lunch."

> Want to go for a walk after your lesson? Turns out I don't have to work tonight.

I stopped walking and read it again, then again, still standing in the hallway outside Dr. Li's door. My stomach did a somersault.

I hadn't even had time to shower that day—I'd had an exam that morning, then rushed to lunch, then had another exam, and then the lesson—an extra one Dr. Li had scheduled even though juries were over. If I were going on a date with Rocky, I would have liked to wear something nice. I was in my comfiest jeans and a Greenwood sweatshirt with a big treble clef on the back.

But going to the dorm meant less time together.

Yes! I typed, then deleted it and just wrote:

> Sounds good:)

> Cool. I'm outside the music building

I went into the bathroom and rubbed some lipstick into my cheeks, then pulled my hair into a bun on the top of my head. I didn't want to look like I'd tried too hard.

"Nice sweatshirt," Rocky said when he saw me.

Rocky was wearing a Greenwood hoodie, too, and glasses with

rounded black frames. People said that you could get away with wearing sweats during final exams if you wore clothes from the Greenwood school store.

"I didn't know you wore glasses," I said.

"Only when I don't feel like putting in my contacts. And it's supposed to be better for my visual health, or something?"

We walked through the courtyard and past the academic buildings, and then we were at the main entrance of campus, at the same spot where we'd all met to go to dinner with Dr. Li. Rocky held the gate open for me.

I hesitated. "Don't we have to sign out on Guardian?"

Rocky shrugged. "You can if you want to? It's such a pain to type in your Greenwood password that's, like, three capital letters and a special character, spin around three times, then tap your nose to the space bar, and *then* wait for the automatic phone call and press Yes, just to announce that you're going, like, less than a mile away."

I laughed. "You don't press Yes. You just press pound."

If you were caught off campus without having signed out, you'd get detention, and I wasn't about to take my chances with it. Rocky waited for me to do it on my phone, sighing exaggeratedly when I mistyped my password the first time. Then he asked how my lesson had gone.

"Well, she told me to keep practicing every day, which is exactly what she told everyone else, so I guess it went well."

Rocky made a face.

"And she put on the earrings I gave her."

"You gave her earrings?"

"It's Christmas. I gave all my teachers gifts." To be fair, the gifts I'd given all my other teachers were pretty lame: small and generic gift boxes of fudge from Crispin's, but still.

I expected Rocky to tease me—to say I'd do anything for an A, or that that was why teachers liked me more than him—but instead he stopped walking and said, "But you didn't give all your teachers jewelry."

"Not all my teachers got me an accompanying gig and listened to me play piano for over an hour a week."

Rocky started to say something, then seemed to think better of it. We passed the Silver Spoon, where a long line snaked out the door—people were stocking up on holiday treats. We walked past the Hideaway and a couple boutiques, and the trees lining Main twinkled with white lights.

"I have a theory about Li," said Rocky as we passed an art gallery, "but you're gonna think I'm wrong."

"I already do, so it's not like it'll change anything," I teased.

"Wu, take me seriously!" Rocky looked around, as if to make sure no one would hear us, and I couldn't tell if he was joking. "I saw her the other day at the coffee shop on Main, the one with the gift shop inside?"

"Café Arvo?"

"Yeah, that's the one. From far away, but obviously it was her."

I couldn't help feeling jealous. I never saw Dr. Li outside of campus. "And?" I said.

"She was sitting at the bar, and she was crying."

I stopped walking for a second and looked at Rocky, to make sure he was telling the truth. His face was completely serious. I couldn't imagine Dr. Li openly weeping in public—or anywhere, for that matter. She was always so composed. "She was . . . crying?" I asked. "Like, was she okay?"

"I don't know, Wu. Does she seem okay to you? She has, like, an inferiority complex, is what I think."

I thought of all the theories from the dancers, the stories Jenny and I had made up while exploring Dr. Li's house. That she was having an affair, or had a long-distance "lover," or had been fired from her previous teaching job.

"And to some degree, I guess I get it," Rocky continued. "If she was a really big deal, wouldn't she be teaching at a university instead of our school? But instead she comes here and tells us what to do, and shows off at a fancypants restaurant, and dresses to the nines every day."

I thought I heard a glimmer of pity, maybe even recognition, as Rocky spoke.

"Doesn't that make you feel bad for her, just a little?" I said.

"Well, no. She needs to get a grip! Whatever shit she's going through, she shouldn't take it out on *us*! You think other teachers don't have their own stuff going on? They pull themselves together."

"She usually *is* pulled together," I said. "I mean, it's not like she knows you saw her in the café."

I felt embarrassed that Rocky had caught her in a private moment like that, and I felt sorry for Dr. Li. I pictured her house in the middle of nowhere, and all I could think about was how she lived alone and ate alone and spent weekends on campus, alone. Inadvertently I shuddered, remembering the note in her bedroom. *Lone Li.*

Rocky and I walked onto the suspension bridge over the Weepy River, where a street musician with an acoustic guitar was sending cheesy Christmas carols out over the water. Someone on Rollerblades glided past us.

"I think you're being too hard on her," I continued. "Everyone has times when they feel down, and who knows what happened? She could have even lost someone close to her."

"Maybe. Honestly, she . . . in some ways she reminds me of how my dad used to be. You could never get anything right with him, you know? Like it didn't matter if I played really well—he always heard or *thought* he heard something that could be better. Which was incredibly bullshit stupid, because he didn't even play piano!"

I stopped. Rocky mentioned his dad so rarely that I sometimes forgot all about him. "That *is* incredibly bullshit stupid," I said.

"We only talk, like, once a year, and even then, it's like he has to say things to imply that I could be so much better—as a pianist, as a person. It's always a few days after my birthday, because he never remembers *on the day,*" he said. "God, how hard is it to put a date in your calendar? I'm only seventeen and I tell people happy birthday more accurately than my dad. It's not like you have to memorize birthdays. That's what Google Calendar is for."

I shook my head. "I'm sorry. That's really dumb."

A couple bicycles whizzed past us. We went to the railing, our shoulders touching as we leaned over the water. The guitarist was playing "Lo, How a Rose E'er Blooming."

"When did he leave?" I asked. "I mean, you don't have to talk about it if you don't want to."

"When I was in the fourth grade, he started leaving for just a few days here and there, saying it was related to work. Then it was two weeks at a time. Then two weeks went by, and another week, and another—and I knew he wasn't coming home again. My mom, though, she kept waiting, and setting out his dinner plate, and holding out hope. . . ."

"I'm sorry," I said softly.

Rocky shrugged. "I don't want much to do with him now, so talking once a year is fine by me. And honestly, with everything I have going on, it's like, I don't want to even think about him, you know?"

With that last sentence, his voice became bitter, unlike I'd ever heard it before. I felt that if I said anything at all, it would only make things worse.

We looked down at the water rushing over the rocks, and the guitarist started in on "I'll Be Home for Christmas." Then I felt Rocky's arm around me. For weeks, I'd pictured Rocky doing just that, had imagined the warmth and weight on my shoulders. But now that it was happening I could hardly believe it. It set off a shower of sparks in my stomach. I rested my head on his shoulder and reminded myself to breathe.

"Don't look, but I'm gonna guess this guy is the type of guitarist who only plays in G, but uses the capo to make it sound different."

I laughed. "Oh, come on. He had some pretty good riffs earlier. I swear I heard him go up a key."

"The key change was the capo, too."

A few kids near us threw bread into the water for the two lone ducks in the calm part of the river, despite a sign nearby that explicitly said not to.

"Do you ever wish you had more family nearby?" Rocky asked.

"Oh, for sure."

"Me too. Even one cousin would be nice."

More than once—even though it was useless—I'd pictured a sister: someone I could stay up with and whisper to in the dark. What was it like, having someone who could know you in that way? The same parents and games from childhood, inside jokes that were several years old.

Rocky said, "Then again, do you ever feel like we have it better than white folks at the holidays? I mean, yeah, it's lonelier, but it's, like, the one time of the year when expectations aren't as high. You can just chill."

"Maybe for you," I said. "My mom always cooks up a feast. It's one of the few times during the school year that I'm sleeping at home, and there are no siblings to distract them from me."

Still, I knew what Rocky meant. My Asian American friends were lucky if they had even another relative in the States. Jenny's family's house was always packed during the holidays because her family lived within driving distance. I'd been sort of jealous of that, until Jenny told me that she had to share a room with two cousins then, and that all the adults got drunk and usually argued about one thing or another.

"Well," said Rocky, "at least we don't do all this over-the-top shit." He gestured to Nellie's, which we could see from the bridge. The storefront was covered in tinsel garlands, and an inflatable Santa by the entrance held a few wrapped boxes. "What happened to good taste, a few candles here and there?"

I laughed. "Do you guys decorate at all?"

Rocky gave me a look. "You clearly don't know the restaurant business. Or my mom. It's okay, though—it doesn't matter to us. We're going to cook up a storm, eat as much as we want, and then we're going to ride our bikes in Sykes Park. It'll be great. I feel like some of our best conversations are on bike rides."

I thought it was sweet how Rocky and his mom were so close. "That makes sense. I think my parents and I talk best when we're in the car."

"In the car? With you in the back seat? But you can't even see them then."

"Exactly."

Rocky laughed. "I can't figure you out, Wu. Sometimes you seem like a little goody-goody who adores her parents and does everything they tell you—"

"That's basically me."

"—but other times you say something like that." He shook his head. "You're more of a mystery than Tina Li."

Without speaking or taking his eyes from the water, Rocky took my hand in his. His hand was surprisingly warm, and I felt my insides go warm, too, as if I'd just drank something hot.

For a while, neither of us spoke. Then I said, "I'm not, though."

"You're not what?" said Rocky.

"A mystery."

He turned to look at me. It felt at once both comforting and unfamiliar to be looking into eyes that were so similar to my own. I had looked at many of my friends with their pale blue irises, their green-gray eyes that seemed to change color depending on their clothing—a quality that I had envied as a child. But his were dark brown pools.

"Okay, Miss Not-a-Mystery," Rocky said. "Can I call you over break?"

Chapter 18

THE NEXT DAY, THE DORMS WERE FLOODED WITH PARENTS. Mothers squeezed shoulders and smoothed hair and pressed their cheeks to ours—all the physical affection they hadn't been able to express for so long. Fathers asked if we'd seen that article in the *Washington Post* about how musicians made excellent doctors. In the dorm lobby, my own mother took me in her arms, mashing my face against the buttons of her blouse. "Oh, Claire," she exclaimed. "It's been so long." Then she stepped back, inspecting me at arm's length. I hoped that there wasn't some telltale sign on my person that I had been hanging out with Rocky, and that we had held each other a long while before saying good night, and that when I got up to my room, he called me to talk until I said I had to go—Jenny and I needed some time before we left for break, too. But my mother asked, "Have you been eating enough fruits and vegetables?"

I'd mostly been eating bananas, due to all of Dr. Li's talk about nerves and potassium.

During the flurry of exams and the preparations before leaving campus, Ghostwriter managed to sneak in just one more note, left outside my dorm:

> Don't think too hard about her over break.

I shoved the note in my pocket and rolled my eyes—I hadn't been planning on thinking about Dr. Li very much at home.

Rocky's mother appeared, and he threw his arms around her. She seemed embarrassed at her son's embrace, and when they parted, she stood with her arms crossed, lips pursed, shoulders drawn in. She was so much smaller than Rocky that she'd had to reach up to hug him. Rocky had told me that this weekend would be some of their few days together away from the restaurant. I could tell Mrs. Wong had been pretty once, but she put little effort into her looks now, as if she couldn't be bothered. She wore loose jeans and a large jacket, her hair in a short braid at the nape of her neck, wisps of it framing her face. Under her eyes were dark circles that she'd made no effort to conceal. The only makeup she wore was a swipe of ruby lipstick that clung to her mouth unevenly, making clear exactly where her lips were chapped. Rocky himself had his backpack on and was carrying a stack of music books and fantasy novels with raised lettering on their covers. Mrs. Wong's eyes widened at the stack of books. She told him, in Mandarin, to leave some behind, and Rocky sulked, but in a joking way. He went back to his room to do what he was told. With everyone else, Rocky was sarcastic, a smart-ass. With his mother, he was different.

Then Rocky came downstairs, and, like every other Greenwood

couple (*were* we a couple?), we hugged for a long time, but not too long—to avoid our parents' questions—in front of the cars that were slowly pulling away. Like every other Greenwood boy, he said he would call, and I made sure my parents couldn't hear, and then we said goodbye and I watched him climb in beside his mother—eager to be behind the wheel after months of Greenwood's no-car rule—and drive away.

♩♫

Over the break, my mother spoiled me with her cooking, and trips to the mall and the movies. I practiced piano in my pajamas and decorated the tree with my parents, who had waited for me to come home before doing that. And I loved it, every second of it, so much. But I also felt the pull of Greenwood, missed my friends, missed the great and collective feeling of productivity and joy. I wondered what Dr. Li was doing while I was playing board games and going to lunch with friends from my old school. I hoped she was enjoying New York during the holidays, which always looked magical in Christmas movies. She'd mentioned that the holidays were hard; now I wondered if that's what she'd been upset about when Rocky saw her. Rocky and I wrote each other long emails every day, sometimes twice in one day, and called each other every few days, too.

"Emails?" Jenny said. "Who are you guys, Tom Hanks and Meg Ryan in *You've Got Mail?*"

For once, it was my turn to roll my eyes at Jenny, who had been on a nineties kick all year.

But I loved getting messages from Rocky. They were funny and sweet and full of questions for me, from how I thought I'd changed since my first year to what I'd eaten that day. He sent me songs he loved and a photo from the park. I was glad to see him looking so happy—glad he had a chance to relax even while feeling so stressed. He also sent me the link to the spring application for Asian Student Society. *Try again!* he wrote. *Rooting for you.*

Since he was working at the restaurant most days, we talked late into the night. I held the phone to my ear in bed and spoke with my face toward the wall so my parents couldn't hear. We talked about our families and Dr. Li and our friends from school, and we talked a lot about the future. Most auditions were in February after Showcase, and I could hear Rocky's anxiety, his panic, in his voice. Often, he spouted his thoughts—about schools, about his playing, about his mother—into one long, frantic paragraph over the phone, going on and on so much I could hardly get a word in.

Then we received our grades. I'd gotten all As except for physics, and Dr. Li had given me an A for my jury. "I almost never give As," she'd said. "You're lucky if you get a B." So I considered myself very lucky.

Rocky, however, wasn't as pleased. "How?" he said. "How! How could she give me a B-plus on my jury? I played everything perfectly! Unless, I'll tell you what it is, it's probably because I didn't do it exactly how she told me to. But you can't give someone a *grade* for their interpretation. That's just stupid!"

"You think I got an A because of my interpretation?" I asked.

"Look, she wanted me to play the development in the Prokofiev with less pedal, and I didn't agree with her, so I played it with

212

lots of pedal—which, by the way, is how Raekallio plays it. And I'm sorry, Wu, you're obviously amazing at piano, but you also do everything that Dr. Li wants you to do, which is probably why you got an A."

I took a breath, telling myself to let his comment go—that Rocky was just ranting. But I was also annoyed. I said, "Isn't that how grades work, though? Doing what the teacher says to do?"

"Why do you have to defend her all the time?" he snapped.

I was so surprised—and hurt—that I fell silent.

Then I said, "Well, I should probably get going."

"I'm sorry, Wu," Rocky said quickly. On the other end, I could hear him release a long sigh. "The B-plus brought my piano grade down to an A-minus, which is going to look so dumb to colleges."

"It won't matter once they hear you play, though."

"Maybe you're right," Rocky said.

Usually, I was glad to be Rocky's sounding board, but the conversation put me on edge. When we talked the next day, though, we both avoided talking about Dr. Li.

When I practiced at home, it was different. My mother folded laundry right in front of me, or sometimes dumped the contents of the hamper onto the couch and, if I stopped playing for even a second, told me to do something useful, like fold everything myself. My father would sit and read and then ask me to play the "fast song that he liked," which was the last movement of my Beethoven. I did listen to myself in another light. I made friends with my old enemy, the Bach fugue, a slow and deliberate meditation on the notes themselves. *Play like someone is listening to you on the other side of the door,* Dr. Li always told us, and it was hard to do that when you had been inside a tiny cubicle of a practice room for God knows how long, and you knew no one was listening to you because they were too busy listening to themselves. But at home, knowing that I had an audience made me sound better.

Via email, Dr. Li scheduled lessons for us—*preliminary lessons,* she called them—before the official start of classes. She wanted to meet with each of us for a half hour on Monday night right after the break, so that we could "hit the ground running" at our actual lessons. The Student Showcase was in February, and we all had to be ready; she didn't want us to embarrass her.

At the end of the break, I hugged both of my parents very hard and my father said they were very proud of me, and all of a sudden, I was sad to leave home. Greenwood, although it seemed like a place where you could never get time alone, felt incredibly isolated, and piano practice was a lonely way to spend one's time.

Chapter 19

ROCKY MET ME OUTSIDE THE DORM WHEN I RETURNED TO school. The first thing I noticed was that he looked thinner in his hoodie, maybe even a bit haggard. When we hugged, his body felt different in my arms. I wondered if I ought to ask about it—if anything, I'd thought Rocky would *gain* weight at home eating his mother's cooking—but it seemed too much, like the type of question that my mother would ask one of my friends out of the blue. And maybe he just got to exercise more at home. We had dinner by ourselves in the dining hall, and I didn't notice anything unusual about how much he was eating. Out of the corner of my eye, I saw Leo carrying his tray over to us, then Daniel furiously gesturing for him to sit elsewhere. Toothpick and Amy passed by our table with approving glances. I even saw the Society members sitting together and couldn't help feeling pleased that Rocky had chosen to sit with me instead of them—although I also wouldn't have minded if he brought me to their table. Afterward,

Rocky and I walked to the music building, where we finally parted ways. I was going to have my preliminary lesson with Dr. Li the very next day.

"You let her schedule it for tomorrow?" Rocky said.

"Well, she originally wanted to do it today."

"But what about what *you* want?" he said.

"What I want is to start practicing now, so it goes okay tomorrow." I smiled. "So I think that means we need to say goodbye now." I opened the door to my practice room.

"You have to stand up for yourself, Claire."

"It's really not a big deal," I said, making as if to close the door.

"Text me when you're out of your lesson," he called after me. "We can get dinner."

But the next day, Dr. Li kept me late, past dinner. By the time I left her studio, it was almost eight o'clock and I was starving. I looked at my phone and saw I had a missed call from Jenny, and a text from Rocky saying he was at the usual table, and another asking if I was skipping dinner.

What, does Li want us to fast now?

That had been half an hour ago. I figured I'd grab something and eat in my room, and made it into the dining hall just as Barbara was about to leave. "Whatchoo want, baby? That new teacher holding you up again?"

There was no one in the dining hall except us. Barbara made me a sandwich and gave me the code to the pantry behind the hot bar and told me to take whatever I wanted. Then she left. I headed to the pantry for fruit, walking across the same tiles where Dr. Li had stood when we first saw her, in front of the empty metal trays. I punched the code into the keypad and opened the door.

Rocky was sitting on the floor, his legs splayed out in front of him like one of the dancers. I wasn't that surprised: Rocky knew the campus like no one else. It wasn't uncommon for him to study in a room in the library that no one else knew about, or to find Ms. Shelley's box of caramels that she used to replenish her candy bowl, or to be able to get from the science wing to the painting studios without having to go outside because of a passage he'd discovered in the basement.

Rocky jumped when the door opened. "Oh, hey, Wu!"

"What are you doing in here?"

"I have the same question for you."

"She let me out late and now I'm famished."

He reached for an apple and threw it to me.

That was when I saw what he was doing.

He held a black pen in his left hand. Pieces of paper lay scattered on the floor around him.

He looked from the notes to me, and when our eyes met, I couldn't speak. Evidently, neither could he. He didn't make any moves to cover his work, just looked up at me. There was nothing he could do anyway: the evidence was all around him, and it was clear. I opened my mouth, but no sound came out.

Before then, I'd heard of the phrase *shaking with anger,* but I'd never experienced it myself. But as I stood there, I realized that was what was happening to my arms.

"You?" I said finally.

He sighed. "Me," he said.

I was more than angry, though. All my fears about being stalked, about someone watching me, listening in, came rushing back. Inadvertently, I took a couple steps away from Rocky, toward the door. He would never hurt me, physically—or would he? I felt like I didn't know him anymore, couldn't trust him at all.

At the same time, it made so much sense that I didn't know how I couldn't have known. Rocky knew my schedule, and he'd held a grudge against Dr. Li all this time. I thought of all the notes—taped to my window, left outside my practice room door, written in chalk on the pavement, in handwriting I recognized now, just *slanted slightly left*—and anger coiled in the pit of my stomach. All those times of being scared, confused, feeling like I was being watched, not to mention being afraid on Dr. Li's behalf.

I couldn't believe this was happening. The only thing I could think was that I just wanted to leave, to run away from the dining hall, and maybe even from Greenwood. *How had this happened? How had I gone from being in love to . . . not knowing at all who Rocky really was? How had he hidden this from me?*

I wanted to scream and throw things. I lifted the hand that was holding the apple, and Rocky instinctively covered his head. But I only threw it at the floor, where it made a dull smacking sound and rolled to the corner. Then I grabbed another and threw that one, too.

Rocky said nothing, just watched me grimly. I fought the urge to grab him by the shoulders and shake him. Then I found my voice again.

"What . . . are . . . you . . . doing?" My voice sounded cold and unfamiliar. I couldn't help thinking it sort of sounded like Dr. Li, when she was disappointed in us. I could only look at him in shock and disbelief, fear. I wanted nothing to do with Rocky Wong anymore.

Rocky didn't say anything.

"And *why*? Why the hell would you do this? You *asshole*. Do you know how creepy it is to wake up and have a note on your window, or leave a lesson and find a pile in the hall? How scary it is to feel like you're being *followed*?"

Rocky hung his head like he was a child being yelled at. He looked at the floor for what felt like a long time. I was glad he wasn't moving, glad I could just say everything I needed to. Then he reached forward and started gathering the paper to himself. He crumpled it up and stuffed it all into the recycling bin, pushing it underneath some collapsed cardboard boxes that had once held cans of green beans. Then he looked at me. "I'm done with that. Really, I—that was fucked up. I feel terrible."

I thought of saying something like Jenny would: *What, you want me to thank you now?*

Instead, I turned around and headed for the door, already resolving never to speak to him again.

"Claire, wait."

Rocky dropped his pen into his backpack. He rubbed his hands together and held them out to me, palms up, like he was making a peace offering. "I'm so, so sorry, Claire."

He looked so sorry that I almost even felt bad for him. But then that made me want to scream. "That doesn't make up for what you did! I thought someone was stalking me. I mean, you basically were! You even . . ." The memory reared itself in my head, unprompted. "You even called it that yourself, when you, you wrote a note to *yourself*!"

"How else was I supposed to warn you? I kept trying to, and you kept brushing me off. But it scared me. The way you're so obsessed with Dr. Li? You take everything she says like it's gospel."

"I scared *you*?" I repeated, taking in the words. I was pretty sure anyone would agree that *I* hadn't been the one behaving irrationally. I opened my mouth to say so, but Rocky beat me to it.

"You still have no idea," he said. "You're so enamored with her, you can't see what she's doing." His voice started to take on a sense of urgency, like he needed me to understand, to agree. "She's dangerous. She's going to ruin your life the way she ruined mine. I can't sleep, I can hardly eat. I can only skate at night, and I hardly have time for that. And for what? Instead of my playing getting better, it's actually getting worse. The way she suddenly took us out to dinner? To"—here, he made air quotes with his fingers—"'celebrate the holidays'? *Pfft*, yeah, right! I know what she's doing. Plotting and planning. I know she doesn't like me, and she wants to see me fail."

"That's ridiculous," I nearly spat. Hours ago, I wouldn't have dreamed of speaking to Rocky that way, but now things were different. Then a chill ran through me. It wasn't only about what Rocky was saying—it was about how he looked like he believed it was all true. And the fast way he was talking and interrupting, the way he had talked when we were in the garden, and on the phone over winter break. He was looking me straight in the eyes—his face concerned for me, convinced that he was seeing things the right way. He ran a hand through his hair, but it wasn't in the cool, smooth way I usually liked. It was a gesture of distress. Sitting on the floor, he looked unlike his usual self. I saw dark circles under his eyes.

"You think she's trying to sabotage you," I said.

"Oh, not just me. Why do you think she gave you the accompanying gig? She's trying to control you! I mean, look, you didn't even want to do the accompanying, did you?"

"Not at first," I admitted slowly.

"You told me yourself that she just dropped the music into your bag."

I put my hands on my hips. "You could have just, like, told me . . . what she was doing. You didn't have to leave creepy anonymous notes everywhere."

"I guess. But I didn't want to get us all in trouble! If she found out that we were onto her, and if you told her it was me who told you, that would really screw things up. Plus, I'm not around a lot. It was easier to just leave the notes at night or in the morning before I left for work."

I studied him. He looked absolutely spent, which made sense given the time of year—but still. "You probably should be getting more sleep."

"Okay, Mom. I can sleep when I'm dead."

I punched him in the arm. Then I turned toward the door again. How dare he talk to me like that after everything?

"Hey!" said Rocky. "It's audition season, Wu. My fate will be determined in the next couple *months*. It's like she doesn't even want me to do well. The way she asked me to practice the Prokofiev? It's going to screw up my wrist for life." His jaw was set.

I took a deep breath. Something about the way Rocky was talking was off—really off. I wondered if I should tell someone about him, slip an anonymous tip to Student Health and Wellness. But how anonymous were those? And would that help, or make him even more angry?

"I don't know," I said carefully, "but do you need to, like, talk to someone?"

He scowled. "Like who? Ms. *Shelley*? I don't need to talk to her. I just want to talk to you." Then he leaned forward and slipped his hand into mine. My heart was hammering. Any other time I would have loved it. I'd been looking forward to it all break. I'd pictured our reunion again and again, but it wasn't supposed to be like this. Anything but this. I still couldn't believe that it was really a conversation we were having. I let go.

Rocky dropped his head into his hands. Behind him, on the shelves, I saw all the things we would eat that week: oversized boxes of Grape-Nuts and Raisin Bran and Cinnamon Toast Crunch. Cans of beans the size of our heads, and crates of apples and bananas and oranges. Massive jars of peanut butter, gallons of vegetable oil.

"I wanted to stop," he said finally. "As soon as we met in the garden, and I saw how it was coming across, that I was hurting you—I tried to stop. I really never meant to hurt you, Wu."

I could barely even meet his eyes.

He was looking up at me with desperation. "I have screwed up, majorly. I see that now. I see now that it was stupid. Really, really stupid. But I needed to let you know somehow, and would you really have listened to me if I just told you all that stuff? Wouldn't you have just blamed it on how she doesn't let me skate?"

"Of course I would've listened to you," I said. "I always listened to you." He looked at me then. "You just, like, don't sound like *yourself* right now." That was it, I realized. Rocky sounded so unlike his normal self that, even though I would have loved to hold his hand, had dreamed for over a year about kissing him, something about the way he was talking frightened me. Something wasn't right.

We regarded each other. When I'd pictured meeting up with Rocky, we were walking around Main Street again, eating ice cream in the cold and making each other laugh—not sneaking around inside the pantry, me wondering if I should report him to Student Health.

"I haven't felt like myself lately," he admitted. He held his palms up to me once again. "God, Wu, I'm so, so sorry. How can I make it up to you?"

Tears were stinging my eyes. Was this really happening? I wanted it to all be a dream that I'd wake up from any second. How could it be that sweet, handsome Rocky was Ghostwriter?

Rocky reached out and put a hand on my shoulder, but I pulled away. "Don't," I said. "And don't call me."

He looked on the verge of tears himself. *Fine,* I couldn't help thinking, *he should feel bad after everything he's done.*

"You know what I'll do," he said. "I'll learn your spring dance repertoire and accompany the dancers, but you can keep the money."

Then my tears did spill over—hot, angry tears—and I wiped at my face with my sleeve.

Rocky's face crumpled then. "I'm so sorry, Wu," he said again. "Please let me help you with that, at least."

I shook my head. "Leave me alone," I said, then turned and stepped out the door, not even holding it open for Rocky. It was only then that I remembered why I'd been inside the pantry at all. But I wasn't hungry anymore.

♩♫

After that, I avoided Rocky. I only ever saw him in classes, sometimes with his eyes barely open, or I saw the top of his head through practice room windows. He'd left me several texts and voicemails, apologetic and pleading as I'd never heard him before, but I still wasn't ready to talk with him. Sometimes I saw him eyeing me from across the dining hall or the choir rehearsal room. I only stopped by the MapleMart once, and although I saw him with his arms full, helping a young mother with groceries, I didn't say anything to him. I still thought about him a lot, wondered if he was doing okay. I wanted to talk to him so badly. So many times I'd think, *I need to tell Rocky about this,* and then I'd remember all over again. As I used to before we'd grown close, I caught glimpses of Rocky from afar: skating in the faculty lot and shooting pool in the rec room with the other Society members while waiting for his laundry to finish. But in music history, he sat quietly and, I thought, sadly, instead of goofing off with Daniel. In choir, he tried to meet my eye, but I kept my gaze on my music. Back in the dorm, I read up on anxiety and depression and bipolar disorder, and my heart sank. I didn't know what to do. I didn't need to say anything to Jenny for her to know something was wrong.

But I didn't want to tell anyone about the notes. Jenny would be the only person I'd tell—but how could I? It would turn her against Rocky forever, and she wouldn't keep it to herself; certainly he'd lose all his friends. And she hadn't loved the idea of us together very much to begin with, so it would only make things worse. So when she asked me what Rocky had done, I said our breakup (was it even that?) had been mutual, that it wasn't Rocky's fault.

"Not Rocky's fault?" Jenny said. "Don't even try to tell me this is a 'It's not Rocky, it's Claire' situation, because that just isn't possible. Where *is* Rocky these days, anyway? I could kill him." She punched a fist into her other palm.

I hesitated. Rocky could hardly admit his own struggles to himself. It wouldn't be right, then, to share them with Jenny. On the other hand, I had never kept such a big secret from her before. I often thought of her as the sister I never got to have: We shared a room, and she was the first person I spoke to when I woke up in the morning and the last when we went to sleep at night. We wore each other's clothes, kept each other's secrets, cheered each other on. More than anyone else at Greenwood, she could give me a hard time, tell me honestly when I'd disappointed her, or betrayed her, or made her proud. But if I was going to confide in someone, it made more sense to tell someone who could actually help: an adult. Someone who would know exactly what to do, and who wouldn't judge Rocky for going through this. I'd thought about telling Dr. Li, but given her own relationship with Rocky, how helpful would she be?

Then one afternoon between classes, I was studying when Rocky showed up in the library. He was wearing his glasses, and he looked surprised to see me, but then started talking as if nothing had changed. "See this?" he said, taking a thick hardcover from his bag. "I know Anthony has library duty, and he'll pull this out thinking it's a book, and—" He opened it, showing me that the inside was full of multicolored confetti. I couldn't help laughing in spite of myself.

"Only thirty minutes till the Bach exam," I said. "Shouldn't you be studying?"

"Get out of here, Wu. I know that stuff like the back of my hand." He sounded like his usual cocky self, but I could see in his eyes that he was studying me, trying to figure out what terms we were on now. He crossed one foot over his other ankle. "How've you been?"

"Okay," I said. The truth was, I hadn't been doing very well at all. It was a strange feeling, simultaneously wanting to be around Rocky as much as possible while also trying to understand why he'd made me feel so awful. "Look, I need to study." From the corner of my eye, I saw that the other students were giving us annoyed looks.

He pursed his lips. "First of all, you study harder than most people I know, and second, how much do you expect to memorize in just half an hour? Why don't we sit down somewhere?"

"I *am* sitting down."

Rocky stepped toward me. "Can we just talk, for a minute?" he asked quietly.

For several seconds, we looked at each other. Then I nodded, and he helped me pack up my books and papers, then slipped my bag onto one arm. We went upstairs, into a study room overlooking the courtyard in the medieval studies section, where no one else usually went, and sat at the table.

Rocky said, "I don't really know what else to say, except that—except that I'm so, so sorry. And that—I don't know what came over me. That wasn't really . . . me? If that makes sense." He scratched his head, hopping from foot to foot. "Sometimes I get too worked up and depressed and then I—well, you know—I start to believe things that are, I guess, questionable."

I raised my eyebrows at him. "You figured that out?"

He smiled a half smile. "I went to talk with Ms. Shelley. It wasn't . . . great, but anyway. That's what she said."

I hoped he would grab my hand again. Though we had played the piano several times together, had watched each other's hands land where they needed to, had waited for the other to breathe in—the cue to start—we had never touched until the night at Dr. Li's. Now I knew why it had bothered me so much, why an ache had formed in my chest when Jenny called him psycho. "I know," I said, "I know that wasn't the real you."

He exhaled and put a hand over his heart. "Thank you for saying that. You have no idea what that means to me." Then he grinned. "I've gotta get my book to the book drop before Anthony catches me. And then we have an exam to take."

He was Rocky again: confident, mischievous, handsome Rocky, and we were alone in the library. "If you really know the exam," I said, "which three cities did Bach stop in on the way to Leipzig?"

He laughed and then groaned. "You're killing me, Wu. Ask me a harder one."

"Okay: Describe the difference between *accelerando* and *accelerato*."

He grinned. "That'll take too long to answer."

"Answer it or I won't believe that you actually know this stuff. If you make lower than an A, I'll personally blame myself for distracting you from your studies."

"Oh, Wu," he said, and reaching forward, he tapped my ankle. My stomach went all watery. "Exams are nothing compared to performance. Do I ever make less than an A?"

"You're such an ass," I said, and then I smiled even more, thinking that I sounded like Jenny and that she would be proud of me.

"This is good. You're swearing. I think you're actually, like, growing up a bit under my influence." He reached his hand around my waist and pulled me toward him. His glasses were slightly crooked. Surprising myself, I reached up, took them off, and put them on my own face.

"Now how am I supposed to take this quiz? You realize I'm practically blind without those, right? I can't even see you right now." When he said this, he put his face right up against mine, so our noses were touching. "Now I can see you," he whispered.

Then I could feel his hand, softly, on my shoulder now. Our mouths touched in something not quite a kiss because we were still talking, and because I was smiling so big I felt his teeth tap against mine.

Rocky said, "Okay, I might make an A-minus," and I felt his lips forming the words against my lips, his mouth touching mine as if he were simply suggesting a kiss. And then we were kissing, and he smelled like laundry detergent and something sweet, like apples. I could feel his hand on my neck and then in my hair.

"You still didn't answer the question," I said.

Playfully, he said, "I can't remember it now."

Chapter 20

FOR THE NEXT FEW WEEKS, ROCKY AND I SAW EACH OTHER every day. He had work and I had rehearsals for the spring dance performance, so we met early in the morning and had breakfast together when most students were still sleeping. It was easier to wake up for Rocky than for the 6:00 a.m. practice slot. He met me downstairs and we walked to the dining hall together, sitting side by side with egg sandwiches. Rocky always ate two. Then, in the practice rooms, we listened to each other play. We sat next to each other in music history, holding hands under the desk. Rocky claimed he had such perfect audio recall that he could take notes after class instead, but I never saw him write a thing. At night, after practicing, we walked through the North Campus Garden, using our phones as flashlights since it wasn't well-lit, then ate cereal— Cinnamon Toast Crunch for me and Froot Loops for Rocky—in the dining hall. Or we met in the library or even the practice rooms: the exact places where we were most explicitly not supposed to. We propped a music stand up against the little window in the door when we were supposed to be practicing, supposed to be studying.

Jenny was ambivalent about this new development—and that was putting it lightly. I couldn't help but finally tell her about the notes.

"Claire, God knows I've been waiting for your first love alongside you, but explain this to me again. Rocky was the one torturing you for the past several months, and now you're *dating*? As I've said before, I don't know exactly what you see in him, and now I *really* don't know! Does he have to be quite so cocky? Such a hot shot? So . . . forgive me, obnoxious? And aside from that, I really don't want you to get hurt again."

But Rocky wasn't obnoxious to me, and his cockiness was only part of an act. Now that he was seeing Ms. Shelley on the regular, and now that I understood more about his struggles, I wasn't afraid. To feel his lips on mine was to feel pleasure right away, easy pleasure, so much easier than the forty-times-hands-apart-forty-times-hands-together Bach. It was like the pleasure of the perfect single key, the D flat two octaves above middle C, for Debussy's prelude, "The Girl with the Flaxen Hair." In the practice room, my scales suffered, but my sound—my sound emerged like it was summoned from the dark, a single note, soft and clear, one line descending and ascending, asking a question, then blurring into shapes and colors. Like it was underwater, above water, through the water. Like seeing light reflected off a glass.

It was so hard to concentrate when practicing.

"How should I put this?" Dr. Li said in one of my lessons.

"Somehow, Claire, you're playing more expressively, but it doesn't feel particularly deliberate. You're just playing however you *feel*. If you carefully choose where to show some restraint, your interpretation will be more mature and, counterintuitively, more moving."

"Oh my god," Rocky said when I told him. "I mean, I've never heard anyone tell you that before. She thinks you're overdoing it. And you never overdo it. Admit it, Wu. You're in love."

Rocky had his own lesson later that week, and I could tell as soon as I saw him that it had not gone well. Jenny and I were already in the dining hall—with Daniel, who realized that he'd see his friend more if he sat with us—when Rocky plopped into his seat with three fried chicken sandwiches.

"She said I wasn't ready yet," he said. "Auditions are next month and she said I'm not ready."

The sandwiches were a good sign, I thought. If he still had his appetite, then he was probably okay.

"Are you really going to eat all *three* of those?" Jenny said, wrinkling her nose. "It's gluttonous."

"Could you not comment on my eating habits? Pretty sure there's something in the honor code about that."

"I have to confess something," said Daniel. "I ate two with another table before I joined y'all." He took a sip of fruit punch. "So this is my third one."

Jenny dropped her head in her hands.

"I didn't eat breakfast, and I'll probably take one of these to go. The real issue here, though," said Rocky, "is that I'm not ready."

Daniel slung an arm over Rocky's shoulder. "You *are* ready. She doesn't give you enough credit. If I played cello as good as you play piano, Ferguson would lose his shit."

"What can you do to *get* ready?" I asked.

Jenny often brought this up, how I went into coaching mode every time Rocky said anything about how his life was spiraling out of control in one way or another: "I'm pretty sure this is not how relationships are supposed to work—Rocky always in crisis mode and you always in coach mode?"

"I don't know," Rocky said through bites of his sandwich. "Practice more? I mean, when am I supposed to do that?" he continued. "I guess I can cut some of my hours at the MapleMart? Skip class again? I still need to tutor Schuyler, though. It's good money—and I'm sorry, but the kid *cannot* do chemistry without me."

"Look," Jenny said. "Showcase is coming up anyway. We should *all* be upping our game. I'm going to start getting up as early as Claire does."

Daniel clapped. "Hear, hear," he said, lifting his fruit punch into the air. "Jenny 'I-always-hit-snooze-three-times' Stone is going to wake up as early as the extra-diligent Claire Wu to practice."

I blushed. Jenny knew why I was getting up so early these days, and it wasn't to practice.

♩♫

After that, Rocky and I still met early and walked to the dining hall, but instead of eating breakfast there, we took it to go and then ate during a break in the practice rooms, even though technically food wasn't allowed there. It seemed that as Showcase approached, every other musician had taken up the same habit, and they couldn't punish all of us, as long as we made sure to keep the rooms clean. In music history, even Dr. Hamilton's animated lectures weren't enough to keep some of us from nodding off from time to time. I started drinking coffee, too—this time with more coffee than milk and sugar—and we could always tell it was a bad sign when Rocky started walking into studio class at 4:00 p.m. with a paper cup from the MapleMart.

"This," Jenny said, pointing to Rocky's leg as it bounced up and down. "This is a bad sign. Are you going to be able to sleep?"

"No sleep till Showcase," Rocky said, and took a swig.

"No! Sleep! Till! Brooklyyyyn," JT sang, and picked up his own energy drink.

So I wasn't surprised, but I was still disappointed when whole days went by where the only communication I got from Rocky was a couple texts. At dinner, he grabbed pizza without taking off his coat and headed out again. Jenny and I started doing the same.

Then the days came when I didn't hear from Rocky at all. He skipped music history again and didn't even text me to ask for my lecture notes. I had overheard Daniel asking for Rocky's favorite sandwich—roast beef and provolone on ciabatta with chipotle mayo—and saying he would take it to him. "Everything going okay?" Barbara asked, and Daniel said, "Yes, ma'am," that it was just a classic case of artist's angst and Rocky went through it every now and then just like the rest of us, and that because of auditions he was basically on social lockdown.

Hearing this, Leo shook his head. "The most talented are often the most troubled," he said, as if he knew everything.

"If you ask me—" Jenny began.

"Ah, but no one did," said Leo.

"If you ask me, Rocky sounds like a first-rate diva. Like, really? You can't even step foot in here to get your own damn sandwich? And when he does something stupid, like freak everyone out with his notes, everyone's just like, whatever, typical Rocky, and he gets a pass! Does this school have *any* sense of decency anymore?"

"I completely agree," said JT. "Who puts roast beef on ciabatta? Everyone knows sourdough is what's up." Jenny rolled her eyes as JT and Leo high-fived.

In the music building that week, I heard Rocky swearing through the supposedly soundproof walls of the practice rooms. It was his own fault, said Jenny, that he'd chosen Prokofiev's first sonata and Beethoven's "Appassionata" in the same semester—Dr. Li had warned him about doing this, but he'd insisted he could handle it—and now that his Beethoven was sounding good, his Prokofiev was suffering. Jenny tried to console me, saying that once he saw me in my recital dress, he'd realize what he was missing.

When it snowed—just a couple inches, as it always did once or twice a year in Green Valley—the parking lot developed a thin coat of ice, and all the blue salt made it nearly impossible for Rocky to skate. I wondered if I was doing the right thing by giving him space, or if I should try to talk to him or to one of his friends. I toyed again with the idea of going to Student Health, which I was now sure Rocky would hate. I wondered if maybe, after the Showcase, he'd be better. I thought again about going to talk to Dr. Li—Rocky would absolutely hate that, of course, but she was likely the teacher who knew him best. I even wrote out what I'd say to her if I did tell her. But after thinking about it, I decided against it; Rocky would certainly read it as betrayal. I was beginning to question how long I could sustain worrying about Rocky while taking no action to help him, when one day in late January, there were flowers outside my mailbox, the artificially bright daisies from the MapleMart—such a relief to me that I didn't mind the tacky colors.

♩♫

We practiced and practiced. I marked my music into sections so that if I had a memory slip, I wouldn't have to start at the beginning again, but had several spots I could jump to if needed. I practiced much slower than I needed to and also much faster than I needed to. I practiced with exaggerated dynamics so that nerves wouldn't diminish them. In our dorm, wearing our performance shoes and dresses, Jenny and I rehearsed our entrances and exits and bows, practiced sitting down and standing up.

In studio class the week before the recital, Dr. Li told us her rules for concerts and went over the order of our recital.

"How do we choose who goes first and last, and the order of those in between? Many performers choose to progress chronologically. But a concert is like a menu. Diners come in and you want to start off with something light. Something pleasant." She looked over at JT. "Bach is too complex, too cerebral, to be an appetizer. I think"—and here her eyes fell on Martyna—"the Clementi Sonata Quasi Concerto should begin the show."

Martyna gasped softly and put her hand to her heart, as if

Dr. Li had asked her to be her maid of honor. "I would love to," she said. "Believe me, Dr. Li, I won't let you down."

"Very good. Then, let's see. JT, your Bach Partita would do nicely as the next piece. Jenny, Khachaturian, very exuberant, next. And, second-to-last, Claire, because that Beethoven is flesh and blood. Rocky, your piece is a showstopper: it will end our concert on a bang."

"But Khachaturian—" Jenny began.

"I've been giving this quite a lot of thought, and I believe Rocky should go last," said Dr. Li. She turned to Rocky. "Here is an opportunity to prove yourself and better yourself, to show us that you can play the very last piece, the one that the audience will take away with them. The Prokofiev is longer and, although it's less flashy, it has a depth and pathos that will linger in the mind."

Beside me, Jenny stiffened. "Okay," she said under her breath, "and we want our audience to leave in the depths of despair, obviously."

Martyna was still glowing from having been asked to begin the concert. "Thank you so, so much for putting me first," she said. "I've never played first."

Dr. Li merely nodded. "Rocky's mother, Mrs. Wong, has kindly offered to provide the reception for us," she said.

I thought it was quite something for Rocky's mother to take off work and drive down for the performance, and I was glad she'd be able to see him doing what he loved. I knew Rocky had been chosen to anchor because he was the best pianist. Concerts always saved the best for last, put the showstopper at the end, so the audience would get on their feet and remember that last piece for days afterward. And Rocky couldn't help himself; he was looking at me with a huge grin. I smiled too.

Dr. Li seemed equally pleased with everyone that day: Jenny's Khachaturian and JT's Bach and Martyna's Clementi, which was no longer sloppy but full of playfulness, and my Beethoven, which had the dynamics and depth she'd taught me. The Showcase was only a week away, and we were all playing solidly from memory. Then it was Rocky's turn to perform for us. He began wonderfully. I knew the music as well as he did; I had listened to him practice it so many times. In my mind I saw him approaching the top of the second page, where the rhythm changed. There, he made a tiny mistake, but it didn't stop him. A few measures later, there was another, where he had to stop and start again, and his neck was turning red. I could see beads of sweat forming on his forehead. We cringed as he suffered through a couple more memory slips, a couple more missed notes, Dr. Li's head bent low over the score, when Rocky suddenly leapt from the piano bench and slammed the lid down with such force that we all jumped. Dr. Li's clay mug fell to the floor and broke cleanly in half. The yellow pencils rolled all over the rug. Rocky sprang from the bench to pick them up, and to put the pieces of the mug on the piano. "I'm sorry," he said, looking down at the mug. "I'll glue it back together for you." Then a dark cloud passed over his face. "I'm sick of this piece."

Dr. Li spoke quietly from her desk. "This is unacceptable. You're not happy with your playing? Don't show that to us. If you can't control your temper in my classroom, then I don't want you to be onstage. If your expectations are here," continued Dr. Li, extending her arm above her head, "but your playing is here"—

bringing her hand down to her shoulder—"and you become angry about it, that is arrogance. I will not tolerate that in my studio." She pointed to the door. "Out," she said, but Rocky was already headed to the hallway. Dr. Li made no move to stop him or to return his music books. The door slammed shut behind him.

"*Someone's* upset," said JT. He gestured to Rocky's coffee cup. "I don't think he needs caffeine today."

Dr. Li looked at Rocky's score, where a pencil had made several laps around a particularly challenging four bars. "Let's give him some time," she said. "I'm sure he'll be all right. And this is a lesson for all of you: This is a piano studio, not a therapist's office. Put your feelings into your music, but leave your outbursts at home."

Chapter 21

THE WEEK BEFORE SHOWCASE, I THOUGHT MULTIPLE TIMES about texting Rocky. I cringed when I pictured him having memory slips and missing notes onstage: If he reacted like that in studio class, then what would he do when a couple hundred people were watching him play? But I didn't text him—I had a feeling he wouldn't want to talk about it. When he didn't reach out to me, either, I figured I should give him space. On recital day, Jenny and I didn't talk except to wish each other luck. Dr. Li had told us we shouldn't speak to anyone all day unless it was absolutely necessary. In our room, we pulled our hair back and pinned the loose strands, made sure none would fall forward when we were bowing or, worse, playing. We put on our black shoes that had only the smallest heel—too much and it would get in the way of the pedal. Simple earrings and necklaces: nothing that would distract. We clipped our fingernails, kept our wrists and hands bare, no watches. It was one of the few times all semester that Jenny wore a dress, a black one with small white dots, which was "more serious than polka dots, but not straight-up black—this isn't a funeral," she'd said. I was wearing the wine-red dress that my parents had bought me over the holidays, a dress I'd hoped Rocky would like. It had a tiered skirt and showed off my collarbones. Now I found that I didn't really care what Rocky thought about it. I just wanted him to play well and return to being his usual self.

We were to practice, said Dr. Li, for only an hour that day. We were not to play our pieces at tempo, but very, very slowly. "If you play this part at half tempo for a week before the recital," she had told me, about the allegro in the exposition and recapitulation of my Beethoven, "your fingers will be like fire." So we set our metronomes at half time and practiced especially our beginnings and endings. Practiced walking in and bowing. Practiced rising from the bench and bowing again. Practiced smiling. "With teeth," Dr. Li had said, "as if you are very happy to see the people in the audience, even though with the stage lights, you won't be able to see anyone at all."

That evening in the greenroom, all was silent. Martyna sat in a corner, breathing slowly with her eyes closed. JT was listening to a recording of the Bach partita, his fingers tapping out the notes on his knee. Jenny and I each ate a banana. They were natural beta-blockers, Dr. Li had told us, and we were to eat them about twenty minutes before curtain call for the biggest impact. We were not to have caffeine, because the adrenaline would be enough; no dairy or turkey, because it might make us sleepy. Even Rocky sat calmly with his Prokofiev score in his lap, not saying much. We hadn't really talked for nearly a week, not since his outburst in studio class. I couldn't help feeling simultaneously worried and angry, my mind just as soon wondering if he was okay as feeling indignant about how he'd disrespected Dr. Li—and all of us. *We're all under a lot of pressure, so why do you get to throw a tantrum?* I'd caught glimpses of him in the music building and in class, and one time he'd asked how I was doing and then, looking embarrassed, said, "Yeah, I kind of lost it there." Now his hair was slicked back and he had on his charcoal suit with a loud purple tie, but he was wearing his glasses. He looked even thinner than before—his suit looked slightly big on him.

"Good luck to you all," said Dr. Li when she came backstage a few minutes before showtime. "Remember, if you keep your mind on the music and really listen to yourselves, there won't be room for anything else. Not even nerves."

From beneath the stage door, we saw the lights dim.

"Okay, guys," Martyna said. "Wish me luck."

Daniel, our stagehand for the night, opened the door, and the spotlight sliced across the dark stage. From what I could hear, Martyna's Clementi was very well done: clean, bright, even. When she appeared backstage again, she was all smiles. I was impressed. Clementi was harder in some ways than the Romantics because you had to find ways to be expressive; the music didn't always do it for you.

JT played next. His playing now had the crystalline tone that we had always envied in Dr. Li's own modeling of Bach. He sounded sure of himself—no easy feat with a piece that exposed your every move. In the Allemande and Courante, the arpeggios were clean, the articulation precise. It was such a touching performance that momentarily I could feel my own nerves quieting down: the magical effect of a contemplative Bach.

I gave Jenny a quick hug and then she walked through the stage door. She wowed everyone right away with her percussive opening, and then with the relentless polyrhythms in both hands, the runs and chromaticism. It was a piece of musical extremes, going down to the bottom of the keyboard and up to the highest registers, from *pianissimo* to *fortissimo,* and full of different textures and moods. Jenny's face was red with exertion and pleasure when she appeared briefly backstage, then stepped out and bowed again because the audience was still clapping.

"Seriously? That five-minute Khachaturian Toccata gets two rounds of applause?" said Rocky.

"They know a good pianist when they hear one," I said, glad no one could hear us over the sound of the applause. "Will you get off your high horse? Besides, Jenny can play that thing completely dry, no pedal needed, and it would still be like butter."

"I wasn't insulting *her*—"

But just then Jenny appeared again and we hugged. "Break a leg," she whispered. Then Rocky did get off his high horse. He congratulated Jenny, then threw his arms around me. "I'm sorry," he said, "about everything." I was so surprised and pleased I hardly knew what to do. Then he pressed his lips to my forehead. "You got this," he said.

Relief flooded over me, and whatever anger I'd been harboring disappeared, replaced by affection. He would play well, I was certain of it. And after Showcase, he would nail his auditions, and we could return to how we'd been before. I pulled away from him, took a deep breath, and closed my eyes, the smell of his cheap cologne and hair gel still in my nose. When I opened my eyes, the smattering of claps for Jenny had fizzled out. It was my turn. I walked across the stage as I'd been taught: quickly, as if about to meet a long-distance lover, is how Dr. Li described it (all of us wondering if she'd been speaking from experience). Up there, everything and everyone faded away. I smiled broadly out at the audience, although I could only make out a few people in the front row. I stepped into the pool of spotlight, placed one hand on the piano, and bowed deeply. Then I sat and adjusted the bench. My right foot shook on the pedal; my hands quivered on the keys. But I sank into that first chord, the weight of my whole torso creating the violent declaration in C minor. The next chords created more tension with their staggered rhythms, then exploded from a low rumble into a gallop that ascended up the keys. It sounded exactly as I'd wanted it to sound. My hands stopped shaking, my foot too, and I began to enjoy myself. I could feel that the audience was mesmerized. Before I knew it, I was in the final third already, and my fingers were moving so fast—just as Dr. Li had said they would. Finally, an ending so still and sad that I let my hands float above the keys before lifting my foot from the pedal and placing them in my lap.

"Listen for that silence," Dr. Li had always said. "The longer the silence, the better job you've done of changing the room." Several seconds of silence, and then suddenly the clapping. So much clapping. I got up from the bench with a stupid smile on my face, shaking with adrenaline, gripping the side of the instrument as if to say we did it together, but also because Dr. Li had always told us to do that—so we wouldn't fall off the stage. I bowed again. Looking down, I sang these words in my head: *Have I shined my shoes today?* and coming up to smile: *Yes, I've shined my shoes today.* In choir, Dr. Hebert had taught us to do this for the perfect timing of a respectful bow.

Now I didn't need to remind myself to smile with teeth. There were a few cheers from the audience: my parents, probably, and Jenny and Leo. I practically ran backstage, for just enough time to get a glimpse of Rocky clapping and grinning wildly before Daniel had opened the door again and was gesturing for me to get onstage. I stood near the piano for another bow, relieved I hadn't tripped, relieved it had all gone so well.

Backstage, Rocky took my hands in his. "Best I've heard you play it."

I threw my arms around his neck. "Break a leg," I said.

He looked at me for a beat. His eyes looked so tired, I thought, but determined. At least all this was almost over. "Thanks, Wu," he said.

And then, heart still pounding with adrenaline, I slipped into the hall and took a seat Jenny had found by the aisle.

From the lighted stage door, Rocky stepped across the stage hurriedly, then bowed and sat down with a thump, even though Dr. Li had taught us to sit down as if we were tucking a child into bed. In a gesture that was familiar to all of us, he adjusted the bench and sat for several seconds with his eyes closed. Then he began to play the Prokofiev, and he began with such conviction that it felt as if the entire hall sighed with relief. I felt my own shoulders relax, the way they did when Dr. Li called them out for stiffness during lessons. Watching Rocky play was not unlike watching an athlete—a diver or a skier—and wondering if they would make it in one piece. I could hear the bench squeak as it moved little by little with his exertion. Yet his playing was exactly as it should have been: violent and chaotic, with unexpected melodies full of longing, the feeling that was continuously driving the piece forward.

Then he missed a section. I could see the sheet music in my head like a photograph—there was an especially tricky part in the middle of the piece, about half a page, that he'd skipped by accident. I didn't think anyone else, except maybe Dr. Li, could tell. I was only able to hear it because I had listened to him so many times in the practice room, serving as a mock audience, giving him feedback. Memorizing the piece was difficult: the themes blended so seamlessly with each other that you could leave a part out and still sound like it was correct. We had all practiced what to do if we made a mistake, acting like nothing was the matter if a wrong note sounded, making things up if there was a memory slip—how to recover just enough to get to the next measure that you did remember.

But Rocky, although he was probably trying to employ one of those tactics, was thrown off, and I heard one more mistake: his left hand fumbled and missed a big leap. But there were so many leaps in Prokofiev that again, I was certain I was the only person who knew the piece well enough to tell that it had happened. Rocky had moved on from it so fast that they'd forget all about it. The rest of the performance was so excellent that it wasn't a problem. He ended the piece so passionately, pushing into the keys and springing back, that the piano itself budged. When he stood for the bow, he seemed as relieved as we were, maybe even glad to be done with it. We caught our breaths as he bowed, and then the room exploded. As we clapped, he stood and bowed from the waist, multiple times. Even from my seat I could see that he was sweating some. He dabbed his forehead with his sleeve.

We cheered as if Greenwood had just won a championship sports game against a longtime rival. And maybe that's what it was like, as our school had no room for sports, really—we didn't even have a football team—we cheered for our musicians, our dancers, our actors. Even Leo, who had just lost fifteen dollars betting that Rocky's performance wouldn't be very good, high-fived Daniel over this, the great victory, the comeback, of our MVP Rocky Wong. Dr. Li, proud coach, turned around in her seat, searching for our faces, and she beamed. We clapped so much that our hands started to hurt from it.

Rocky had disappeared from the stage, and still we clapped. He didn't come out again until after we had been clapping for nearly half a minute, and when he did, it was as if Daniel had pushed him. He didn't walk all the way to the piano but only stepped out a quarter of the way across the stage, and his bow then was more like a nod. Even from where I was sitting, I could hear Dr. Li mutter, "What kind of bow was that?" Still, we kept clapping. Even with the tiny mistakes, it had been that good. And when he went backstage, the clapping continued, on and on, yes, there was no question that he was the star pianist this year, probably Juilliard-bound, if he wanted it.

We whooped, we cheered, encouraging him for a third bow,

all of us on our feet. Standing ovations were not given lightly at Greenwood, and we wanted him to see that even the dancers—the dancers, Rocky!—had not only shown up for this recital, but stayed till the end. Toothpick was jumping up and down, cheering in a high-pitched squeal. But he didn't appear. Not after someone yelled, "Get it, Rockman!" or after Dr. Li, in a rare show of frustration, cupped her hands around her mouth and called, "Rocky, please take another bow."

Rocky's mother made her way down to the stage with flowers in her arms, yellow tulips. She held them in front of her as if, catching their scent, her son might appear.

"He's such a bad sport," said Jenny. "A couple missed notes and he's like, wah, I don't want to bow anymore."

"It's not like that," I said. Already, I could picture what was going on backstage: Rocky sitting in the greenroom with his head in his hands, beating himself up over mistakes, not caring that no one could tell the difference, thinking he'd let his mother down even though she was waiting for him with flowers. "It's not like he doesn't want to bow—it's that he's so totally immersed in thinking about what went wrong, he's still at the performance. He's not thinking about bowing at all."

"That's exactly what I'm talking about, though. He can't do that. He has to think about his audience. Being a performer is like being a royal—there has to be this public person who smiles and bows because that's how you say thank you for listening."

We made our way out of Halpern Hall and into the receiving line, which was the best part. Everyone wanted to tell us how good we were. They asked us to sign programs, they congratulated us.

My parents took me in their arms, telling me how proud they were, and they were pleased to finally meet Dr. Li, who congratulated and even hugged each of us, albeit briefly. Then everyone approached the reception and *ooh*ed and *aah*ed over what Mrs. Wong and her friends had set out.

"This is amazing," said Leo, walking past me. "I'm so hungry after these things. Beats what they usually have. Those mini finger foods don't fill me up."

It was not the typical Greenwood spread. Bottles of water, sandwiches, and snack-sized bags of chips had been set out on the table, as if Mrs. Wong had in mind a brown-bag lunch instead of a reception. Despite what Leo had said, I couldn't help feeling sort of embarrassed about it. At other recitals, students' families brought big glass bowls and filled them with sparkling peach punch. They laid out deviled eggs, meatballs, biscuits with fried ham, egg salad sandwiches with the crusts cut off. They set these on tablecloths that they brought from home, delicate white ones with doily-like patterns at the edges, passed down from a grandmother.

Mrs. Wong's reception tablecloth was plastic and still creased. She placed the flowers in the middle of the table, laying them on their side since there was no vase, and beside the flowers, a cake. It was the sort of cake that I'd seen in Chinese bakeries in Atlanta, tall and round with whipped cream and glossy fruit: strawberries, mangoes, blueberries. In the center, chocolate icing spelled *Congratulations*.

I'd never seen so many Chinese people gathered in one place in Green Valley. It seemed like Mrs. Wong had invited the entire Chinese church that Rocky had once played for, and his old piano teacher was there, too. They spoke to each other in melodic Mandarin, patting each other on the shoulder, as if congratulating one another about Rocky's success. I could only understand bits and pieces of their conversation, and heard one of them telling another that I was also a pianist. They both looked at me expectantly. I called them Aunt and Uncle in Mandarin, as I'd been taught, and couldn't say much more.

Amid everything, I hadn't had the time to check my phone since well before the recital started. I had a text from Angela: You were awesome!!!!! Sorry couldn't stay for reception, see you later tonight. There was nothing from Rocky. Quickly I sent him: You were amazing!!! This cake also looks amazing. You coming?

Mrs. Wong appeared by my side, and I shoved my phone into my pocket. She didn't speak that much English, but we'd talked before at other Greenwood events, and once or twice when she was dropping Rocky off at school. At the school functions, she often stood so close to me that every now and then I felt her arm brushing mine, as if she were a clinging friend I'd brought to a party. Once, after a concert, she put her hand on my arm, and I felt obligated to lead her out to the reception as if she were my grandmother. I'd mentioned this to my father, and he said, "Do you know why she does this? It's because she has no other family in this country. It must be very hard for her."

Now Mrs. Wong kept addressing Dr. Li as laoshi, which meant "teacher," while Dr. Li responded to her quietly in English: "I'm doing fine, thanks, it's very nice to meet you, yes, Rocky is doing well, I like it here in Green Valley." My own parents spoke to Dr. Li only in English.

Then Mrs. Wong placed her hand on my arm and, instead of greeting me, gestured to the sandwiches. I picked one up, along with a bag of chips and a brownie. Dr. Li was standing there with her arms across her chest.

"Well? Where is he? We can't stay here all night."

"He might still be backstage," I said, though really, with Rocky, who could be sure?

"You must be very proud," Dr. Li said to Mrs. Wong.

Mrs. Wong shook her head, but she was smiling. "You did a good job with him," she said.

Toothpick and Jackie had come out of the hall, too.

". . . didn't hear a single wrong note," Toothpick was saying. "Not a single one."

"He doesn't have very good stage presence, though," said Jackie.

"Do you think he was nervous?"

"Of course he was nervous."

"I wonder if all that playing makes his hands hurt."

"You know these recitals are graded, right? They're, like, fifty percent of the grade."

I could see Ellie Giang and a couple other members of the Society near the reception table, waiting for Rocky. I wondered if they had any clue where he was. Then I wondered what they'd thought of *my* playing.

Dr. Li adjusted her bag. "I suppose while I'm here I should have a slice of this cake," she said, reaching for a plate.

Mrs. Wong took out a knife and held it above the cake, as if trying to figure out the best way to cut it. Then she looked toward the door. My mother offered to help, but Mrs. Wong declined.

"Where is he?" Mrs. Wong said.

Dr. Li sent JT to check backstage and the men's room, but Rocky wasn't in there, either.

Mrs. Wong's face clouded with worry, and she set down the plate she was holding. "I'm sure she is in his room," she said, making a grammar mistake that my own mother sometimes made when she was distressed.

"He'll probably be here any second," I said, even though my phone hadn't yet buzzed.

After some discussion with Dr. Hamilton, Dr. Li decided to call the dorm.

Dr. Li took out her phone and dialed. "Yes, one of our students seems to have disappeared." She forced a laugh, then said, "It's nothing like that. But we've all been waiting for several minutes and are becoming a bit concerned. We just want to be sure he is safe. Okay? All right, then." She hung up and said, "They're sending someone to check his room."

I wondered if he'd gone somewhere on his skateboard.

Standing between my parents, I took a bite of the sandwich. Turkey cold cuts, lettuce, and tomato were stacked between slices of whole wheat, cut in half diagonally. They were a little too perfectly bland, as if Mrs. Wong had studied notions of American food, and this was the result. While I ate, Dr. Li spoke with Dr. Hamilton, their eyes darting to the door every time someone else entered the room. Daniel had looked all around backstage, and it was completely empty. When a few more minutes passed and Rocky still hadn't appeared, people began to leave, saying they would congratulate him in the morning. I noticed Ellie and the other Society members waiting by the window.

My parents hugged me again and then said they were tired and would head to their hotel, and did I want to go with them? I looked over at Jenny, whose parents hadn't been able to make it after all because of their hospital duties, and I said no, I would see them first thing in the morning, if that was all right with them?

My father looked hurt, but he said, "That's fine, Claire. You want to celebrate with your friends. That's fine." He looked over at my mother. "We've had a long day and need to rest. You did an excellent job. I'm sure Rocky's going to be okay," he added, but it seemed he was saying it more as a comfort to me than anything else.

My mother put her cheek against mine. "That boy is complicated," she said. "You don't need to get mixed up with him."

"We're very proud of you, Claire," my father said. "We'll see you tomorrow morning and then we have the whole weekend together." When we hugged, I smelled the familiar cologne he'd worn since I was a kid, and felt the pleasant scratchiness of his sports coat against my cheek.

They walked through the dark parking lot. Watching the car pull out, I felt a prickle of remorse. I clutched my concert program: months and months of practice, fifteen minutes onstage, hours of driving for the two of them. For a second, I felt myself pulled toward them, watching their silhouettes in the dim light where Rocky used to skate. I knew I ought to go to the hotel. I pictured them driving all the way over from our house in North Carolina: nearly three hours.

But where was Rocky?

Even Jenny said she was exhausted and would see me in our room. "That jerk," she said. "I'll be damned if he's not just playing pool in the rec room." She put her hand on my shoulder. "He'll never be good enough for you."

I texted again. Where are you??? And then I called, twice. Rocky didn't pick up. I saw Mrs. Wong calling, too, looking agitatedly at her phone. Among the few of us who remained, conversations dwindled, and the food and drink sat uneaten. The cake had been cut and distributed onto paper plates, but only a few people were eating it. Someone—probably JT—had taken a few of the strawberries from the top, leaving miniature craters in the frosting. With Rocky missing, it felt wrong to eat it, like eating birthday cake when the guest of honor wasn't there.

"We're all very proud of your son," said Dr. Hamilton to Mrs. Wong.

Mrs. Wong shook her head. "Thank you. You are a great role model for him."

Dr. Hamilton chuckled. "Well, he's both a great scholar of music history and a brilliant pianist. It's a pleasure to have his comments in class."

I thought of Rocky's comments, which were delivered via lip sync with Daniel or were so esoteric that no one else knew what he was talking about. He had been reading about Mozart's financial debt—including a recent theory about how he'd been sued by a fellow Freemason—and would raise the issue every now and then in class.

Mrs. Wong looked at the two men, then at me, then at Dr. Li.

"Where else could he be?" Dr. Li demanded.

"Someone already checked our club headquarters," said Ellie Giang. "No sign of him."

Stefan said, "He wasn't in his room, ma'am. But couldn't have gotten too far: his skateboard was still in there."

Hank said, "I asked on the intercom if anyone had seen him." He looked at Stefan. "Waited a few minutes and no one said anything. But you know, kids sometimes disappear for an hour or two. No reason to panic. For all we know, he could be downtown, having himself a nice meal."

Hank and I met eyes. It was clear that he was just covering for Rocky. I wondered if he knew something, or if he had covered for Rocky before and just figured he ought to now.

Dr. Li furrowed her brows at him. "None of my students would go downtown to eat by themselves after playing in the Student Showcase. They want to celebrate with their fellow musicians." She gestured toward me and JT. "Besides, Rocky knows better than to disrespect his audience like that."

"Ma'am, I know it may be hard to believe," he said, "but it happens. Kids feel pressure, and they gotta"—he whistled—"just get outta this place for a second." Hank frowned. "He got friends that maybe hook him up? Alcohol, stuff like that?"

"No, no," said Mrs. Wong.

"Rocky doesn't drink," Dr. Li snapped. But she didn't know whether Rocky drank or not—or did she?—so it sounded like she just wanted to defend him reflexively. "He's training to become a concert pianist."

Stefan said, "He's got no business being off campus. It being past curfew and all. Besides, I didn't get an alert on Guardian." He was a scrawny guy with long legs that poked out of khaki shorts, like a camp counselor.

"My student is missing," said Dr. Li. "He played his recital piece—brilliantly, I might add—and then he ran off. I couldn't care less about the damn curfew."

I had never heard Dr. Li swear before. I wished Rocky were there to hear it, and to hear how she'd spoken of his playing.

Mrs. Wong's face crumpled into the same distressed expression that Rocky's had when he finished his recital. "What do we do now?"

Stefan rubbed his chin. "Have you called him?"

Mrs. Wong looked irritated. "Of course I call him already."

"Where would he have gone, do you think? A favorite place on campus? Or downtown? Any ideas?"

Mrs. Wong's face was completely blank, and I thought for a second that she hadn't understood. Then I realized she looked that way not because she hadn't understood the question, but because she had no idea where her son could possibly be.

Chapter 22

BY ELEVEN-FOURTEEN, ROCKY STILL HAD NOT BEEN FOUND.
Jenny and I sat on the carpet in our room with our suitemates,
waiting, wondering. My stomach was in knots, and even though
the concert was hours ago, I found myself doing the breathing
exercises Dr. Li had taught us, holding my breath and letting it
out again slowly. It seemed wrong to just be sitting around, but
aside from texting and calling, I didn't know what else to do. The
halls were unusually quiet, as if everyone else were waiting, too,
and our usual late-night talks and Showcase celebrations couldn't
proceed until Rocky was found. Even Hank had admitted that he
didn't know where Rocky was—he just didn't want him to get in
too much trouble.

"Maybe Rocky felt embarrassed," said Miyoung. "I don't like
being in the art gallery when people are looking at my work." She
shuddered. "Too exposed." She'd just gotten out of the shower,
and she gathered her damp hair to one side of her face.

"I don't think Rocky minds the attention," I said.

"That's an understatement," said Jenny. "He loves performing."

"Do you think he ran away?" Angela asked.

"He's avoiding people," I said. What I thought was that Rocky, after achieving something so big, felt disappointed that it hadn't delivered the high that he'd expected. He was wondering what he would do now, how he could outdo himself.

"Yes," said Jenny, "classic Rocky. You know how he gets sometimes."

But what if I was wrong—what if something had happened to him? He might need space for a while, but it was unlike him to just go away and not even respond to texts and calls, especially since his mother was here.

"But why didn't he take his skateboard with him?" I said. "What if something happened to him?" My voice broke.

Jenny put a hand on my shoulder. "Hey," she said, "this is Rocky we're talking about. Nothing's going to happen to him. He's super strong, remember? If anyone tried anything—"

Just then, all our phones buzzed in unison. It was an alert from the Guardian app:

Greenwood School Emergency Alert: This is NOT a drill. All students must shelter in place immediately. Rocky Wong missing two hours ago. Call or text any information to school emergency number.

"What the hell," Jenny muttered. "How are we supposed to report Rocky sightings if we have to stay where we are?"

I grabbed a sweater and threw it on over my dress. "Let's go."

Ordinarily Jenny would have made some quip: Rocky could stay out all night if he had to, or okay, so I was willing to break the rules, but only when it came to Rocky? But instead she started texting furiously.

"Do you have Craig's number?" she asked me. In a matter of seconds my phone buzzed again, this time with a group text from Jenny. The plan was: wait until the dorm parents had checked us in, then take the back stairwell into the basement. There was a door at the end of the hall that opened right up to the dorm parking lot.

At about a quarter after ten, Jenny and I hurried down the stairs. Daniel was already outside, standing in the dark so he wouldn't get caught.

He sipped from a thermos, shaking his head. "Black coffee," he whispered. "I'm gonna stay up all night if that's what it takes."

Anthony Lee and Craig Meyers, Rocky's suitemates, came down too.

"Hey," Craig said, giving me a wave. "You did a really good job tonight."

Anthony was still wearing his button-down shirt and khakis that he wore to the Showcase. "I hope Rocky's okay," he said. "Geez."

We knew campus well enough even in the dark, knew the places teachers wouldn't think to look. We set out toward the center of campus, but instead of taking the path, we all walked single file on the grass so that the lights wouldn't catch us.

I heard Dr. Hamilton calling out, "Rocky? Rooooocky!"

Jenny said, "This is horribly inefficient." We were walking on the path that led from the dorms to the center of campus.

"It's stupid, is what it is," said Anthony. "If they're so worried, why don't they just call copters to come look for him?"

"I mean, that would be pretty extreme, wouldn't it? Plus, bad publicity?" said Craig. "Expenses?"

I tried, desperately, to think as if I were Rocky, after a really good Prokofiev performance with a few mistakes hardly anyone could hear. *Screw this place, I need a break,* I could hear him saying, but even then, wouldn't he be here by now? And he loved his mother in a way that was both guilty and dutiful; he wouldn't have left her hanging without good reason, unless some freak accident had occurred. But what could have happened between the time he'd stepped off the stage and the reception had begun? Most likely he just needed to get away for a bit. Then I remembered how Rocky behaved when he needed space. He went into a study room in the library that none of us knew about, or shut himself into the practice room that everyone avoided, the one with the key that always stuck.

"I know a place we can check," I said.

"Oh?" said Jenny.

"The pantry inside the dining hall." When she looked confused, I said, "Never mind. I'll be right back."

I set off from the dorm to the dining hall, nearly breaking into a run. Rocky was in the pantry—I was sure of it. He needed to be alone, and he knew no one would find him there. No one except me.

The dining hall was completely dark, and none of the staff were around. I used my phone flashlight and stepped behind the hot bar. I entered the code—wrongly the first time, I was so flustered—and opened the door. But it was dark in there, too. I turned on the light and stepped inside, calling Rocky's name for good measure. No one. Just the food, and the floor we'd sat on back in January.

I found Jenny again, who was searching outside the dorm with the others. If he wasn't there, then where was he?

"No sign of him," I said to Jenny, although that much was obvious.

We could hear teachers bickering about whose fault it was that Rocky was gone, others trying to remember where his favorite places were, his favorite things to do. Dr. Hamilton and Mrs. McHeusen had stayed on campus after Showcase. Walking a few feet in front of us, they didn't speak to each other much at all, just desperately called out, "Rocky! Rocky!"

In the library, we wandered in between the stacks and in and out of study rooms, looking and looking and feeling helpless. We went downstairs and started searching in the archives. Then I went into the study room in the medieval studies section of the library. Right there on a desk, I saw what looked to be a letter, on notebook paper, folded into thirds. I knew it had to be from Rocky. As I had with all the notes he'd left me, I opened it.

Dear Everybody,

It's time.

Please don't blame yourself (I know you will). Nothing to do with you, my decision completely.

I tried to be good, even Great. This is my peak. I mean, what's harder than Prok. 1 and the Appassionata? and it wasn't good enough.

As Dr. Schantz always told us about story scenes in English class, it's best to arrive late and leave early. This is something like that.

God knows I tried. The people I love don't deserve for me to be like this.

Forgive me if you're the one who finds this note. If you're the one who finds me. I think that means you knew me? Hardly anyone really did, feels like. So, thank you, and I'm sorry.

Rocky

My entire body felt cold. I couldn't breathe.

I stepped out of the room, clutching the note. Jenny leaned over it, then she grabbed my arm, harder than she ever had before, and dragged me into the hallway. "There's still time. We have to find him."

♩♫

Maybe I would never see Rocky again. The fear I felt was physical, beginning somewhere in my stomach and working its way up to my throat. More than anything, I wanted this to not be happening. I wanted Rocky to walk in, completely fine, laughing this off. A good scare. A horrible thing to do, but at least he was okay. All of a sudden I longed for home, to have never come to Greenwood at all. To be in my bedroom with its striped wallpaper, my mother—a perpetual night owl—working on the computer in the living room, looking up stocks and the prices of houses, the light turning off in the hallway after my father had checked to make sure all the doors were locked, as I lay in bed, falling asleep to the sound of a few cars on our quiet street.

My eyes welled. I felt dizzy.

Jenny gripped my shoulders. "Okay, listen. We have to keep looking. That's the only way we can find him. Okay?"

She handed the letter to the others. No one moved. What had, moments before, felt kind of like an adventure, a game, now felt very real. A brick settled into my chest. For the first time, the school and the town felt huge, unknowable. Rocky could be anywhere, tucked away in some small corner of campus, or out in the sketchy part of town, past the West End market, which was out-of-bounds for Greenwood students.

At the end of the hall, the stairwell door creaked open, and Dr. Li appeared with Mr. Yanko behind her.

"Ah," she said with a sad smile. "Just the place I like my students to be, usually."

Then she saw my face, and I handed her the letter. Dr. Li read it, and her hand flew to her mouth. She looked at us, and we all looked at her.

Dr. Li opened her purse and dialed 911, her voice the loudest I'd ever heard it.

In the library, we flipped on all the lights in the stacks, yelling Rocky's name through the narrow shelves filled with books we hadn't read, stacks that we'd used for making out and for whispering secrets and eating candy that we weren't supposed to have in the library. It felt as though we'd been looking for hours, each growing more hopeless than the next, calls of "Rocky, Rock-o, Rockman" echoing in the silent library.

We ran through the courtyard and went to search the dining hall again, the academic classrooms, the gym. On the dark campus, several flashlights shone here and there. I took the brick path down to the courtyard, the one on which, months before, Rocky had written those notes about Dr. Li in yellow chalk. I walked slowly, pointing my flashlight on either side of the path, but saw nothing except grass. The trees of the North Campus Garden were still bare, stretching above the brick walls covered in leafless ivy. I tried to sidestep puddles, but it was hard to see, and my feet squished inside my sneakers. I shined the light over tables and around flower beds. My stomach hurt. Had there really been no other choice? Had he looked at his life, all its parts, and decided it was better to leave it behind?

Farther up, near the courtyard, I could see Mrs. Wong wringing her hands. My own mother would have gripped Stefan by the collar by now and demanded answers—which is what Cassandra Maverick's mom did when Cassandra got food poisoning from a dining hall sandwich last spring, although the true cause couldn't be proven, and what was she doing eating tuna from the dining hall, anyway? But Mrs. Wong, walking to one spot and then looking over her shoulder, as if Rocky could be behind her, seemed utterly hopeless. She was calling out Rocky's Chinese name, which was Ren-Shu. I knew what it meant because he'd told me once, not without pride: "A bighearted man." Stefan walked beside Mrs. Wong, trying every now and then to comfort her by putting a hand on her shoulder, but it seemed to make her feel worse rather than better. She wrung her hands, calling "Wong Ren-Shu" over and over. Then I heard a rustle just outside the small greenhouse at the edge of the North Campus Garden, and a flashlight winked from the bushes.

"Oh my god!" someone said.

"Rocky!" said another.

We all rushed over. Rocky lay on the ground, beside the winter cabbages that some of us had been tending all semester.

"No," he was muttering, "no, no, no."

Relief washed over me, so strong that tears began to leak out before I could stop them. "Rocky!" I said, trying to get close.

"Stay back, Claire," said Dr. Li, putting a hand up. "He needs space." Dr. Li's hair hung in loose strands around her face, and there was a run in her pantyhose. She grabbed Rocky's shoulders, something we were all accustomed to in our lessons. She knelt over him, saying, "You're all right, you're going to be all right." When he didn't move at all, she bent over him, saying his name, shaking him. I stood desperately close, wanting to see. His face looked strangely white, and it frightened me.

Dr. Li checked his hands, pressing the meaty part of his palm with her thumb.

"*Mm,*" he said. He gave a small shake of his head. She tested his fingers, then made sure he could rotate his wrists. He didn't wince through any of it—just let her handle his hands as if they were in a lesson.

"Wiggle your fingers," she commanded, but by then Rocky had faded, his head tilted back, his eyes seeming to gaze up at the dark patches of sky amid the darker trees, and then they closed.

The ambulance came with sirens even though the streets were empty of traffic. When the ambulance arrived, it pulled all the way onto the narrow campus path, its tires flattening our perfect grass, its lights casting a red glow on our faces and the buildings. The door opened, and two paramedics, a man and a woman, leapt to the ground in their navy-blue uniforms. They pulled a stretcher out and lifted Rocky onto it. He lay crumpled like a marionette, his purple tie wrinkled and loose, his shoes black and still gleaming. The woman took his leg by the ankle and laid it out straight.

Daniel came running toward us, saying something about pills, and then Mrs. Wong started screaming, not in Mandarin or English, but something that was no language at all. I had never heard that kind of screaming before. I wished I weren't there, wished I hadn't seen any of this. I regretted not going to the hotel with my parents. I would have lain between them on the bed to watch TV, the British detective shows that my mother liked.

I wouldn't have found out about anything until morning.

The female paramedic said to Mrs. Wong, "Ma'am, he's going to be okay. Ma'am, the sooner you get in, the sooner we can get him to the hospital."

The male said, "Y'all step away now."

Dr. Li put a hand on Mrs. Wong's shoulder with some force, the way she would right before we were due to play, and spoke to her quickly and softly in Mandarin. Mrs. Wong, crying now, climbed into the ambulance after her son, and as she did so, she thanked Dr. Li over and over again, xiexie, laoshi.

Chapter 23

"CLAIRE?"

My mother's voice. Off and on throughout the morning, I'd heard the sounds of my parents getting ready for the day: the coffee maker percolating, the hair dryer whirring, the bathroom door opening and closing. I hadn't been able to sleep that night in the hotel, or the night before in my dorm bed. Now I buried my head into the pillow, curling my legs up to my stomach.

"Claire," my mother continued, "it's almost nine. You'll miss the whole morning." She sat on the edge of the bed and stroked my hair.

"I don't feel well."

"You'll feel better if you get up."

No, I thought, *I won't feel better. Whether I get up or lie here all day, I won't feel better.*

"We'll go to the art galleries today. They opened an hour ago already."

That, I knew, was my parents trying their best to help, since they themselves weren't really interested in walking through Green Valley's open studios.

I resented my mother's use of *already*.

"It'll be a good break for you," she continued. "Get away from the stress, the pressure. Get away from feeling sad."

"I *am* away," I muttered into the pillow. "I just want to sleep."

I wasn't away, though, not at all. I couldn't stop seeing what I'd seen. Rocky lying there on the grass, helpless, pale, looking nothing like the person I'd kissed in the library. And even though a couple of days had passed, I couldn't stop feeling what I'd felt—so raw and heavy it was as if it had just happened—picking up that note, reading what he'd written, knowing he was somewhere on campus and possibly dead.

Possibly dead.

We hadn't used that word the other night: *death*. No one had. Not even Dr. Li, when she'd called 911. She'd said Rocky was unconscious after having attempted to end his life.

"If you sleep too late today, you won't be able to sleep again tonight," my father said now. "Take a shower. That'll refresh you."

Rocky had been rushed to the hospital, his stomach pumped. He was going to be fine, the doctors said. The Green Valley police had come to talk to us last night, had asked if Rocky had seemed depressed. Now Rocky was at a mental health care clinic in Columbia, a little over an hour away. It was supposed to be the best in the state.

I couldn't stop my heart from racing. It wasn't like the greenroom: no number of deep breaths could calm it. The night of the search, I was so intent on finding him that my own feelings hadn't really surfaced. *If I were Rocky,* I kept thinking, *what would I do? Where would I go?* I couldn't come up with an answer.

And for that, I could not forgive myself.

Did I even *know* him?

My mother was putting her earrings in now, and she'd laid my clothes out for me like I was in grade school. I slid out of bed and headed to the shower.

To not have known he was feeling so hopeless—that was what really hurt, what created an ache in my lungs that wouldn't go away. And he must have been thinking about it for a while. He had to have been, hadn't he? Was that how it worked? I wasn't sure. I pictured Rocky: thinking about ending his life as he grabbed pizza from the dining hall and walked away from us, believing he needed to be alone. Thinking about it as he showed up late to music history bleary-eyed because he couldn't sleep the night before. Why couldn't he see himself the way I did? Why couldn't he see that I loved him, and that his music was great, even Great?

Even if I had known, what then? There was nothing I could have done that would have made things better.

I should have listened better. I should have been around more. There were nights when Rocky didn't sleep and then crashed, crashed so hard he slept through half a class, on a blanket in the practice room, head on his folded arms in the library. Other seniors crashed that way, didn't they?

I bit my lip. How had I missed it?

When I came out of the shower, my parents looked as if they'd been talking to each other and had stopped. My father announced that we were going to lunch at the Hideaway, which again I knew was more for me than for them. At the diner, my parents both had barbecue plates and sides. I got a pulled pork sandwich, reciting my order without thinking and without feeling hungry.

"Claire, eat," my mother said.

I took a bite.

"Your friend is going to be okay," said my father. "It's over now. He's fine, and he's in the best place to be."

I felt my mouth tremble. I didn't want to cry in the restaurant, at this table with the red-and-white-checked tablecloth and the sauces in their plastic squeeze bottles. At this place where we'd had so many good times.

My parents took me to buy toothpaste and snacks and laundry detergent, a couple new books. I felt like I was wandering the town in a haze, unable to really see where I was going. Later, in our hotel room, my mother flipped through channels on the bed, a luxury I usually looked forward to, since Jenny and I didn't have a TV. But now I couldn't focus on anything; my stomach was in a knot from the moment I woke up until I went to bed again.

♩♫

The next morning at breakfast, my mother said, "Maybe you should speak to a counselor. It could be helpful. Do you want me to make an appointment with someone? Or talk to Ms. Shelley next week?"

But I didn't want to talk to someone who didn't know Rocky,

and—although I knew it wasn't right, I was angry at Ms. Shelley. Wasn't it her job to catch the signs? All I wanted was to see Rocky.

I said, "I was wondering if we could go to Columbia. It's only an hour away."

My father put his newspaper down and looked at my mother. "Columbia?"

"I want to visit Rocky."

My mother looked at me. "We're in town for such a short time."

"I know you care about your friend," said my father. "But how will you being there help him? What are you going to say to him?"

"He's exactly where he needs to be," said my mother. "He'll receive good care."

"But he's all alone there!" I burst out. I thought of how Rocky hadn't been able to pack his comic books, his skateboard, if he would be able to skate there at all.

My father asked me if I wanted some water. I said no. He got up and started filling a cup anyway. My mother reached across the table and smoothed my hair.

I didn't bring up Rocky again. I let my parents tell me gossip from home, plans for our summer trip to California. In stores, my mother brought me clothes to try on, skirts and dresses that made me feel older than I was. But all my former daydreams about concerts and teaching—which I was hoping to do in the summer— seemed so foolish, now. Before they left, they each hugged me for a long time, and assured me that we'd see each other soon. Then I stood in the parking lot and watched their car pull away from the school. I stood there for a long time, and then I headed up the path to the dorm.

♩♫

On campus the next day, dining hall conversation never rose above a murmur. People smiled at each other in the hallways, sad smiles that didn't show teeth. Jackie Lund, standing in front of me in the lunch line, actually handed me a plate and silverware on a tray, even though we never did that sort of thing. On Rocky's dorm room door, other boys spelled out *WE MISS YOU ROCKY* in sticky tabs meant to mark books.

In music history, there were no random cricket imitations, no one holding their tuner up to one ear to try to memorize the sound of A440 so they could have perfect pitch. Dr. Hamilton, who usually stood so straight, had his arms on the podium and was leaning toward us, looking at each of us with tired but very serious eyes.

Without using the whiteboard or any slides, he told us that he was there for us, that we could tell him, anytime, if we were ever feeling like the world was too much for us to handle. "I love my students. I really do—I want to make sure you all know that. I care for you very much. If you come away from here knowing anything, know this: we love you and believe in you, dammit. That's what keeps us teaching here. Playing music—you all already know this or you wouldn't be here, but I want to make absolutely sure you know this—playing music is an act of love. Listening to it is also. And teaching it, well, teaching it is love itself."

He loved us. Did we understand that? Well, did we?

We all nodded.

"Good," said Dr. Hamilton.

Then he told us to open up our books to page 127. We were learning about Frédéric Chopin, who'd died young of tuberculosis and left behind his brilliant, sensitive music.

♩♫

Classes continued as usual, except that our teachers told us before class and after class, some of them even during class, that we could talk to them if we wanted to, that if there was anything we wanted to ask, or share, we could talk to them. As far as I knew, no one really did. They said also that we could go see Ms. Shelley whenever we wanted. A few people who'd hardly known Rocky went to see Ms. Shelley because it made for a good excuse to get out of class. Unlike the other teachers, she was terribly earnest, and had framed cross-stitched Scripture verses and motivational posters on the wall, the kind with kittens that said, *You are purrfect just the way you are!*

At night, in the dorms, we speculated.

"Do you think he really meant to?"

"Meant to what?"

"You know. Kill himself."

"Or what? He just wanted attention? You always think he just wants attention."

"That's not what I'm saying, but sure."

"You think it was because of auditions?"

"I mean, I knew he was feeling down, but—"

"He had friends. People liked him, girls liked him. I don't get it. Kids you read about are usually way worse off than him."

"It's not *about* that. He was sick. He should have been on meds, but he refused to see someone."

"I think it's selfish. It's like even when he's planning his own death, he has to go and—"

"Shut *up*."

♩♫

One night, I lay awake listening to the air conditioner: it would turn on for several minutes, then just as suddenly shut off, then turn on again. I pulled the blanket between my knees and lay on my side, facing the window. Was life so awful, I wondered, that Rocky would want it all to end completely? Did nothing or no one give him hope? Had he thought of ways to do it: Drowning himself in the Weepy somehow, or throwing himself from the tenth floor of the Avery? Tchaikovsky had wanted out, too.

How did it feel to swallow that many pills, what happened to your body, and wasn't he scared? And why hadn't he come back onstage to take that final curtain call? I remembered his lips against my forehead, how he'd said it was the best I'd played it. Last words. As if that was the most important thing to say. And what kinds of things did they talk about at a mental health clinic after something like that? I couldn't picture Rocky sitting in a circle doing group therapy, talking about his feelings.

When the air conditioner stopped, I heard a sound from Jenny's bed—at first I thought she had stirred in her sleep, but then I realized she was crying. I climbed out of my own bed, crept in the dark across the narrow space between the sink and our desks that I knew so well, and climbed up. She said nothing, speechless for the first time in our shared life. She made room for me and gave me her other pillow. We slept like that until morning.

♩♫

Nearly two more weeks passed, and Rocky still didn't return to school. When we asked how long he would be gone, no one could tell us. "As long as it takes for him to recover," they said.

In my lesson with Dr. Li, she took her time, awkwardly, to ask me how I was doing and to say she wished she had more information she could give me about Rocky, but she knew only as much as the other teachers. She herself didn't look so great—as if she hadn't been sleeping. And while I was playing, she seemed preoccupied, looking out the window instead of at my hands and posture.

Somehow, Rocky had taken me down with him. I couldn't play music. I moved through scales as fast as I could, distracting myself with the repetition, or else sight-read through new pieces in a noncommittal way. When it came time to play repertoire, everything felt dull. A few times, I tried to pray, something I hadn't really done since arriving at Greenwood, and found I didn't know what to say. *Please be with Rocky*, I'd think. That was all I could come up with.

♩♫

That Tuesday night, while Jenny was working on a group project, I went into our room and closed the door. Then I sat down at my desk and looked at the new application for the Society. *Why,* the application asked, *do you belong in the Asian Student Society?* I didn't really know what I was doing, but I started to write. Maybe I would hand this to them, and maybe I wouldn't, but I needed to write it down. I wrote about how far away I felt from my parents. I wrote about how Rocky had been in so much pain and couldn't tell anyone, couldn't tell me. I wrote about that night, finding the note he'd written, the way my heart had launched up into my throat and my stomach had bottomed out. How fiercely you could love a person, how badly you wanted to make everything okay. I wrote to Ellie that I was so deeply sorry about her mother. I wished there was more I could say or do, but wasn't that all we could do? To be there, to give attention? Be there the way I would be for Rocky, the way Rocky had been there for me? I wrote that I'd seen Ellie's mother walking around the art galleries last spring, looking at her daughter's work, that her mother had been luminous, and so clearly happy, even though she knew she would only live a few more months.

I had marveled at it ever since.

I folded the letter into thirds and walked to the art studios. I had never been down there before, because I hadn't had a reason, but I knew where they were, in the basement of the gallery. Inside, the air was cool and damp and smelled of paint and plaster. Ellie was in the far right corner, molding one of her faces. When I came into the room, she looked startled to see me. I dropped my letter on her table and left.

♩♫

In studio class that week, as she had for the past few weeks, Dr. Li looked exhausted, and her eyes had dark circles under them, like Rocky's had. Still, we went through the usual rituals. We listened to Richard Goode playing the late A-major Beethoven sonata. Dr. Li made some comments on the first movement and invited us to do the same. But we didn't have much to say, only wanting to listen. Last semester, this was the piece that Rocky had put words to, singing with Daniel: *Greeeeenwood School will kick your ass. . . .* No one mentioned that now.

I gave a first performance of the Schubert sonata that I had loved for years. Its delicate music box melody was too sweet now; all of its harmonic tensions were resolved within measures. I played it without much feeling, my fingers knowing where to go but saying very little, and afterward there was a smattering of claps and then silence.

Even Dr. Li's teaching wasn't the same. "Thank you, Claire," she said after I'd played. Under normal circumstances, she would have given me a long list of what I needed to do. Instead, she said, "You know what you need to work on." Then she called Jenny up to play, and instead of being critical, she told Jenny she could hear a lot of improvement in her Mozart. It was true that Jenny's playing was more tender now.

Then Dr. Li did something she had never done the entire year: she dismissed us at the time that all other Friday afternoon classes were let out, at exactly five-thirty.

We gathered our things and walked to the dining hall. Leo joined our table, looking solemn, holding a chocolate chip bagel in a napkin.

"Hey," he said. "How are you guys holding up?"

When we didn't say much, he continued. "You know something? Schumann tried to kill himself once. He was angry about Brahms, you know, because Brahms was hitting on Clara? So Schumann threw himself off a Rhine River bridge, but it didn't work out. Then he wrote the Ghost Variations."

That didn't exactly line up with what we'd learned in music history, but for once, nobody told him to shut his mouth.

Leo sighed. "Poor Clara. He sent her the Variations after he was rescued."

"I've never heard of those," Jenny muttered.

"Yeah," said Leo, spreading cream cheese on his bagel. "I listened to them one time last year, when I had a crush on Jackie and was kinda depressed, and it was, like, two a.m. and I couldn't sleep." He shuddered and shook his head. "Shouldn't have done that. They're really creepy."

To my surprise, Jenny laughed. And then so did JT, and then Martyna, and then I was laughing, too.

Then, as she was reaching for the salt, Martyna said, "Isn't that Rocky's mom?" We looked at where she was pointing. Through the windows behind the cereal dispensers, we could see Mrs. Wong sitting at one of the courtyard tables, with the purse she'd brought with her to Rocky's recital, and a suitcase.

Dr. Li was making her way across the courtyard. She stopped in front of Mrs. Wong, took her suitcase from her, and led her over to the faculty parking lot. Later, when I asked in my lesson, Dr. Li told me she had invited Mrs. Wong to stay with her— Mrs. Wong's team at the restaurant was covering her for at least another week—so she wouldn't have to stay at a hotel. When I said it was kind of her, Dr. Li said that it wasn't out of kindness but duty. It was simply the right thing to do.

What they talked about those nights when Mrs. Wong was staying with her, or if they talked at all, we didn't know. Maybe with Mrs. Wong there, Dr. Li spoke Mandarin, or even Taiwanese. Taiwanese was a language that was not written. It existed only in sound, and it was songlike to me, full of vowels and dynamic range. Maybe they talked about Taiwan, but most likely they talked about Rocky. In class, Dr. Li didn't say anything about her guest except that Rocky was improving, and that Mrs. Wong had made some delicious dumplings and would we like to keep some in the dorm kitchen? But they looked depressing to me. The neat rows and pinched creases were reminiscent of all the time Mrs. Wong was spending away from Rocky and away from work, with nothing to do but worry and cook and worry some more.

During class, we'd been quiet. Martyna had played a short piece by the twentieth-century composer Villa-Lobos, which was supposed to be bursting with hectic energy, but because she played it under tempo, it came out sounding not like a flashy encore but a warm-up exercise. JT had played a Scarlatti sonata with too heavy a touch, and Dr. Li had told him he was overemoting. "You can feel all the emotions you want," she'd said. "But your playing deserves more nuance than simply pouring them out into the piano."

Now Dr. Li regarded us. She pulled her chair out so that she was within our semicircle instead of speaking to us from the piano or behind the desk. "You're not doing very well. I can tell from your playing." She glanced over at Jenny and me. "And from your critiquing."

"Well, I feel pretty terrible," said Jenny.

"Me too," I said.

"I understand," said Dr. Li. She sighed. "It may be hard to tell at times, but the whole school is sad along with you. Including me. It's a normal response. It would be strange if you were not upset. You will get through this. Did you see how the daffodils have started to come out, almost overnight, on Main Street?"

At this, Martyna's eyes spilled over and she said yes emphatically.

Dr. Li got up and handed her a box of tissues. "You all are incredibly good friends to Rocky. Things will get better, with time. For Rocky as well."

We all nodded.

Then she said, "This is what I want you all to do: I want you to do something fun."

We all looked at each other. It wasn't typical of Dr. Li to encourage us to have fun. It took away from the time when we should have been practicing.

"You're sad, and maybe angry, or maybe you don't know how to feel. I understand that. But please, Rocky wouldn't want you to just be sitting around moping."

I considered. I wondered if, on the contrary, moping because of his absence was exactly what Rocky would have wanted us to do.

"There must be *something* you need to do away from campus. Preferably outdoors?"

"We could go shopping," said JT, putting a hand each on Jenny's shoulder and mine.

"I've been needing new shoes for forever," said Jenny.

"I could go for a frozen yogurt," said Martyna.

Only I hesitated, not really wanting to go, but also not wanting to be alone. If Rocky were here, he would have said something snarky: *Shopping is for capitalists,* or *Froyo's moment is over.* But Dr. Li was nodding and smiling, gesturing for us to go out, and then Jenny grabbed me by the elbow and pulled me into the sunshine.

When we arrived at Nellie's, it appeared that everyone else had had the same idea. Toothpick was monopolizing the full-length mirror. "Is this Daisy Buchanan enough? Scott and I are going to prom as Gatsby and Daisy." She wore a white dress with fringe at the knees. Jenny rolled her eyes, and JT said, "Fabulous. Absolutely fabulous. You'll need something for your hair," and went in search of it. Even Leo was at the store, deciding between bow ties and trying to figure out when and how to ask Jackie to prom.

We went out for dinner that night at the Hideaway and made it just in time for curfew. I was even starting to feel a little bit better. When we got to our dorm, I realized there was a voicemail on my phone. It was from a number I didn't recognize, down in Columbia. My friends from home didn't call during the day, and no one at Greenwood left voicemails. It was easier to text, or even just talk to a friend of the friend in the hallway; the message always got to them. I washed my face, brushed my teeth, and changed into my pajamas. Finally I checked the message.

A tired but familiar voice said, "Hey, Wu. I hope you're doing okay. I wanted to let you know that I'm okay." Rocky cleared his throat. "You can call me at this number. Just ask for me. If you want."

My stomach clenched. I felt my hand holding the phone go sweaty. A smile pulled up the corners of my mouth—it was Rocky, after all, and he was okay—but seconds later, tears sprang to my eyes. I pictured not calling him back. Leaving him hanging, wondering, hurt, as he'd left me. He'd be waiting by the phone. He'd wonder if he'd missed any calls from me. It was mean and I knew it was, but I couldn't help it. I'd spent the last few weeks feeling sad, and now what I felt was anger.

How could he?

At the same time, I wanted to talk to him so badly.

I took the phone into the bathroom, where Jenny and I usually went to make private calls (even though you could still hear most of whatever was said).

"Palmetto Mental Health!" a woman's voice said, a little too brightly. I asked for Rocky.

"Hang on just a second, hon," she said. After some shuffling, I heard Rocky thank her.

"Palmetto Mental Health!" he chirped.

I rolled my eyes and hoped he could hear it over the line. "Rocky, it's Claire."

"Wu. I'm sorry. I'm, like—I'm so, so sorry. I heard that you found the note."

I stiffened. I hadn't expected him to bring up the note right away. I tried to picture him. Did patients wear scrubs at mental hospitals? Jenny said they took your stuff away and watched you all the time.

"I found it, yeah," I said. I wished I knew the right things to say, the right things to ask. "I didn't realize that you were feeling so bad. How are you doing now?"

Was that an okay question? Rocky obviously wasn't doing well. But what else could I say?

"Not great, but . . . better. I'm getting better."

"That's good," I said. I took a seat on the edge of the tub.

"You won't believe this, Wu, but it's worse than the dorms here. They have to check on me every fifteen minutes. Can you believe it?"

"Sounds pretty terrible."

Rocky chuckled—a forced laugh, I thought, which was rare for him. "One good thing, I don't have to deal with Giambalvo's late-night philosophizing. How is he, by the way?"

When I thought about it, I hadn't really been paying any attention to Daniel, or Rocky's other friends. Poor Daniel, I realized, was still sleeping in the room they shared. "I think he's hanging in there," I said, resolving to talk to him as soon as I could. "I didn't know you were feeling so bad," I said again. "I wish—you know you could have told me, right?"

It was as if I could feel Rocky's discomfort over the phone.

"What did I say in my note? It has nothing to do with you." Rocky was quiet for a second, and I thought I could hear a TV in the background. "Besides," he said, "if my mom ever found out I was talking to a shrink, I mean, you know how it is with her. There's still a stigma around this stuff. Worse than a stigma. She denies that it even exists. There's no way that my mother's only son could have mental health issues."

I hadn't thought about that. I wondered what Mrs. Wong thought now that Rocky talked to shrinks pretty much all day.

"She just wants you to be okay," I said.

"I had a nightmare about Li last night," Rocky said. "She was yelling at me, saying I wasn't good enough."

"She's worried about you, too."

Rocky huffed. "Yeah, worried I'm not practicing."

I took a breath. "Listen, Rocky," I said gently. "She's not thinking about that at all right now. She said you played *brilliantly* at the Showcase." Student Showcase felt like it'd happened ages ago.

Rocky paused. "She said that?" Then, "But you heard what went wrong at the Showcase, didn't you?"

"It sounded amazing to me."

"But still, Wu—"

"I heard it, I heard it. It was tiny and you handled it beautifully. No one noticed, and even if they did, they wouldn't have cared." I wanted to add, *I don't even care about it,* but I stopped myself.

"Well, apparently the conservatories care."

"What do you mean?"

"I didn't get into Peabody."

"So what? That's just one school. They can't take everyone. Maybe they already had enough pianists."

"What do you mean, so what? It's like, man, if you can't even get into Peabody, how can you expect to get into Eastman? I couldn't face my mom after I got the letter. And after what happened in the recital. She knew that piece inside and out after hearing me play it for her over break, like, two thousand times."

I doubted that Mrs. Wong had caught his mistakes, but I wasn't about to argue about that. "Listen, you could go to Eastman for grad school. I've heard it's easier to do that."

"I don't want it to be easier."

I took a breath. "Then that means you haven't reached your peak, doesn't it? That means you still have plenty of work to do. That means you care! I mean, you said it yourself, 'What's harder than Prok 1?' But you know what, Rocky? *Lots* of pieces are harder than Prok 1. It's, like, not even that hard!" That was when my voice broke, and I started to cry. I wiped my eyes, slightly embarrassed at my hiccupping sobs and runny nose, but unable to contain them.

There was silence. Then I could hear Rocky sniffling, could almost see him swiping his face with his sleeve.

For a while, we both just cried.

"You have to understand," he said, "it wasn't some freak decision. Everything finally collided and made a big mess."

"You were burned out."

"Yeah. And I just, I didn't want to be a burden on you."

"Don't say that. You could never be a burden. Don't you say that. Ever." I wished there were some way I could touch him, could shake his shoulders, press my face to his. On the phone, I heard him take a breath. I blew my nose into a few squares of toilet paper.

"I don't even know how I managed the recital," he said. "It's amazing how the adrenaline just takes over and your fingers just,

like, do what they need to. I love that. It's weird. I haven't practiced in a few weeks now. But it feels like so much longer. I miss
it. I really do."

"You didn't think you would?"

"When you're doing something every day like that, I don't
know. I didn't know why I was doing it. Even if I become the
best at it, what then? It's still not perfection. But even if it is, what
comes next? I practice and practice, try to make something really
good, and for what, another recital? What's the point?"

"When you feel better, we could—we could talk about that
stuff sometime."

"Oh yeah? You want to be my therapist?"

In spite of everything I could feel myself smiling. Rocky was
still himself.

"I didn't want to hurt you, Wu. I—I care about you, and I
know you care about me."

And why couldn't that be enough? I wanted it to be enough
so badly I ached.

"I'm still here, aren't I?" said Rocky. "And you're still here. I'm
in this stupid hospital, but god am I glad I'm here at all."

Chapter 24

I LEFT THE PRACTICE ROOMS JUST BEFORE DINNER THE DAY it happened. I was in the courtyard, halfway between the music building and the dorm, walking through campus in the warm spring air, when I felt a tap on my shoulder. Three taps, to be exact. When I turned around, Ellie Giang was already walking the other way.

When I called her name, she didn't turn around, didn't even stop walking, and that was when I knew. Then she spoke, so softly that I wouldn't have caught it if I hadn't been listening so hard. "Midnight, hallway." That was all she said.

That night, I kept my lamp on long after Jenny had gone to bed. I tried reading *Persepolis,* which I'd borrowed from Miyoung, but found it hard to concentrate. A few times, I thought I heard movement in the hallway and wondered if there was any chance that I'd heard Ellie wrong. My stomach was churning, sliding between elation that they'd chosen me, and doubt, thinking they'd made a mistake. Finally, at midnight, I eased out of bed and slid into my shoes. I closed the door as gently as I could, shivering in my pajamas. At the end of the hall, Ellie was waiting, using her phone's flashlight. I walked toward her.

She said nothing, but I'd pictured this so many times in my head, I knew that all I had to do was follow her to the secret meeting place. I was about to do just that when she opened her arms and hugged me—briefly, but still. It was a strong, comfortable embrace, the kind given by mothers or close friends. When I put my arms around her waist, I accidentally touched her hair—it was that long. Then she let go, turned, and went down the back staircase. I followed her, careful not to let my shoes make a sound on the steps. I winced when the door creaked open, but Ellie was sure of herself, guiding it closed. We walked to the common room, messy with the remnants of late-night studying or partying, it was hard to tell which. Half-empty bags of chips and cans of soda littered the couch and table. Ellie climbed onto the sofa and I followed suit. "This opens super smoothly," she whispered, lifting the window, "because Rocky greased it up with Daniel Giambalvo's beard balm."

The breeze blew into the room. I climbed through the window and landed on soft soil: flower beds. Since the dorms were at the very edge of campus, they were surrounded not by other buildings but by grass. In the dark, it was hard to make out anything or anyone.

"Stand still a minute," Ellie said. "I'm going to tie something around your eyes."

"You're going to blindfold me? I can hardly see as it is."

"You can't know where this place is. Not until we're sure."

"Sure of what?"

"Your dedication."

Dr. Li talked a lot about dedication, too. Some of us had it and some of us did not—only time would tell if we were in love with music, if we would love it till the end.

With a scarf around my eyes, I had the particular sensation that I was depending on Ellie for everything. I had never walked in pitch blackness for so long, what felt like several minutes. She didn't say anything except for "Watch out here" or "Step here," so I didn't say anything, either. Just smelled the Greenwood spring smell of wet grass and new paint.

"You're hesitating a lot," she said after a while. She put her hands on my shoulders. "You have to trust me, Claire."

Ellie stopped walking. Her hands dropped from my shoulders and I heard her opening a door. A light clicked on. I could see the shapes of people moving.

"Sit here," Ellie said. I heard a chair scraping the floor. I sat, and she lifted the scarf from around my eyes. The room burst into applause and laughter. JT was there, draped on a beanbag. Miyoung Kim, Angela Chung, and Lily Zhang were sitting on a couch. Lily was wearing sweatpants, which I'd never seen her in before, and without all her usual makeup, I saw she had freckles.

We were in a shed of some sort, a clean, tidy, and decorated shed, but still a shed. A pair of worn pointe shoes hung from an old ceiling fan, and the walls were covered in dusty old sketches. In the corner were an electric bass, a cajon, a guitar, and a keyboard.

Ellie pointed to the shoes. "Alyssa Park graduated ten years ago. She dances for American Ballet Theatre now. The sketches are by Bruce Tong, class of eighty-seven. I know you know his comics."

I gazed up at the shoes, which had frayed ribbons and holes at the toes. The sketches, mostly of Bruce's hometown of San Diego, were unframed, on thick paper, done in pencil and ink. The current Society members had their art on display, too: one of Ellie's plaster faces sat on a shelf, a collection of Greenwood concert programs were tacked to a bulletin board, and a painting by Miyoung hung on the wall.

Ellie pointed to one of the programs. "Your Beethoven," she said. "It wasn't just good—right notes, right dynamics—it was masterful. There was something in it, something real. It was . . . well, it was frightening. We could hear your fear, your sadness. We could hear *you*."

I remembered that night. It was before everything had happened, but even then, I could sense something about Rocky was off. As if she could tell what I was thinking, Ellie said, "We miss Rocky, too. He'll be psyched to know you're here. Psyched, but not surprised."

I said, "He always teased me that I wasn't Asian enough."

Ellie looked me in the eye. "You don't have to *do* anything to be Asian. Being Asian is in your blood."

Ellie had me kneel on a worn cushion. She took an old violin bow, which had belonged to Allison Khong, a violinist who now played for the New York Phil. "I hereby declare Claire Wu a member of the Asian Student Society," she said, tapping my shoulders with the bow as if she were knighting me.

"Thank you," I said.

"Don't," said Ellie. "Family doesn't thank."

Everyone cheered.

"The most important thing we do at the Society is listen to each other. But tonight is your turn to speak, Claire," said Ellie. "Speak from your heart."

It reminded me of how once, during a lesson, Dr. Li had said, "I know you can make a melody sing better than that." She had touched her fingers to her sternum, where a long necklace lay. "It has to come from in here."

We all sat in silence for a while, not unlike the silence that followed listening to a recording in Dr. Li's studio. I thought for a while about what I would most like to talk about with them, the members of the Asian Student Society—my fellow members. And then I told them about what it was like growing up. I told them about how once, when I had invited a friend from school over for dinner, my mother made ginger beef rice, my favorite. It was a dish you couldn't order at restaurants, and my mother made it with expensive cuts of beef for us, a type of ginger that we could only get at the Asian grocery store nearly an hour away, so thinly sliced (my mother standing over the cutting board, the beef, then the ginger) and cooked down for so long that it lost its bite and you could eat it along with the rice. But my friend looked at it skeptically, pushed it around on her plate. "I'm still really full from lunch," she said.

Later, I'd overheard her telling other girls at school about it. The weirdness of the rice, the purple pieces of ginger. My parents padding around the house in slippers. But worst of all, how she couldn't understand what my parents were saying. "Maybe that's how they talk in China!"

The other girls had laughed.

The thing was, my parents had been speaking English the whole time. She couldn't understand them even though they were speaking English to each other. The accented but fluent English that they used every day with the mail carrier, their bosses, the next-door neighbor who asked us would we please water her begonias while she was in Florida over the weekend.

Later, one of the friends had come and found me in the hallway. "It was just a joke. She's not a bad person." She paused. "You know, she's friends with Juanita Gonzalez."

"So?" I said.

"So she's not racist."

I'd felt sick to my stomach.

The members of the Asian Student Society nodded. There was no expectation that they had to say anything in response. All I heard was the sound of their breathing, the occasional "*Mm.*" But that was enough.

So I went on, remembering something from fourth grade. One weekend, Olivia and I were riding our bikes through the neighborhood. It was quiet; we could hear birds. Then two boys from our school, the Taylor twins, started calling out, "Chinese! You're Chinese!" As if it were a bad thing. As if they needed to yell it to warn the neighbors. We didn't stop, didn't respond other than to look at them, in shock, while we pedaled past, and then we rode away. They kept shouting it until we reached the end of their street.

When we got home and told my father what had happened, he looked up the Taylor family in the neighborhood directory. He dialed their number.

"This is Aaron Wu. My family and I live in the neighborhood, and my daughter is saying that something happened with your sons. Do you have a minute?" Mr. Taylor must have said yes, because my father said we would be there in five. We got in the car.

I couldn't remember anymore what my father told him, or what the Taylors' father said to us. But I was proud of my father that day.

The other members of Asian Student Society snapped their fingers. My whole body was warm, and I felt the best I'd felt since the night Rocky had gone missing, and more comfortable than I ever felt when speaking up in a group of people. They all shared, too: Ellie, about how she felt she could never be good enough for her mother, that it was something she had to process even while her mother was dead, and JT, about how he still hadn't come out to his parents yet, "and I feel like I'm lying to them every damn day." We listened to each other and cried together, passing around a box of tissues. I felt spent, but somehow in a good way.

Afterward, as if on cue, everyone got up and picked up musical instruments: Ellie began tuning her guitar, Lily took a shiny silver harmonica out of its case, JT sat on the cajon ("Rocky usually plays this," he said). Then Ellie stood and, lifting the cover off a little keyboard, said, "All yours, Claire."

I walked over to it, inspecting it. The keys felt light to the touch, and there were so many buttons. I hadn't played standing up before. I'd have to get used to it, but I knew I'd enjoy doing that.

"Okay, everybody," said JT. "We're in G tonight. Who knows where we'll end up." He shook his hair out of his eyes, his hands slapping the box, and called out, "One, two, three, four!" Ellie came in on the electric guitar, loud and wild riffs that were nothing like the strumming she did on the grass with her acoustic. Then Lily, the harmonica bright and sharp, then me: somehow, from listening, I knew which chords to play. I had to listen in a different way than I did when I accompanied the dancers, and I had to trust my ears to make things up when I wasn't completely sure. The drum pounded in my ears and the bass thumped in my chest. I thought, *This is what music is for.* We had showed each other our pain, and now we were celebrating our joy: creating it, even. Looking around at the others—some of them with big grins, some of them with eyes closed—I felt lighter and lighter still. We were sweating from exertion and our hands hurt and our chords fell off beat. But we were still listening.

Chapter 25

THAT SPRING, WE STUDIED FOR OUR EXAMS, WENT TO THE Silver Spoon for ice cream sandwiches, and ate picnics out on the grass. We took yellow school buses to prom, the windows painted by the art department with rough reproductions of Van Goghs in blues and greens, tripping over our skirts and sliding into the seats in our gowns. After dinner—a three-course affair that still couldn't rival the one Dr. Li had taken us to—Jenny and I danced with each other, screaming lyrics in each other's ears.

Adeline Felts and Scott Dessen were crowned prom queen and king, surprising no one. When Toothpick took the mic, she announced that she would be joining the American Ballet Theatre as a member of the corps that summer. We all cheered. Later, she came up to me at the drinks table. "Pianist!" she exclaimed, looping her arm around my neck. "If you're ever in New York, come sleep on my couch." I was pretty sure that she wouldn't care about me by the time I made it to New York, but it was nice of her all the same.

At the after-party, we watched a movie on the projector in the math room. Jenny, Martyna, and I all went to our dorm, and Jenny and I stayed awake talking until we couldn't keep our eyes open any longer. I couldn't help thinking it had been a nearly perfect day, that the only thing that would have made it more perfect was for Rocky to have been there.

♩♫

When I woke up the next morning, late, Jenny and Martyna were still sleeping. There were some things that the Society wouldn't change; although Ellie had called us family, Jenny could still be my sister. That wouldn't have to change, I decided. More than one person at Greenwood could be family.

When I sat up in bed, I saw that there was a note taped to my window on a torn-off piece of notebook paper. I recognized the handwriting at once: blocky, slanting slightly left. The note had only one word:

BREAKFAST?

In the breeze, the paper flapped, hanging on with just one piece of tape. I put my hand up to the glass, my heart quickening. When I tried to get up, I nearly fell out of bed from excitement. I pulled on my clothes, tiptoed around Martyna (who'd fallen asleep on a pile of blankets on our floor), and nearly ran to the dining hall, smiling like an idiot all the way.

When I got there, Rocky was getting cereal.

"You actually don't have to hurry," he said. "The dining hall extended their hours since I guess you guys stayed up so late last night. Something very typical, very cliché. I think it's called prom?"

I was grinning so widely my cheeks hurt. "You would have really liked it."

"I know for sure that I wouldn't have."

"You don't know anything for sure."

"I know I got into Indiana with a full scholarship." Before I could respond, he said, "I know I love you."

I threw my arms around him, and he pulled me into his chest and kissed me all over my face. We stood there, holding each other, until Barbara asked were we planning to eat anytime soon, and did Rocky know that he was spilling milk all over her sparklin' clean floor?

♩♫

I had my last lesson with Dr. Li the next week, and at the end of it, we talked through new repertoire for next year: Brahms, Scarlatti, Grieg, Ravel. She asked me about my plans for the summer, and I told her about my family's trip to California and going to the beach with Jenny, who was really close to getting her driver's license. Rocky and I were going to visit each other as much as we could, and I was helping to plan events for the Society in the fall. Otherwise I foresaw long days of volunteering at the library and in a nursing home near our house—which my mother had said would be character-building—and my plans to teach piano lessons to a few neighborhood kids.

Dr. Li raised her eyebrows at that one. "You're starting early. I don't think I taught my first lessons until college."

"I'm nervous about it," I admitted.

"You'll be just fine," said Dr. Li. She smiled. "I think I've prepared you well."

We talked about schools: about the professor at Juilliard who had a glass eye and put it on the piano to watch you as you played your scales. About the massive donation that Indiana had just received from a music-loving billionaire, and how Rocky would do so well there. About Jordan Hall at New England Conservatory, how beautiful and intimate it was.

"And who knows?" Dr. Li said. "Maybe you'll end up at one of these schools yourself. Your playing has come a long way, Claire. Watching you and the other pianists learn, and practice, and perform: it has been a joy." She smiled at me.

"For us too," I said, although I knew I couldn't speak on behalf of Rocky or Jenny. "I'm glad you came here."

Dr. Li looked out the window. "But you know . . . ," she began. She fidgeted, as if wanting to say something but wasn't sure how or if she should. Then she said, "I failed Rocky, as a teacher."

"Oh, no, Dr. Li—"

"I know I did. I didn't see what he needed, didn't realize he was mentally unwell. He was playing so much and he lost sight of why he does it. And you know, with"—she looked physically pained as she said this—"his father being gone, his mother doing everything—I can imagine the amount of pressure he's under."

She paused. "I pushed him hard, but he pushed himself harder, to an unhealthy place. I didn't see that he wasn't keeping up."

If she had said those things just a few months ago, I would have been surprised, but I wouldn't have believed her. Rocky? Not keeping up? He was made of drive, of stamina. But now, listening to Dr. Li, I was beginning to understand. That Rocky had buckled under pressure—intense pressure—this one time didn't mean he couldn't handle things, but that he'd miscalculated. That in the frenzy of trying to be the best—to get into the best school, to play the best recital—he'd forgotten why he played music in the first place.

I hadn't meant to, but I started to cry. I cried for Rocky, for the enormous load he carried always, and how I was powerless to help. Dr. Li brought me a box of tissues, and to my surprise, she sat down beside me on the bench and put her arm around me. I felt her silk blouse against my cheek. We sat like that for a while, and I wiped my eyes with my shirt.

"I'm sorry," said Dr. Li. "I didn't mean to make you cry."

I shrugged. "I've been crying a lot these days."

"And of course I—I shouldn't blame myself."

I shook my head. "You shouldn't. And I shouldn't, either." When I thought about it, everyone close to Rocky could do the same: his mother for inadvertently pressuring him, Greenwood School for not giving him more scholarship money, his boss at the MapleMart for being such a stickler. We could all blame ourselves.

Dr. Li smiled. "Look at us. Now you're the one telling me what I shouldn't do."

"I'm sorry—"

She put her hand up. "It's what I needed to hear. Thank you, Claire."

Then Dr. Li sat back and regarded me, appraising me like my mother or an aunt.

"You've grown up this year," she said. "When you first came into this studio, you were eager to play for me, of course, but I could see you were terrified. Now look at you. You're so much surer of yourself. You don't need me to tell you who you are." She smiled, and so did I, in spite of myself. I thought of how scared I was the first day we'd come into her studio. The way she'd pushed me to say what I thought. She'd called on me as if she knew I was the one who was least likely to speak up. I thought of the first day we saw her in the dining hall, how regal she seemed, how unknowable. And at the assembly, waiting and waiting for her.

"There was a question we wanted to ask you, at the Annual Assembly," I said.

She nodded. "I remember. About success, right?" She crossed her legs. "You should know this: There is no mountaintop moment. You think you've made it, once you play that recital or land that gig. But the truth is, the very best part of playing music is what you already have. It's what you do every day." She gestured to the piano. "It's right there between you and the keys. There's nothing better." She shook her head. "The goal of the music department here . . . it shouldn't be to churn out a bunch of concert pianists, although that is a wonderful thing. It should be to foster a deep love of music. That's what I should have realized far, far earlier.

"I kept holding Rocky—and all of you—to higher and higher standards. I didn't want you to become complacent about your playing. I didn't realize that, even before I arrived, you were all so ambitious. But I was hardest on Rocky. He reminded me of myself at that age. So sure that I had what it took. I felt I had to stretch him, see what he would do, what he could do, if I pushed him the way my professor pushed me."

She sighed. "The pressure at Juilliard, it was everywhere. You could smell it. And in New York, there are thousands of musicians just as talented, all just trying to pay rent. The truth is, Claire, I had a breakdown myself. I ended up taking a year off from school. I was so burned out, I didn't even like playing anymore. For a while I could hardly stand to even listen to classical music. All it did was make me feel worthless, guilty."

"I'm so sorry," I said.

Dr. Li took a deep breath. "So when I got here, I thought, I should be hard on all of you now, because if you don't have what it takes, it's better for you to figure it out when you're still young. I didn't want you to end up like me, having that wake-up call at a conservatory. But obviously, I was wrong." She laughed ruefully. "If there's one thing I'm learning here at Greenwood, it's that you can be kind *and* challenging. You can seek your students' well-being and have high expectations for them at the same time. I guess I'm still so old-school."

There it was again, Dr. Li trying to use slang the way my mother sometimes did.

"So how did you get started playing again? I mean, *really* playing?" I asked.

"What brings any of us back?" she said. "Beauty, right? And the comfort of it, the challenge." Dr. Li's eyes shone. Then she said, "I lucked out when Greenwood asked me for an interview."

I considered this. If anything, I'd always thought that it

was the other way around, that Greenwood had lucked out by getting Dr. Li. "You don't wish you were at Juilliard or anything?"

She looked at me. "Not at all, Claire. I was very lucky to get to teach here." Then Dr. Li smiled. "Besides, why would I want to teach college when I could be spending more years working with students like you? I've been too hard on you at times—that's clear to me now—but you've been great students. You're great kids."

She had never called us that before. *Kids.*

"I wonder, sometimes, which of you will still be playing, oh, I don't know, ten years from now. Hopefully you all will be, in one way or another."

I couldn't picture any of us stopping. "I will be, for sure," I said.

"I think you're right. It can be a lonely life, though."

I wondered about that word. I wasn't lonely. Or was I? I had friends who loved each other fiercely, and even if I ate breakfast alone and dashed through lunch, I could always count on a full table at dinner and Jenny in the dorm. How could she know that despite all that, I sometimes felt something like loneliness, especially walking from the practice rooms at night, chilly air settling in, clouds of my own breath in front of my face, the path lighted by lamps. That close to curfew, you saw everyone coming out of the art studios, the library, the practice room, one by one. Each having been lost in a secret world of their own.

Then she looked into my eyes. "Rocky may have been the

most talented; Jenny the bravest, the most outspoken. But you, Claire, are the most sensitive. And that sensitivity—to people as well as sound—will take you far."

She leaned over and patted my hand with hers.

"Now it's time for me to stop filling your head with these things, and fill it with something truly noble." She stood and slid two books out from the B section of the case, placing one at each piano. Then she took a seat at the Steinway, the piano I sat at week after week. She gestured for me to do the same at the Kawaii. "You have been playing all year for me," she said. "Now let us play something together."

"Wait, what?" I said, even as I took a seat.

Dr. Li said, "You take the melody. I'll accompany *you* this time."

I looked up at the music. Then I counted, "One, two, three." I took a sharp breath in—there was Dr. Li's cue—and we began to play. What we played together wasn't flashy, and it wasn't Beethoven, although she had called him the greatest. It was one of the Brahms waltzes for four hands, in A major. The piece was at times thoughtful and at others lyrical and sweet, even playful. The bass line was slow and calm, nothing like the Beethoven we had heard her practicing through the vents at the Annual Faculty-Student Assembly. Above it, I played the melody, as gentle as a lullaby. My own playing had depth and tenderness both. In the upper registers, it sparkled and sang, and during the final variation, we both took our time as we arrived at the ending. Even though neither of us was speaking, we were deep in conversation.

A Playlist for <u>The Notes</u>
(in order of appearance in the book)

Piano Sonata in E Major, op. 109, no. 30, by Ludwig van Beethoven
(Richard Goode)

Piano Concerto No. 2 in G Major II. Andante non troppo, by Pyotr
Tchaikovsky

Nocturne in B Major, op. 9, no. 3, by Frédéric Chopin
(Emanuel Ax)

Piano Concerto in A Minor, op. 54, "Allegro affettuso," by Robert
Schumann
(Martha Argerich and the Vienna Philharmonic)

Piano Sonata in C Minor, op. 13, no. 8 (Pathétique), by Beethoven

The Sleeping Beauty, Op. 66, Act 1: Waltz, by Tchaikovsky

Piano Sonata in F Minor, op. 1, no. 1, by Sergei Prokofiev

Arabesque No. 1, by Claude Debussy

"The Girl with the Flaxen Hair," by Debussy

Piano Sonata in F Minor, op. 57, no. 23 ("Appassionata"), by Beethoven

Toccata by Aram Khachaturian

Waltz in A Major, op. 39, no. 15, by Johannes Brahms

Acknowledgments

A standing ovation for Chad Luibl and Roma Panganiban: I could not have asked for sweeter or savvier agents. You picked me out of the slush pile and made my dream come true. Thank you so much for listening to me, going to bat for me, and seeing something in this story, for taking a chance on this debut and having such a great vision for it. Special thanks to Roma for intelligent line edits and encouragement when I needed it (which was often).

Brava and *encore* to my superstar, genius editor, Phoebe Yeh, whose insights and questions transformed this book. Thank you for your incredible warmth, passion, curiosity, and generosity. I always love talking with you, and not only about writing.

A round of applause for Daniela Cortes, Melinda Ackell, and the rest of the team at Crown Books for Young Readers for everything you did to bring this book into the world. Thank you to Hsiao-Ron Cheng for the gorgeous cover design that so captures the spirit of the novel.

To the MFA community at Boston University: thank you to Leslie Epstein for caring so much for your students, for loving classical music, and for your continual championing of this book. Thank you to Ha Jin for teaching me how to truly read a novel, and to Sigrid Nunez for teaching me how to revise. To Chris Amenta and Cara Bayles: thank you for patiently, persistently reading draft after draft.

Many thanks to Josh Cook and the Porter Square Books Writers in Residence program. You saw something in this manuscript's earliest chapters and provided the space, community, and coffee to write it.

To Marina Lomazov, my first and best reader: thank you for teaching me how to listen and how to tell a story, both through the piano and on the page. Dr. Li would not have come alive without you. Thank you for your precise, perceptive comments throughout the years.

Many thanks to Dr. Hoyt for geeking out on music history and teaching me to do the same.

To my writing teachers Ben Greer, Bret Anthony Johnston, Matthew Salesses, and Nancy Somers: thank you for your guidance, good questions, and generous encouragement. To Johnny Miles, for graciously reading my earliest stories and telling me to keep at it.

Much gratitude to the Kundiman family, especially Duy Doan, for having a poet's heart and ears.

To Scott Ruescher, Steve Seidel, and the Arts in Education cohort at HGSE (2010): thank you for listening so well.

To Raynetta Gibbs at Choate Rosemary Hall: thank you for your invaluable expertise on teen mental health. Thanks to my EN 200 students (2021 and 2022) for your smart suggestions and boundless enthusiasm.

To the South Carolina Governor's School for the Arts and Humanities: thank you for a magical two years. To Stephen Buck and Tien-Ni Chen: thank you for teaching me to fall in love with the piano. To Govie besties Heather Carey and Megan Murph for the music and mischief.

To many folks at Church of the Cross in Boston, especially Ryan Ruffing, and to the Boston Fellows arts cohort: thank you for the nourishing conversations on art and faith, and thank you for reading. You kept me going when I didn't know what I was doing or why.

To my FWB Bstuds: thank you for many years of loyal friendship, for loving me, listening to me, praying for me, and cheering me on. Special thanks to Kate Danahy for reading.

To Matthew "Locker" Lockerman: I wouldn't have finished this without our early morning writing sessions and pacts. Thank you for holding me accountable and asking the right questions.

To Dr. Emily "PLP" Fine: thank you for reading my work and for your pragmatic wisdom in situations both social and imagined. To Dr. Nicole "Nip" Wilson Hanna: thank you for working out and hosting literary fetes. Thank you to Daniel Leonard for reading and listening, and for many years of friendship. Aubrey "Aubs" Goio and Elizabeth "Eliz" Sliwa: thank you for adventures at the University of South Carolina School of Music and beyond. Thank you for being excellent friends and for loving both me and my stories.

Thanks to Emily and Dan "Mama and Papa" Morse for your encouragement and for always providing tea and a table for writing. I finished the first draft of *The Notes* at Morseland the day after Thanksgiving 2019, when I probably should have been helping to clean up.

A deep well of thanks to Mom and Dad for your constant love and support, for piano lessons, and for not getting mad when I lost my dorm keys multiple times. I would not be a writer (or a musician) without you. To Elizabeth "El" Con Linehan, thank you for our lifelong friendship, for literary and culinary tours of New York, and for your ceaseless enthusiasm for my writing.

And thank you, Pete, for everything: your patience, your belief in me and my work, and your good counsel and comfort in the face of various writerly neuroses. Our life together with Libby is the best story.

About the Author

CATHERINE CON MORSE was one of the inaugural Writers in Residence at Porter Square Books. A Kundiman fellow, she received her MFA from Boston University. Her work has appeared in *Joyland, Letters, HOOT,* and *Bostonia. The Notes* was shortlisted for the *CRAFT* First Chapters Contest and is her first novel.

Catherine attended the South Carolina Governor's School for the Arts and Humanities, a public arts boarding school, where she was as intrigued with her teacher as Claire is with Dr. Li. Catherine continues to play and teach piano today. Most recently, she taught English at Choate Rosemary Hall. She lives in the Connecticut River Valley with her husband and daughter.